pirates

the orgone
chronicles — book two

by nobilis reed

PIRATES

The Orgone Chronicles – Book Two
by Nobilis Reed

ISBN: 978-1-905091-91-1
Paperback Edition
© 2011 by Nobilis Reed

Published in the United Kingdom by Logical-Lust Publications 2011
www.ll-publications.com
57 Blair Avenue
Hurlford
Scotland
KA1 5AZ

Edited by Rachel McIntyre
Additional editing by Zetta Brown
Book layout and typesetting by jimandzetta.com
Cover art and design by Helen E. H. Madden www.pixelarcana.com © 2011

Printed in the UK and the USA

the orgone chronicles

by nobilis reed

SCOUTS

(2011 Finalist – EPIC eBook Awards)

pirates

Hunters

ACKNOWLEDGEMENTS

A really good book requires the efforts of many people. So did this one. It would not have been possible without the support and encouragement of my writer friends, Michele Bekemeyer and Ann Regentin, and my wife, Dee. Just as important, the tremendous work of my editors, Rachel and Zetta, have been instrumental in making this book what it is.

dedication

To all my awesome friends, who inspire me.

chapter one

Challers, Port

VALKA PANTED, her body hot with fever and soaked with sweat, while I knelt at her feet. According to what I had been able to learn, the proper vessel in which to receive an Ovor egg as it was laid was a shallow ceramic bowl. There was a stack of them next to me, enough for the seven eggs Valka was expecting. I was as ready as I could be.

Only, it wasn't going well. Over the past week, Valka had developed a fever, and when she started feeling contractions, she sent a panicked call to my cubicle.

I had crossed the hall to her pod without even bothering to put on clothes. I couldn't believe how bad she looked. Didn't the doctors care what was happening? They were supposed to be taking care of her, vack them all! And now the eggs were coming.

"Portcon! We need medical attention here!" I screamed.

The floating holographic head that represented the interface to Port's main computer system said simply, "Medical assistance is en route, Ward Challers Dizen. Estimate four minutes until arrival."

Valka gave another grunt, pushing words past her teeth. "Too late."

I saw a dark mass pushing out of her body, squeezing through. I held my hands up and took it in my hands as Valka's muscles expelled it.

The thing smelled terrible. None of the recordings I had found mentioned that. I swallowed to keep the bile where it belonged and set the egg in a bowl with a white cloth over it. The next one wouldn't be long.

"Medical team has arrived," said Portcon. "Opening pod access."

The door opened, revealing a middle-aged woman wearing a greenish coverall. "Come on out, make room for us."

"She's having her eggs now!" I shouted. "Someone has to stay with her!"

"They'll be fine," said the medic. "Come on out."

I hustled to the door, and watched as the medic took my place. Another one squeezed in alongside Valka's reclining chair. The second one took out an injector and put it to the inside of her elbow. Valka's breathing immediately became less ragged, and she relaxed back down onto the chair. I could hear a wet squelch as another egg was born. My stomach took another tumble.

The smell only got worse. I knew something was wrong when the medics frowned and shook their heads.

"What?" I cried. "What's wrong?"

"Ward, you'll need to either keep quiet or go back to your pod."

I took a deep breath. "Okay. Okay."

The medics worked in near silence, occasionally exchanging a word or two of medical jargon that I couldn't understand. Finally, they piled all of the eggs into one bowl and began packing up their gear. Valka was still and quiet, her only movement was the slight rise and fall of her blanket as she breathed.

"Is she going to be all right?"

"She'll recover. Nasty infection she got there."

"And the eggs?" I didn't want to care about those eggs. They were a legacy of the Scouts and the forced breeding program they had imposed on Valka. But Valka cared about them. No matter how it had happened that she was bearing them, they were hers, and she had been looking forward to this day ever since we had arrived at Port. She cared about them, so I did too.

"Dead," said one of the medics. "That's what gave her the infection."

"Dead? But how?"

"You two are the new kids—ex-Scouts, right?"

"Yeah."

"You get in any fights while you were escaping?"

"Yeah. There was some fighting when we left."

"Use the jump drive?"

"A few times."

"Hyperwarp and jump drives aren't the cleanest forms of propulsion. No good for developing eggs. That's probably what did it."

I didn't know what to say. Part of me wanted to be glad that Valka wouldn't be burdened with seven eggs to tend, but I knew that learning what had happened would devastate her. Finally, I just asked, "How long will she be asleep?"

"The drug will keep her out for four hours or so. After that, she'll sleep naturally. You should probably get some too. Do you need a tranquilizer?"

"No, I'll be okay." I stumbled across the hall, through my door, and collapsed onto my chair. With the adrenaline of the evening starting to burn off, I was bone-tired. "Portcon?"

"Yes, Ward Challers Dizen?"

"Wake me up if Valka Parl wakes up, please."

"I will do that, Ward Challers Dizen."

I pulled the thin sheet over my body and tried to let the blackness of sleep wash over me. One thought kept intruding, however. How would I tell Valka? What would she say? I tried to comfort myself with the knowledge that whatever happened, I would be there for her. It didn't feel like enough.

Nothing was going right. We had all expected something to change when we reached Port. We had expected there to be a tremendous outrage that innocent human lives were being used as power sources for the new weapon system being used by the Scouts, the one we were calling "egg missiles."

Robert had tried to get the word out, convince people that something had to be done, but it seemed like everyone was convinced that it either didn't matter, that the Scouts were despicable for a dozen other things anyway, or that we were lying to try to stir up trouble. Robert said it was a credibility problem; he had been away for too long, and nobody remembered him. The rest of us were complete unknowns.

VALKA'S RECOVERY took a long time. By the end of the second day, she was alert and awake again, though not really strong enough to come out of her pod. She was well looked after, with medical monitors installed in her pod and daily checkups by human medical staff. I looked in on her often, but when she was resting, I went back to my pod.

My interest in history, which I had gained during my studies at the Academy, became a need during those days of waiting. It was the only way I could distract myself. There were many, many things the Scouts had never told us, things the Pirates knew and were more than willing to share. I spent hours scanning the archives, sorting through events I had never even heard of in school, and it was better than fretting about things I couldn't control.

One thing that particularly caught my attention was the true origin of the Scouts. During the Great Diaspora, after the discovery of orgone and faster-than-light travel, mankind's government fragmented into a thousand individual colonies. Nobody had the strength to hold all of the colonies in one entity. There was a constant, low-level conflict throughout this era.

According to my studies at the Academy, the Scout Service appeared at this time as a force that sought to quell the constant fighting with diplomacy and trade. The records I found here, however, told a different story. One group, known as the Incorporates, started conquering systems one after another. They had mastered a technology for direct interface between brain and computer that allowed them much greater control over their warships. Not only that, they were able to command absolute loyalty from those they conquered by means of this interface. Whole populations were reduced to blissful, mindless slavery.

Once the rest of the galaxy learned what the Incorporates were doing, the reaction was immediate. The horror of it shocked them into action. Resources were marshaled, technologies were shared, and great warfleets were dispatched to erase the Incorporates from the galaxy. It was in this conflict that the Scouts, Fleet, and Merchants were founded.

When the war was over, the leaders of the three services decided to remain in power. They said it was to preserve galactic peace, but of course, it also preserved the "emergency powers" they'd been given in the war.

After fifteen days, Valka had gained strength to wake me with a kiss on the lips. I smiled. "Good morning. Feeling better?"

"Yeah." Her face was bright, but there was an edge of darkness to it.

"I guess you know what happened to the eggs," I said.

"I asked Portcon."

"I would have told you, you know."

"I know, but...I guess I didn't see the need to involve you. I'm sorry. I should have let you tell me."

I sat up and put my arms around her. "It's okay. I'm sorry."

When I let go, Valka's features had taken a hard edge. "Seven more crimes the Scouts are responsible for," she said.

"I have a feeling they're not going to worry." I sat up and hung my feet off the side of the chair to make room for her. "Portcon? Breakfast, please. The usual?"

"Oatmeal with fruit is available, Ward Challers Dizen."

Valka hopped up on the chair and snuggled up next to me. She caught my eye as I stared down at her. "What?" she asked.

"I guess I'm not used to seeing you without that belly. It seems strange."

She smoothed her coverall over her stomach, frowning. "I'm still kind of overweight. All this sitting around isn't good for me. I got more exercise back on Stakroya Station. I also ate less."

I leaned down and kissed her. "You know that doesn't matter to me." It was the truth. It was Valka that I loved, not her body. The Scouts had transformed her into an Ovor, a four-breasted race designed to produce large quantities of eggs, but that didn't matter to me.

"It matters to me. I feel like a lump."

"Portcon says that the nutritional content of the food is calibrated to keep you healthy."

"Yeah, well, that may be true, but these pods are orgone collectors, right? They probably want to keep us a little fat, because more mass means more basal orgone."

"I guess."

"You guess? Look what they do to Merchants. Challers, you can't trust these people. Everyone is looking out for their own interests."

I looked down at my own body. I had to admit that the muscles I had gotten during my training with the Scouts were not as defined as they had been. "They've got a gym up on the Boulevard. We could go together."

"Yeah, have you seen what it costs? I know I have a lot of credits with the Port, but I can't spend it like that. I'm just going to have to be more careful about what I eat. Ooh! It's almost ten. Put your screen on. I want to see the Morning Summary."

"Hmm?"

"It's a program they put on every morning to show you everything interesting that happened overnight."

"Portcon, please display 'Morning Summary.'"

Portcon's face disappeared, replaced with a rotating logo and a dramatic voice. "Welcome to Morning Summary for day 842 of cruise fifty-six." The logo was replaced by a long list of names, grouped in fours and fives under titles like *David's Destroyers* and *Madden's Marauders*. "Please choose the Worthies for your report," the voice continued.

"What is this?" I asked.

Valka snuggled close, holding my arm. "I discovered it last week. Those people we saw patrolling the Boulevard? They call them *Worthies*. They have cameras following them around all the time, and folks can watch what happens. Pick David's Destroyers."

I reached out to the hologram and waved my finger at that section. The screen cleared, and an image formed of a man in a baggy white shirt and black pants lounging in a comfortable, armless chair. He swirled a drink in one hand and smiled at a short-haired woman who had just walked into the scene. She was similarly attired, though neither wore the weapons we had seen Worthies wear up on the Boulevard.

A disembodied voice accompanied the scene. "The romance between Krinna and David has continued since she signed up for his crew. It's a good thing he convinced her to join up, since with only two members, his crew would have been delisted this morning. As it stands, he still has only ten days remaining to get back to four members and keep his crew going long term."

David took her hand and pulled her down for a passionate kiss, which she returned with enthusiasm. She reached behind him and pulled out the knot that held David's shirt together, and unfolded the two triangular flaps to expose a hairless, muscular chest.

"Are they going to have sex right there where everyone can see?"

"Uh-huh." Valka squirmed closer and put an arm around my waist. "He's been romancing her all week."

We watched Krinna run her hands over David's chest, and the camera zoomed in to show the effect her caress was having on his nipples. When it zoomed out again, she was shrugging out of her shirt, revealing a back almost as well-muscled as his chest. Soft music began playing in the background, a light tune that heightened the affectionate tone of the scene.

"You like this guy," I said.

"Hmm?"

"I mean, you like watching him."

"Oh, yeah. I mean, his crew is about to be officially disbanded, and he's completely not concerned. In control. You don't see that kind of confidence all the time."

The point of view shifted again, this time coming down from above—a perfect angle to catch David taking one of Krinna's small breasts into his mouth and the look of pleasure that came over her face as she arched her back.

I started off watching David, trying to figure out what it was that Valka saw, but Krinna soon had my full attention. I had never seen a woman who looked like that before. Even my mentor in the Scouts, Shirley, wasn't as muscular as this woman. I was attracted and repulsed at the same time. Something inside me said it wasn't right for a woman to look so masculine, but then I remembered the hermaphroditic Chevalier newgens I had met at Scout Headquarters. I pushed that thought aside.

As Krinna reached down into David's pants, Valka slid her hand past my waistband and squeezed my swelling cock. "I've been thinking about you all week," she said.

If watching David got her this worked up, I wasn't going to

complain. "Why didn't you come over?" I moved my hand from her shoulder down under her arm to cup one breast through her shirt.

"I didn't want to come over until I was ready."

"Ready for what?"

"You know." She pulled her shirt up over her head and threw it aside. "This." Her four Ovor breasts were full and round, tipped with thick, dark brown nipples. She did have a bit of extra weight on her, but I barely noticed. By the time both of us were fully naked, the couple on the holoscreen were naked too, rubbing their bodies together as they kissed.

Valka leaned back on the chair, letting her legs fall to either side. "I want you to pleasure me while I watch."

I smiled and climbed up onto the chair, between her legs. Her pussy lips, which had been kept hairless while we were at Scout Headquarters, were covered with fur. I ran my fingers through it. "I don't know if I still know how," I said with a smile.

"Mmm, I'm sure you'll figure it out."

While I explored with my fingers, I heard the sounds of Krinna and David's encounter over my shoulder. Judging from his encouragements and her muffled responses, she had something important in her mouth. I took it as my cue to get my own mouth involved.

I pulled her pussy lips apart. It had been too long since we had been this close. Valka's advanced pregnancy had made a lot of sexual activities difficult or tiring, and I was elated to be able to do this for her again. I licked slowly, playing with her inner lips, flicking them lightly with my tongue. As I gradually moved up towards her clit, I felt tension building in her thighs.

"Vack, Challers," she said between deep breaths, "I missed this."

I chuckled. "So did I." I hadn't performed this act on Valka too many times, but I knew how to pay attention to her reactions and adjust. With a light touch, I placed my lips around her clit, drawing only just enough suction to be felt. She made a soft, contented noise and touched my head, not pushing down or pulling back. She was simply acknowledging that I was there.

I sucked harder, flicking my tongue at the tiny bud of flesh between my lips. "Ooh, too much," she gasped, and I backed off, licking along the sides of her clit.

"Sorry."

"It's okay. That's much…mmm…much better."

I slipped one arm under her body and drew my hand up to stroke the lower part of her cunt. A brief flash crossed my mind of a black, sickly egg. I pulled back to look. Except for the hair, it hadn't changed all that much since I had seen her last, making it easy to dispel the image from my mind.

The sound of David and Krinna's sexual encounter changed. I looked over my shoulder to see Krinna straddling him, flexing her thighs as she rose and fell, impaled on his cock. I wanted to fuck Valka too, but I could wait until she'd had an orgasm. I went back to my task with the goal firmly in mind.

Slipping my fingers inside her, I searched for the firm knot of flesh on the upper wall of her channel. It was there, where I had found it once before. I hoped the result would be as spectacular as the first time. With quick little strokes, I rubbed the spot with my fingers while I licked the hood of her clit in the same rhythm. I imagined a kind of circuit between my hand and my mouth, with Valka's body strung between. When my tongue started to get a little sore, I switched to using my nose for a few seconds while I gave it a rest, and went back. When my fingers cramped, I switched hands.

She did not disappoint me. Her thighs clenched around my shoulders as I worked, and growling cries escaped her throat. I could feel her pussy tensing around my fingers and even smell the musky change in her scent.

And then I noticed that the top of my head was wet. I pulled back and looked around.

Milk dribbled down from all four of Valka's breasts, and droplets were scattered all over her stomach. She looked down at me, grinning sheepishly. "Sorry," she said, when she'd gotten her air back.

I laughed. "Don't be. I think it's great. It's like you're ejaculating too."

"I guess I am." She took the lower pair in her hands and squeezed. Streams of milk sprayed out. "They got sore after the eggs came and this made them feel better. Ever since then, I've been milking myself. Port said that most women who get sick during pregnancy never even start lactating, but Ovors might be different. The information wasn't complete."

I climbed up her body, licking the droplets up as I went. "I could have helped, you know." The milk was sweet and warm, with just a hint of salt from her sweaty skin.

"I know. I guess I didn't want you to see me that way."

"I want to be with you no matter what, Valka. I don't mind seeing you weak or sick. I want to take care of you."

"Okay. I'm sorry. I think I like the idea of you taking care of me."

I sucked on the hard nub of her nipple and got a tiny squirt of milk. "Does that feel good?"

"Mmm, yes."

"Good. I like doing it." I sucked some more, and gradually felt the tightness in her skin recede. I switched to the other.

"Mmm, that's much better," she said.

I went from breast to breast, gently draining her of the offending fluid. My hard cock bumped her thigh, and when I finished, I shifted position to enter her.

"Oh, Challers." She put a hand on my chest. "Please don't."

"Why not?"

"An Ovor is always fertile. I don't want to go through that again." Her eyes pleaded with me. "Please."

I hung over her. If I pressed the issue, I could probably convince her to let me fuck her, but we had both been through too much for me to even consider it. I sat back on my heels, my cock jutting up from between my thighs.

"Here. Let me do this instead. Lie down." She climbed off of the seat so I could take her place, and then she climbed back on, straddling my knees. She transferred some of the copious lubrication from her pussy onto my cock before wrapping her lower pair of breasts around it with her hands. "How does that feel?"

"Mmm, that's not bad. It's not as good as being inside you, but it'll do."

Above her head, David and Krinna were cuddling on their chair. She sat on his lap, sitting crosswise with his arm supporting her shoulders. Their soft demeanor contrasted with the hard edges of their bodies. They both seemed too tough for such contemplation, but there they were.

I returned my attention back to Valka. Her upper breasts bobbed hypnotically as she moved. I brought my hands up to them, stroking their soft skin as she continued pleasuring me. "They've gotten bigger, haven't they?"

"A bit."

I watched my cock disappearing between her breasts. "Seems like a lot more...mmm...than a bit to me."

She looked down. "I guess."

I gasped as the first jet erupted from my cock, arching over my stomach to land on my chest. It was so soon it caught me somewhat by surprise. My stomach and Valka's breasts were splattered with semen.

"Feel better?" she asked.

I laughed. "Yeah. Thanks."

Valka got a washcloth from the hygiene station and cleaned herself off. "You really like me this way?"

"Yes. Of course, I do. Why do you ask?"

"I want to save up to get enough to use a gentank." She climbed up onto the chair and sat cross-legged, facing me, and handed me the towel.

"How much does it cost?"

"The price seems to fluctuate for some reason, but it's usually something like a hundred thousand."

I whistled. "Where are you going to get that kind of money?"

"Well, you know you don't have to stay in your pod all day. That pays your basic life support, but if you want to accumulate credits, you have to do more than that. I've been looking around and there are a few jobs I could do."

"How much would you get?" I finished wiping myself off and tossed the cloth into the recycling hatch.

"Well, there's a job as a data wrangler that would pay twenty-five an hour. If I work ten-hour days, then I could have enough to use the gentank in about two hundred days, given what we're starting with."

"Could you do it from your pod?"

"No, this would be at a data center a few decks down."

"So you'd have to pay life support while you were away. Valka, that's not two hundred days. That's a lot more. It might take years."

Valka groaned. "I hadn't thought of that."

"I don't mind."

"I do! I don't like this body. I don't want to have any more eggs!"

"Maybe there's a drug or something that will stop that."

"There is. It costs ten credits a day."

"That's not too bad."

"I don't like draining our savings like this. I'm not making any income, and it costs life support any time we visit."

I looked up at the screen where David was walking along the Boulevard with Krinna and another Worthy whose name I had missed.

"How much do Worthies make?"

"I don't know."

"Portcon," I called. "How much do Worthies earn?"

"A Worthy earns shares of all the crisis and transcendent orgone that is generated while being observed by Wards."

"And how much is that?"

"It varies widely, but most Worthies earn between two thousand and five thousand credits in a day."

I turned to Valka. "That's it, then. We need to become Worthies."

chapter two

Renedy, Stakroya Station

"RENEDY JAWMET, please report to the command deck." Captain Shaunson's voice echoed through the hallway around me.

Mrs. Blanchak, standing at her accustomed post, threw me a stern look. "Young lady, the elevator is that way." She nodded at the hatch behind me.

"Yes, ma'am," I said, trying to slip past her.

She stepped to one side and blocked me. "That was Captain Shaunson. I don't believe there's any other errand which should take precedence over his polite request?"

"Actually..."

The voice returned. "Renedy Jawmet, report to the command deck immediately."

I rolled my eyes and turned around, grumbling under my breath.

Mrs. Blanchak called after me, "An attitude like that is not going to land you a decent husband, Miss Jawmet!"

The elevator doors closed off any further abuse from my busybody hall-watcher. I had moved out of my parents' apartment in order to get away from people like her. My own place was my eighteenth birthday present to myself. It cost most of my surplus credit allocation, even after agreeing to take on two extra hours of work a day, but what else was there to do on Stakroya Station anyways? The communications cluster was more entertainment than anything I could afford to buy—at least, when I was allowed to do my job.

The doors opened. Consoles stood in a four-meter ring around a central pedestal where Shaunson sat in his command chair, already facing the elevator. His expression was stern and cold.

"Miss Jawmet," he said, making a steeple with his fingers and uncrossing his legs. "I've just had a rather unsettling report from your superior."

I couldn't help rolling my eyes. I grunted so he'd know I heard him. Mr. Greel was the only thing worse than a slimy, leering bachelor-boy looking to take advantage of an available girl like me—and that was a creepy, leering married-guy looking to get a little extra after his ration at home ran out.

"He says that you have been accessing private communications channels."

I glanced away, over at one of the empty consoles. It wasn't going to do much good, but I had to put up some kind of defense. "I haven't. He's lying."

"The system logs are unequivocal, Miss Jawmet. You have been caught accessing private holocams without authorization. After three violations and three disciplinary actions from Mr. Greel, and no change in your behavior, he had no choice but to refer the matter to me. Do you know just how much trouble you are in, young woman?"

"Captain, let me clue you in on a little secret Greel left out of his report. He probably wrote down that he's staying late into my shift for 'special supervision.' What he didn't tell you is that 'special supervision' involves loading pornographic holos onto the main data viewer and making suggestive comments while it's running. Not exactly the best environment for a working relationship based on trust."

"I have received several complaints from you to that effect. A search of the system logs revealed no corroboration for your claims."

"Who do you think keeps those system logs? Of course there's nothing in there...Greel purged them. Same as the logs that show me accessing private holos. It was him. He just switched over the access logs to say it was me."

"These are very serious accusations, Miss Jawmet. If they're true, it's reason enough to have Greel thrown to the void. If they're false..."

"If you think they're false, I'll be the one that's vacked. Since I'm vacked either way, why not?"

Shaunson took a deep breath, scowled, and shifted in his seat. "You will notice that I decided to have this meeting in private. No recordings, no witnesses. You're a good woman, Miss Jawmet, strong and spirited. I want to give you a shot at a decent future. It comes down to this: I'm willing to receive your resignation, and your acceptance of the offer of marriage that has been posted for you. Clearly, the work environment is not going well for you. Hopefully, you will make a better wife and mother."

I snorted.

He pulled out a doc tablet and held it out to me. "This is my offer. Will you take it?"

I looked at the list. Everything was there, waiting for my signature. "I don't like this guy," I said. "He's just so...dull."

"Liking him isn't required, Miss Jawmet. There aren't that many men your age looking for wives in the first place." He glanced at the chrono on the wall. "And your meal shift is about to start. Think about my offer, Miss Jawmet, and consider where your path is leading you." He took the doc tablet back, touched a control on his console, and the elevator doors opened behind me.

I stared at him. "You do know that he really is doing all this to me, right? You're not that stupid. You know."

"Your meal shift is starting, Miss Jawmet. I wouldn't want you missing it."

I fumed all the way down the elevator, through the meal line, and to my regular seat. The room was crowded, but my usual table was empty, as it always was. Nobody wanted to sit with me. It was like they could smell failure.

"Hey, sweets."

I looked up. Everyone, that is, except Starholder Massey, who had just sat down across from me. "Sure. Why not." I looked down at my soy cubes and poked them with one of my eating-sticks.

"So..."

I looked up and glared at him. I did not want him to start a conversation, and I hoped he would get the message. He didn't.

"How did it go with Captain Shaunson?"

"He said I had to quit the communications center and get married."

"Really?"

He could at least have had the good grace to look disappointed. "It's all vack-yack," I said, grumbling into my bowl. "Greel is setting me up to take the blame for his vacking games."

"Well, that's not fair."

I looked across the room, catching sight of a happy couple with their newborn twins. "The Scouts really do grab the best and brightest, don't they? This place got a lot darker when Challers and Valka left."

Starholder nodded, completely missing the insult. I shifted my gaze to the empty chairs next to me, finally finding enough motivation to put one of the soy cubes in my mouth.

"So what are you going to do?"

"I'm not going to resign and marry you, if that's what you're asking, Starholder. I like being single."

"But...Captain Shaunson..."

"Captain Shaunson can jump out the airlock. I'm not quitting. I'm going to get evidence on Greel, good evidence, and make it stick."

"How?"

"Somehow." I tapped the eating-stick on the table. "I need to get access to a camera. I mean a real one, not one that's part of a console."

"Captain Shaunson has one. That's how he gets the holos for the news reports."

I snorted. "Yeah, right. Like he's going to let me borrow it."

"I can get it. What do you want to do with it?"

"I want to get a recording of what Greel does. I want to prove what a burner that guy is."

"You just leave that to me. I'll get you the camera."

"You'd do that for me?"

"I wouldn't have registered the marriage proposal if I didn't like you."

"I thought that was your parents."

"They just told me to register one, not who I should register it for."

I paused and looked him in the eye, but I couldn't see past that stupid smirk he always wore. I shook my head. "I don't want to be obligated to you. It's a big risk."

He shrugged. "I don't mind."

"No, it has to be a trade. What do you want?"

He started to shake his head again, but smiled shyly instead. "A kiss."

I frowned. "Starholder..."

"Too much? Alright, then if I get you the camera, just call me Star."

It occurred to me that I was the only person I knew who called Starholder by his full name. Even his instructors called him Star, and probably his parents too. "All right. Get me the camera for long enough to use it and I'll do that."

"Done." He stuffed the rest of the meal down his throat as quickly as he could eat it, then rose from the table. "Sorry to eat and run, but I've got a mission. You'll have that camera before your work shift starts."

I DIDN'T THINK he would be able to do it. After all, he had only minutes to accomplish it. But he caught up with me just as I was getting on the elevator to the communications cluster. Holding out a small optical block, he said, "Here you go."

"This is it?" I asked, turning it over in my hand. It didn't look like a device at all. There were no lenses, no knobs or buttons or other controls that I could identify. "How does it work?"

He pointed out a slight depression on one flat surface. "Hold your finger there and put your eye up to the edge. You'll see the controls. You slide your finger around to select them and tap to activate. It's Scout tech. Stuff we can't build in the fabricators here."

I did as he instructed and a faint orange glow appeared inside the gray translucent block. When I peered closely, it resolved into a ring of familiar symbols and icons. "Got it. Thanks...Star." I hesitated a moment, then got up on my tiptoes to kiss him on the cheek and quickly dodged into the elevator. "I gotta run." The elevator doors closed before I could see his reaction.

In spite of its advanced design, the symbols and commands seemed to be the same as on our own technology. I set the thing to record images and audio continuously until someone shut it off or it ran out of memory. I doubted the latter would happen.

When the doors opened again, Greel was at his usual station, leaning back in his chair, boots up on the console surface. Greasy hair the dull color of asteroid dust clung to his blotchy scalp. He glanced up from his console and leered. "I'd have thought you weren't coming back, girlie. Guess you just can't get enough of my quality entertainment." He hooked his thumb over his shoulder at the big screen on the wall.

I rolled my eyes. "I come here because it's my job, sir. Not because of you or those stupid holos you put up." I set the camera down on the top of my console where it had a good vantage point of the whole room, including the big screen. I thumbed my console and logged in, settling down into my seat. "Mr. Greel, I have the information watch."

"Scheduled data warehouse maintenance complete, nothing to report," he said, and I saw the indicator come up on my console to tell me I was, indeed, the one responsible for the communications cluster now. Sure enough, as soon as the formalities were observed, he started with his same old routine. "Well, take a look at this. Looks like Keelie and Dack are at it again." The holoscreen lit up, throwing pale orange light over the whole room. The sounds of energetic sex filled the room. "They sure are a pretty couple, eh?"

"Sir, I really don't want to watch this."

"Now girlie, what you need to do is relax."

I shuddered, hearing his boots drop to the deck, the chair squeak as he stood up, then his heavy footfalls as he crossed the room. Hands came down on my shoulders, squeezing and kneading.

"Please stop, sir," I said, holding down the bile with the hope that his violations were being recorded. With luck, this would be the last evening I was forced to endure them.

"I said relax, girlie." His fingers dug deeper into my flesh. There was nothing relaxing about his touch.

I hunched my shoulders, gritted my teeth, and closed my eyes. *Last time*, I told myself. *This was the last time.*

"You wouldn't have convinced Shaunson to let you come back to work if you didn't want to be here," he said, bending down to whisper in my ear. "You wouldn't have come back if, deep down, you didn't like it. Why don't you just admit what you really want?"

I said nothing, concentrating on the block of optical plastic sitting on the console. That was my salvation, my hope. I could endure one more shift. Just one, then I would bring the recording to Shaunson and he would have to believe me.

Then his hand stopped moving. It left my shoulder. "What the vack is this?"

I opened my eyes and looked up. He had the camera in one hand, turning it over with a puzzled expression on his face. "How in the void did you get your hands on Captain Shaunson's cam?"

I grabbed for it but he snatched it away, stepping back into the middle of the tiny room. "I see your game now," he said, waggling it at me. "I see your game! Well, it's not going to work, girlie-girl. Not going to work." His words were defiant, but there was panic in his eyes. He suspected that his actions had been recorded. He could smell trouble coming.

With increasing urgency, he turned the block over and over. "How does it work? Tell me! Tell me how it works!"

"Vack you, Greel. You're done hurting me. You're done humiliating me. It ends now."

He was looking for a way out, only there was nothing he could do. So he took the only option available to him.

"Erase it!" he shouted, grabbing my arm. His panic-fueled grip was painfully strong. "Erase it now!"

I spat in his face. "Forget it, burner." I grabbed the cam and yanked it out of his hand.

He screamed, locked his arm around my throat, and we fell to the deck. The impact knocked the breath from my lungs and, with his arm across my windpipe, I couldn't draw another. My head swam, my eyes exploded with stars, and consciousness quickly slipped away.

chapter three

Challers, Port

"I REALLY DON'T think you're ready for it, Challers." Robert was speaking more clearly than when we had last talked to him. Either the paralysis that had slurred his speech was lifting its hold on him, or he was learning how to speak in spite of the disability. Talking to him through a holoscreen across Port's internal communications wasn't as good as seeing him face to face, but even so he seemed a good deal stronger than when we had seen him last.

"Why not?"

"Have you watched the Worthy programs? You know what they do?"

"Yeah, it looks like they spend most of their time enjoying themselves."

"Hah. Be more specific."

"Going to parties, chatting, having sex, and occasionally dueling."

"You see, this is why I don't think you're ready, Challers. The environment the Worthies live in is one of constant maneuvering for position and status, and if you can't see the subtext, then they're going to take you apart."

Valka spoke up. "All right, then teach us what we need to know."

"I can't. It's not that simple. It's something you just have to pick up."

"So you think we can't be Worthies without knowing how, and we can't learn how without being part of it."

Robert groaned.

"We're doing this, with your help or without it."

"All right. All right, I'll tell you how it's done. First, you're going to need to buy your gear. It's expensive, but if you haven't completely blown your reward from the plunder we brought back from Scout Headquarters, you should have enough credits. Talk to Portcon, that's a pretty simple matter. Once you make that order, though, that's when everything's going to start happening. As soon as you put on the orgone belt, you'll officially be a Worthy."

I shrugged. "Is that all it takes?"

"Officially, yes. But the other Worthies are going to want to size you up. Figure you out. You're going to get invitations to at least two gatherings. It doesn't really matter whose invitation you accept, because the same folks are going to be there no matter which one you go to—it's going to be all the ship captains looking for more crew to fill out their roster. Because of your training with the Scouts, you're going to be in high demand."

"That sounds like a good thing."

"It is, but it means you're going to have to be doubly careful about being maneuvered into a position that's not in your best interests."

"I see."

Robert sighed. "I doubt it. Challers, do you even know how the Pirate economy operates?"

"Economy?"

Robert shook his head in frustration. "How orgone flows through the society."

"Sure," I said. It seemed pretty obvious. "Port collects basal orgone from the Wards and uses it to propel it through space, just like a Merchant ship. And Portcon said something about Worthies getting a share of crisis and transcendent orgone?"

"That's true, but you're missing a critical element in the system." Robert raised a finger to punctuate his point. "Crisis orgone is released when someone feels hate or fear—transcendent orgone, when someone feels sympathy, love, or connectedness. They don't just happen, they happen because of things that happen to you."

I could see what he meant. I was missing something. "Don't you have to use it as soon as it's generated? If you wait too long, it just dissipates. That's why Scouts have sex in order to activate their jump drives, and why the Fleet has huge gladiatorial arenas in their battle cruisers."

He nodded. "That's right. But the Scouts don't know how to build orgone accumulators. We can store orgone. That's why our little raiding ships can stand up to their battle cruisers, and that's why we can exchange orgone as money."

Now I understood. "Okay, so the orgone that the Wards make gets channeled to the raiding ships, which are used by Worthies to go out on raids to bring stuff back."

He lay back in his chair and closed his eyes for a moment. "Exactly. That's the core of it. And it's the Worthies' job to inspire the Wards to make orgone. The more they inspire, the more often they can go out on missions."

It made sense. I nodded in appreciation. "And they inspire it by having sex and getting into fights."

"Yes, and by setting up a framework of drama around the sex and the fighting to give it all context. That's why they're constantly inventing reasons to form alliances, make promises, break them, betray, seduce, abandon, reconcile, and go through it all again. It's an unending cycle of emotional turmoil, and even though you know it's all an act, it still wears on you. That's why I went on that deep-cover assignment with the Scouts. I just had to get away from it all," Robert explained.

"So what you're saying is that the more drama, sex, and violence I'm part of, the more credits I'll make?"

"Pretty much."

"That doesn't sound too bad, actually. The fights aren't lethal, right?"

"No, but they can be damn painful, and humiliating if you lose."

"I've had worse. Robert, you rescued me from a Scout prison. You know what I've been through. So far, everything you've described is a walk in the park in comparison."

He smiled with the good half of his face. "I guess I'm underestimating you again, Challers. So why do you want to get into this in the first place?"

"Valka doesn't want to be an Ovor anymore. We're going to save up for a session in the gentank."

"Well! You better earn those credits quick."

"What? Why?"

"The only reason that's on the market at all is because we came back with a mostly unused gentank from one of the two Scout ships. As soon as that gentank gel is used up, there won't be any amount of money that will buy it. It just won't be there until someone brings back more of the gel and the Scouts control it. Very hard to get hold of."

"How long do you think it'll be available?"

"No idea. I've been away a long time. I'm sure there will be people maneuvering to get enough credits together."

I scowled. "And we're starting from behind."

"How much have you got left from your share when we arrived?"

"About two hundred thousand between us."

"Don't worry about that, then. Even after buying your gear, you're already strongly in the running. And what's more, the other Worthies won't know what you're after, as long as you don't tell anyone after you get your belt."

He shook his head and continued. "That's another thing I should warn you about. Once you get your belt, your privacy is over. Wards will be able to see you, listen in on your conversations, pretty much anywhere you go, and Wards talk to Worthies all the time. Anything you say will almost certainly get back to your enemies. Once you start, you're pretty much on your own. You can promise each other that you're going to stay a team, but it's damn hard to keep secrets in that environment."

I nodded. "We'll figure out a way."

"You do that." He didn't look convinced. "Just as long as you understand, if you think you're going to go into this and stay a couple, you're going to have a really hard time of it. People are going to try to break you up, get between you. Talk about this before you start. Lay down some rules, rules you can live by, to show that you're holding on to your commitment to each other, because everything is going to be different after you put on your belts."

"Robert, we were Scouts. We've been through the whole jealousy thing."

"This is different. But I guess that's all the help I can give you right now. I'm getting tired. Take care, and stay in touch."

"We will."

The link cut off and Valka and I were left alone. She climbed up onto the foot of my chair with her legs hanging off one side. "You don't mind that people will be watching us? I mean, all the time?"

I smiled. "I look pretty good, and you...you're drop-dead gorgeous. We have nothing to be ashamed of. Is that what worries you most? Having sex with people watching?"

"I've never even imagined it."

I swung my feet down to sit next to her, nuzzled her neck, and put my arm around her waist. "Why don't you imagine it now?"

"That there's someone watching us?"

"Lots of someones. Imagine there are cameras all over the room, recording our every move." I felt her body stiffen. "There might be, you know. There might be cameras here right now." I took her earlobe between my lips and felt her tension ease a bit.

She ran one hand through my hair. "You don't know that."

"Pretend. Remember when we were kids? We played pretend all the time."

"We were children."

"And I hope we never lose touch with it. Come on. Pretend." I slipped one hand up under her shirt and played with a nipple, making it turn hard in my fingers.

"Mmm, you're distracting me."

"I bet the Wards are going to love seeing those big, juicy breasts of yours. Let's take off that top and show them off." I pulled back to give her room and saw a bright flush creep up onto her face.

She pulled her shirt up and off, releasing her breasts. She crossed her arms over them, but with four there was more going on than she could really hide.

"Gorgeous," I said, bending down to pull one hand away so I could kiss the chocolate tip. "They're going to love seeing you."

"Challers, hold on a moment," she said in a serious tone. "This whole 'people are watching us' thing? It doesn't really do much for me."

"No? But it's so sexy! Just imagine..."

"No," she said. "It's not. Not for me. But I can see that it's sexy for you. You like the idea of showing me off, showing off what we can do, maybe even showing yourself off."

I drew back. "What are you saying?"

If she didn't want to become Worthies and the whole affair was a big waste of time, then it would be a very long time before we would be able to fuck again.

"What I'm saying is that I think you've got it backwards." She hopped off the chair and pulled my pants down as she knelt, letting my half-hard cock free. "What they want to see is this." She wrapped her hand around the base and squeezed, making the head immediately swell up and turn purple. She licked it. "Tastes marvelous." She inhaled. "Wonderful aroma."

I snickered.

"It is to me. And everyone watching is going to miss out on that. But they won't miss out on seeing my man get the blowjob of his life." She engulfed my cock with her mouth, eagerly running her tongue up and down the length as it swelled.

She had called me her man. The thought sent a surge of warmth through me and I wanted her more than I could remember ever wanting anything.

"Have you started taking the pills?" I asked, feeling my breath getting a little tight.

She paused, said, "Yes, but it says to give them seven days to have full effect," and went back to her task.

"Then I'll just have to...ah...wait, won't I?" The thought wasn't nearly as awful as it had been a few minutes before.

She reached into a pocket, pulled out a tiny metal sphere, and held it up to me.

I somehow managed to squeeze it open, revealing a small roll of some kind of film. "Huh?"

She stroked my cock with her hand. "It's a 'condom.' Here, let me show you. She pulled the little film from my hand and rolled it down over my cock, and then kissed the tip. "It keeps your semen from fertilizing me. If you were an Ovor too, it would be almost certain, but even so I don't want to take the risk."

"Neat." I watched as the membrane sealed itself tight against my skin, except for a small pocket on the end.

She ran her hand along my shaft. "How does it feel?"

"It's like there's nothing there."

"Oh, good." She stroked my shaft. "Because your audience wants you to feel everything." She gave me another lick. "Absolutely everything."

Instantly, my mind was thrust back into my fantasy world with dozens of anonymous spectators just beyond the walls of my pod, watching our every move. She put her lips and tongue to work, teasing the tender spot just under the knob, and pushed it down her throat for a deep, satisfying thrust. I had to hold myself back from grabbing her head and pushing in.

She stood up with a satisfied grin and turned to bend over the chair. "Go ahead. I know you've been waiting. I've been waiting too. I want you inside me."

I wondered, briefly, what it would be like to have sex this way with her after what she has been through, but I didn't need to worry. She was as hot and wet as ever, squeezing around my cock as I thrust in.

"Vack, I've missed this," I breathed. The power of the act washed through me like a wave and I found myself thrusting as hard and as fast as I could, heedless of anything but getting to orgasm as quickly as possible.

A little voice in the back of my mind scolded me for not seeing to Valka's pleasure before getting my own, but I could feel her fingers dancing between her legs, and knew I could trust her to do what she felt was best, and to tell me if she needed anything from me. Within a minute or so her own moans and cries were joining mine in the tiny room. When I stiffened and felt the sweet flood of release, she was not far behind. As I steadied myself through a wave of post-orgasm dizziness, she made a long, low growl and her pussy fluttered in climax against my cock.

I pulled out and inspected the condom. The bulb at the tip had grown, filled with my milky fluid. I tried to get a grip on it to slip it off, but nothing happened.

"Hey," I said, "it won't let go."

"Hmm?" She turned around to look. "Just wait until you're fully soft. It should just slip off then."

I caught sight of her breasts, dribbling milk down their slopes, and getting soft again suddenly was something of a question.

She giggled and shook her head. "You get aroused by just about anything, don't you?"

"No," I said, leaning down to kiss her tenderly on the lips and caress one damp breast, "just anything associated with you."

She swatted me playfully on the chest. "Come on, we need to talk." She got some washcloths from the hygiene station and handed me one. "I've been thinking about what Robert said."

"What, while we were having sex?"

She smiled crookedly, glancing at the floor as she sponged the milk off her chest. "In spare moments."

"Okay, so what have you got?"

"Robert said we should have some ground rules. Things we can do to show that no matter what else happens, we're still first with each other. How about if we agree not to have sex with anyone we haven't both met?"

I nodded, finally able to get the condom off of my cock. It hung from my fingers in an elongated teardrop shape. "That sounds like a good idea." I dropped the condom in the sanitary disposal. "And how about if, when we're at a party or something together, we don't split up unless it's agreed by both of us. Check in first."

"Agreed." Valka pulled her clothes back on. "That'll show everyone that we think of ourselves as a couple. And we have to make sure, every day, to fill each other in on anything that we've done. When folks figure out that we don't have any secrets from each other, maybe they'll treat us as a team."

"I'm not sure I really want to hear too much about that," I said, cleaning off the spooge. The condom had certainly made cleaning up a lot easier.

"Well, it doesn't have to be too detailed if you don't want it to be."

"Are you saying you want to hear all about it when I have sex with other people?"

She made the coy smile I knew so well. "You were always the jealous one. I think I'd like hearing about it when you're having fun. It would get me going."

"Really?" I gathered up my clothes and put them back on.

"Really. Sometimes, back at Scout Headquarters, when it was bad between me and Masters, I would imagine you with Shirley." She snuggled up close, drawing me into a gentle embrace.

I wondered what had happened to Shirley. She had come with us when we escaped from Scout Headquarters. In fact, it had been she and her copilot, Masters, who had rescued Valka. I hadn't heard from her since we arrived.

"You miss her, don't you?" Valka was looking up into my eyes.

"Uh, no."

Valka smiled. "You're a terrible liar, you know that, Challers Dizen? You're going to have to do something about that if you want to be a Worthy." She patted my chest. "It's okay if you miss her. I know you're not going to discard me for her."

"I am the luckiest guy in the universe, you know that?" I leaned in and kissed her.

A playful sparkle lit in her eyes. "Yes, I do."

chapter four

Renedy, Stakroya Station

I WOKE UP to docking clamps locking and unlocking on my skull over and over again.

At least, that's what it felt like.

I groaned and looked around, squinting. The lights were out except for some emergency illumination strips around the door, but I could tell I was in the infirmary. The soft beeping I could hear was a machine measuring my heartbeat.

There was another bed next to mine, and two more above those, but they were all empty. I was alone in the small room. "Is anyone there?" I asked. My voice felt scratchy and sore, and talking only made my head feel worse.

"Just a minute, Miss Jawmet, just a minute." A door opened, letting a stream of blinding light into the room. I knew the voice. It was Dr. Klane. The few times I had been down to the infirmary, he had always been nice to me, so it seemed very odd for him to be inflicting that terrible light on me.

The door shut, and he shuffled over to the bed and put his hand gently on my wrist. "And how are we this evening, Miss Jawmet?"

"I don't know about you, but I feel ground up and recycled."

"Well, that's to be expected. You had a nasty fall there, miss."

"It wasn't a fall," I said. "Greel tried to kill me. Choked me." My voice still wouldn't work right.

He grunted and felt around my head, finding a spot on the back of my skull that hurt even worse than anywhere else. "Choking doesn't give you a concussion, miss. Do you remember anything else?"

I moaned and lay back down on the bed. "I want to talk to the captain."

"He's already on his way, miss. Just relax. Everything's going to be just fine."

"How did I get here?"

"Don't you worry about that, miss." He patted my hand and

smiled. "We will take very good care of you."

I wasn't going to get any answers, so I just lay back onto the mattress and closed my eyes. It made my head hurt a little less. There was a faint, muffled ring from the next-door chamber, and Dr. Klane shuffled out. The light was a lot less painful with my eyes shut, but I still burrowed under the sheet rather than endure it any longer than I had to.

The door opened again, and there was another voice. I couldn't quite make out the words, but I knew who it was—Captain Shaunson. After a minute, the door closed.

"Miss Jawmet."

I groaned.

"Renedy."

I poked my head out just far enough to squint at him.

He spoke slowly, as if each word were individually selected and decided upon in strict order, according to arcane procedures of captaincy of which only he was aware. "It has become clear to me that you and Mr. Greel cannot work together under any circumstances, and that the fault lies, at least in large part, with Mr. Greel himself. I have transferred Mr. Greel to new duties. He will not be causing you any further difficulties."

"Difficulties," I said.

He waited a few seconds. "Yes."

"He's the one who bashed my head against the deck, isn't he?"

"As I said, he has been dealt with."

"Dealt with. If he's still drawing air, it's a waste of good oxygen."

"I understand you are in a great deal of pain, so I will ignore your attitude."

I closed my eyes. "Just tell me if I get to keep my job."

"Yes. As soon as you are able, I expect you back at your position. After all, someone will need to train Mr. Greel's replacement, and as the senior communications specialist, I see no one else qualified for the job."

I relaxed. "Thanks."

"I'm going to assign Starholder Massey as your trainee."

I tried to keep my expression neutral, but he must have sensed my doubts.

"He will surprise you, Miss Jawmet. I'm certain. Now, rest up and heal. I need you back as soon as you are able so you can get started on Mr. Massey's training. But you must agree not to speak to anyone about what happened."

I shook my head and squinted at him. I couldn't believe my ears. "What?"

"I am willing to retain you in the communications cluster if you keep quiet. If you don't, there will be repercussions."

"All right. All right. I won't talk to anyone."

"Good. I'm glad we understand one another."

There was definitely more going on than I could get my head around, especially with the docking clamps still going off. I crawled back under the covers. After a few minutes, Dr. Klane came back, there was a pinch in my arm, and darkness crept up on me again.

As soon as I was able to get around on my feet again, Dr. Klane declared me healed and Captain Shaunson put me back on the duty roster. I still had headaches, but the bruises were healed and my job didn't require that much moving around anyways.

"You know," said Star, throwing his elbow over the back of his chair, "the communications cluster is where Challers and Valka always used to come to get away from everyone."

"Yeah. I know. Can we focus on the task, here? We've got a hundred reports and logs to assemble before the Scouts come around again. If we don't get moving, we're not going to have them ready in time. Nothing was encrypted with the right keys, and the formatting is wrong on about half of them."

"Right. Later." He clicked his tongue, turned back to his console, and tapped on some keys.

I hoped he was actually getting something done rather than just making noise. I also hoped that whatever work he was doing actually accomplished something. I had a solid suspicion that the misapplied crypto keys were his fault.

The intercom lit up on my console. "I've got it," I said, activating the circuit.

Pardik's voice came through. "Hey, I heard you had some trouble down there. Need some spare processing power? I got a backup server I'm not really doing anything with right now. You could take it for a few hours if it'll help you make your deadline."

His voice was just enough like his brother Challer's to make me remember him all over again, and the thought made me wince. "Thanks, but that's not exactly regulation and I don't want you to get in trouble."

"I'm the one making the offer, aren't I? I know the risk. If you need it, take it."

"I can't, Pardik. This has to be done on our own systems. It's a security thing."

My stomach gurgled.

"Uh...then maybe I can bring you something?" he asked. "Like maybe some food? Have you had lunch?"

"No. Or breakfast either."

"I'll be down in a minute." The connection closed and the room went quiet again except for the ventilation fans.

A file appeared in my work queue. I shook my head. I was having a hard enough time making a dent in the pile of work already in it without more arriving.

Then I saw the ORIGINATOR tag. "Star? Why are you sending me more vacking work?"

"It's not work. I thought you'd want to see it."

I tried to access the file. "It's garbage. Toss it."

"I don't think so. I found it in one of the memory spaces Greel supposedly scrubbed last week. It didn't have an entry in the directory, but when I did a base-level scan, there it was."

"Why are you poking around...wait." I tapped a few keys and sent a command after the mysterious file.

DECRYPTING... appeared on the screen. I went back to work while it processed. After a few minutes, I checked on it. FAILURE.

"What was that?" asked Star, looking over my shoulder.

"That was Greel's encryption key. Shaunson gave it to me when I took over the comm cluster."

"Hunh."

"Wait...vack." I tried again. This time, I waited and watched the progress as the program did its work.

DECRYPTING...SUCCESS.

"Which key was that?"

"Mine. The burner had my key. He was probably using it to encrypt hidden files to throw off suspicion if anyone found it." I queried the decrypted file. It was a holocam recording.

"You going to open it?"

"Yeah. Yeah, I think I gotta."

"Maybe you ought to show it to Shaunson first."

"No. No, if I do that, I'll never see it again, and nothing will change. This is Greel's work, but it's got my keyprint on it. I gotta see what it is." I opened it.

The small holoscreen to the right of my console lit up. It was a recording of an entire room, a big one, maybe twelve square meters in size. There was a big bed, a sitting area, and a private galley. The door opened and two figures entered. The first was Shaunson. The second, I didn't know. He had on baggy black pants and a shirt belted at the waist, and there was a weapon I didn't recognize slung over his shoulder next to his long black braid.

"I don't have anything for you," said Shaunson. "The new guy in the organization. He's watching too close."

The stranger grunted. "So I came all this way for nothing."

"My hands are tied."

"Mine aren't, Billeck. If it makes it any easier for you, I can shoot up the place a bit on the way out, make it look like the real thing."

"You know that's not going to work."

The stranger walked up behind Shaunson and wrapped his arms around the captain's chest. "I'm sorry," he said. The gesture was familiar, affectionate...erotic. He whispered something too faint for me to make out, and then Shaunson turned and they kissed, passionately, desperately.

We watched, mesmerized, as the two men stripped off their clothes and tumbled into the bed. I couldn't tear my eyes away. The man who had been talking to Shaunson—and who I was watching receive expertly delivered fellatio from him—had to be a Pirate. There was no other explanation for his outlandish dress and their cryptic conversation.

"Oh, vack," said Star.

"Vack is right. This must be why Shaunson was so reluctant to make trouble for Greel. He had this hanging over Shaunson the whole time. If the Scouts ever got hold of this..."

"He'd be in big trouble," said Star.

"Dead counts as big trouble, yes."

As the men writhed and moaned and kissed and sucked and gasped, I found myself filled with more emotions than I could name. Fear stabbed through me. Fear that I now knew something I was not meant to know, something that made me dangerous and therefore made Shaunson dangerous to me. Alongside that was the thrill of being privy to a deep, dark secret.

And yes, I was getting hot. I could feel my flimsies getting squishy and a swelling in my sensitive bits. This was the main reason I kept watching.

When the Pirate groaned and threw an arm over his face, Shaunson crawled up next to him and caressed his chest, running his hand over the thick hair sprouting from that muscular torso.

"Come with me," said the Pirate.

"I can't. I have duties here. If I go with you, these people will suffer."

"They will suffer anyways."

"Worse, if I leave."

The Pirate kissed him. "Always a man of duty."

"These people are my family," he said. "They depend on me."

"I understand."

"I might be able to shake something loose," said Shaunson. "How long have you got?"

"An hour or so."

"Then I had better get to it. Check Docking Bay Three before you go." He planted yet another passionate kiss, and then rose from the bed. He dressed in silence and, while I couldn't quite see or hear enough details to say for sure, it seemed like he was crying.

I sniffled in sympathy.

The recording came to the end and the projector popped off. "That explains why Greel isn't dead for what he did to you," Star said. "He's probably been holding this over Shaunson for years. We need to tell him we found it."

"No, are you crazy? We can't do that. If he knows we've seen this, he'll get rid of both of us."

"He's not that way."

"Star, you poor naïve boy. Everyone is that way when they think they have no way out. We are each going to need a copy, stuck somewhere that the other doesn't know where it is, that we can get to if we need to."

I started typing commands to make my own encrypted copy of the file using Greel's key, back-dating the history tags to before the old bastard had been removed from his post. I certainly wasn't going to leave my own fingerprints all over it.

Star sighed and ran his fingers through his hair. "All right."

chapter five

Challers, Port

IT TURNED OUT that we couldn't just order the orgone belts and have them delivered to our pods. We could only schedule appointments with the technician who fitted them. There was a workshop one level down from the Boulevard, near one of the major elevators. Valka and I walked in to find a spacious waiting room with a dais half surrounded by mirrors at the far end.

A woman immediately strode out of a side door with a big smile on her face, dressed in a black coverall decorated with shiny bits of chain and sparkling clasps. Her broad, infectious smile lit up the room. "Welcome, our two newest Worthies!"

She took our hands. "My name is Vivian Muse, but you can just call me Viv." She gently pulled us toward the middle of the room. "And don't you look fabulous? Oh, they are going to absolutely eat you up. Now, you followed my instructions, yes?"

Valka nodded. "Yep. No sexual activity of any kind for twenty-four hours and no holo programs. Meditation and quiet all day."

Viv gave me a raised eyebrow. "You too, right? I'd hate to have to reschedule you for tomorrow."

"Me too." I glanced around the room nervously. "Wasn't easy."

Viv chuckled. "I'm sure." Then her smile vanished. "Now, before we start, I just want to remind you that this session is going out over the public net. Officially, your lives became matters of public interest as soon as you came through those doors. If you want to back out, now would be the best time."

I took a deep breath and looked down at Valka. "No. We're doing it."

Valka nodded.

Viv smiled again. "Wonderful. Let me explain how this is going to work. You'll stand here," she said, indicating the dais, "while we do a preliminary fitting of the base garment and put on the calibration framework. We'll be able to measure exactly where your energy flows are strongest and place the collectors at the most advantageous positions. Now, who's first?"

Valka looked at me, and I stepped up onto the dais.

"Very good. If you'll just strip down, please?"

I quickly pulled off my clothes, which Viv took and set aside. When I stood up straight again, I noticed Valka smiling at me in the mirror. She winked and I smiled back.

A delivery panel opened just to the side of the mirrors, and Viv took a band of elastic material from it and wrapped it around my middle. It ran from just under my ribs down to my hips and was tight but very well fitted. It was finely textured and roughly the same color as my skin. The closure ran along my belly, a seam so skillfully made I could barely see it.

"How do I take it off?"

"You just run your finger down the front. It'll recognize your body energy."

"Can I try it?"

"Certainly. Once you get your own belt, you will want to keep it on most of the time. It's quite difficult to damage, and if you take it off, you'll lose the stored orgone."

I ran my finger a short way down the closure and it opened easily. I closed it up again and looked down at Viv. "Good, so what's next?"

"Next, we calibrate the crisis orgone." She took a black mesh band and wrapped it over the belt, closing it up similarly to the first.

Suddenly, I was plunged into darkness. The only light came from beyond the mirror panes, which had suddenly become windows onto a hallway where flames roared out of vents and doorways. I gasped and pulled back, glancing around for somewhere to escape.

The lights came up again and the holocaust ended. My heart hammered in my chest.

Viv moved up, holding a small tablet. "Good, good. We've got a good reading there. Now for the transcendent orgone."

Valka giggled behind me.

I turned and scowled back at her. "What are you laughing about?"

"Oh, the look on your face. Sorry."

Viv pointed a finger in her direction. "You, my young Worthy, can now pay him back for that. Can you give him a quick little orgasm? For the calibration, of course."

"Of course." Valka walked up to the dais with a playful smile on her face. The dais was just high enough to bring her face even with my crotch, so she simply took my hips in her hands and sucked my cock into her mouth.

I looked down—first at Valka, and then over at Vivian. She

pretended to ignore what Valka was doing, seemingly concentrating on her tablet instead, but when I glanced at the mirrors, I caught her watching our reflection. She saw me catch her and a twitch of a smile graced her lips. I smiled back and Viv's gaze fell downward. Her eyes moved back and forth between my face and Valka's, checking in with me in the mirror every few seconds.

We were being watched.

It was every bit the charge I hoped it would be. Electricity shot up my spine and it seemed like the top of my head was going to fly off, I was so hot.

And then there were the people who would be watching from their pods. The Wards, scattered throughout the ship, would be watching the holograms coming from this very room to get their first look at Valka and me.

I didn't last even two minutes before I threw my head back, made a growling groan, and filled Valka's mouth.

Viv handed us a couple of towels, and then stripped the belt from my abdomen. "All right, now while we get that ready, let's get your lady-friend here fitted up."

Valka pulled off her clothes with a matter-of-fact air and mounted the dais.

"We don't get many Ovors here," said Viv, bringing a second belt over. "I don't think there's been a recruiting raid on an Ovor station in years."

"Oh, I wasn't born an Ovor," said Valka. "The Scouts put me through the gentank."

Viv fitted the belt around Valka's waist. It came up just below her lower pair of breasts. "Really? Well, how do you like it?"

"It's pretty nice, actually. And Challers likes boobs, so that's a double bonus." Her lie had come out without a moment's pause.

Viv clucked, smiling. "You better be careful. Too many puns will get you challenged to a duel."

Valka chuckled. "That wasn't on purpose."

I asked, "So how are you going to do the crisis orgone calibration? I mean, she's got to know what's coming." I needed to change the subject before Viv's questions got too close to our reason for becoming Worthies.

The lights went out again, and the lightshow appeared behind the mirror panes. I heard Valka gasp, and when the lights came up again, she had her hand between her breasts, her eyes wide with shock.

"Like that," said Vivian with a sparkle in her eye. "The black piece wasn't necessary. We can do the calibration just with the base garment. All that's necessary is a little scare."

"So, why did you use it on me?"

Viv shook her head. "So your lady here wouldn't be expecting it now, of course. I hope you don't mind a bit of theater." She stood away from the dais. "Would you care to do the honors, then?"

"Gladly."

Valka sat down on the edge of the dais and spread her legs for me. "Standing up wouldn't be a good idea," she explained. "I always get all weak in the knees."

I gave Vivian a wink. "By the way, we're going to need more towels."

I knelt at Valka's feet and took her in my arms for a deep kiss and moved down slowly, leaving a zigzagging course of kisses across her chin, her collarbone, her shoulder, meandering to one breast, and then another. By the time I brought my mouth down towards her mons, she was already warming up, already breathing deeply, already becoming nice and slippery wet.

I parted the folds of her pussy and applied my lips and tongue with careful precision. When Valka lay back onto the dais and began stroking the top of my head, I glanced up to see Viv looking down at us, her hands holding her tablet to her belly, a slight flush coming to her cheeks.

I imagined she had taken this job for just this reason—to get to be there and watch when new Worthies were made. I wondered what happened when she needed to calibrate the transcendent orgone collectors and there wasn't a second potential Worthy near at hand. I imagined she would gladly provide the service herself. Would she break that professional demeanor? How far would she go?

Before I got a chance to find out, Valka shuddered and let out a trembling cry, arching her back and pressing her pussy into my face. Tiny fountains of milk sprang from her breasts, leaving little droplets scattered over her chest and the top of the dais. They pulsed a few times and slowed to a dribble as her orgasm faded.

Valka took a big, fluffy towel from Vivian's hand and wrapped it around her chest to absorb the milk that still flowed from her breasts.

"Well! Quite a strong reading there. Very good." Vivian tapped on her tablet. "And your belt is now ready, Challers."

It didn't look any different than it had the first time, except for a few hard knots running up the spine, and here and there under the surface of the fabric. She put it around my waist and closed it up. At the top of the closure was a small tube that ran through a set of clips around under my left arm.

"This is your transfer tube. This allows you to transfer your own personal orgone to the orgone banks for credit, or to transfer it to someone else." She pointed to a Y-connector at the end of the tube. "This is the outflow tube, and this is the inflow. Depending on how you connect it to someone else's belt, you will either give all your orgone to that person, or accept it all for yourself."

"Yes," Valka said. "I saw that on some of the duels I watched. Losers have to give up all the orgone they collected during the duel."

"That's the usual result, yes."

The delivery panel opened again, revealing Valka's new belt, plus a couple of bundles of black and white fabric. After helping Valka into her belt, Viv took the bundles of fabric from the panel and handed one to each of us. They turned out to be the Pirate "uniform" of loose white shirt and black pants. We put them on and Viv stood back and smiled.

"Congratulations," she said. "You are now full-fledged Worthies. Now remember, keep the belts on at all times; if you take them off, you forfeit your status as a Worthy and half your orgone credits." Her serious tone turned cheery again, and she cocked her head to one side and smiled. "Have fun!"

FROM THE ORGONE belt shop, our next stop was the Boulevard. According to everything we had seen, a Worthy never went about unarmed and the Boulevard was where we would find our dueling weapons.

The shop had a wide variety of shapes and styles—from tiny holdouts all the way up to huge shoulder-slung cannons—but all the weapons operated on the same principle. They fired an intense infrared laser pulse, powerful enough to instantly vaporize the surface layer of whatever they struck, causing a tiny explosion but very little thermal shock. This blast was the vehicle for doing damage to the target, rather than the laser itself.

The weapons generally had three settings: "tag," "stun," and "kill." Set on "tag," the beam was wide and would feel like getting slapped. On "stun," the beam was narrower and had the force of a hammer blow. Set on "kill," the beam was needle-thin and could burst holes in a person's flesh. For serious combat, each of the weapons also had a receptacle for the orgone belt's transfer tube, allowing them to be powered by crisis orgone—and thus become far more powerful on the "kill" setting.

The only places on the body where the "tag" or "stun" intensity would risk serious injury were the eyes and ears. For that reason, the weapon shop also sold various styles of hardened protectors. Many of them also served as microphones and cameras for Port's entertainment network to allow "Worthy's eye view" reports from duels.

Most of the holsters for these weapons were low-slung hip holsters designed for quick draw rather than comfort, though some of the smaller weapons had cross-draw holsters that kept them higher on the hip. Valka opted for the smaller type with a sleek, silvery design on the holsters. It ended up looking more like a piece of jewelry than a weapon.

For myself, I chose a decent-sized item that looked intimidating enough without being clumsy or looking like I had something to prove. The shopkeeper said it was a reliable, well-respected unit. I chose a fast-draw holster that hung low on my thigh. Valka and I took the opportunity to practice drawing them and putting them away, plus we took a few turns at the target range to get a feel for how they worked.

I thought I was ready.

chapter six

Challers, Port

WHEN WE CAME OUT of the range, a small robot rolled up and projected a hologram in the air in front of us. "Welcome, Worthies!" said the transparent figure of a friendly looking man in the familiar Pirate uniform. "Your first big party is starting! We're all waiting for you here at the Blackguard Club."

The man winked out and was immediately replaced by a woman in similar gear. "Congratulations on becoming Worthies. Would you mind stopping by the Lonely Asteroid for a drink? We'd like to get to know you."

Before a third could pop up, Valka squatted down and addressed the robot. "Give me a Portcon interface, please."

The familiar, nondescript head appeared in the holographic projection and nodded. "What can I do for you, Worthy Valka Parl?"

"Tell me, how far is the Blackguard Club?"

"The Blackguard Club is forty-two meters forward."

"And how far to the Lonely Asteroid?"

"The Lonely Asteroid is thirty-seven meters aft."

She stood up and smiled. "The Lonely Asteroid it is."

I chuckled. "Because it's closer."

"We've got no other way to evaluate them. Might as well go with the shortest walk."

She looked down again. "Robot, please show us the way to the Lonely Asteroid."

It beeped and rolled away, staying a couple of meters ahead of us as we strolled. Valka put her arm around my waist and squeezed, and I put my arm around her as well. It was a little awkward to walk that way, but it felt good to have her there beside me.

A small crowd of Wards formed around us pretty quickly, shouting questions and waving to get our attention. Above their heads, camera-bots hovered on little air jets, pointing at us from several directions. Most of the questions were fairly innocuous—like "Are you a couple?" and "Whose crew are you going to join?" But some were just plain rude: "Who do you think you are?" and "Don't you think you're kind of scrawny to be a Pirate?" and "Do you take it in the ass?"

Valka just shook her head at most of the questions, and I waved people away, but they wouldn't go. Finally, I stood up on a bench and addressed the crowd. "All right, listen, people. I'd love to stay and answer your questions, but this is no way to go about it."

The crowd stopped and grumbled.

"You can get a better look watching from your pods. I'm not answering any questions in the street."

A few stubborn stragglers shouted anyways, but when it became clear that we weren't going to answer any questions, they quieted down and most of them drifted away.

"Nicely handled," said a Worthy leaning against a nearby rubbish-collector robot. She fell into step beside me as we walked. "Some new Worthies have had to shoot a couple of them before they'd leave off." She had long blonde hair drawn into a loose ponytail.

"Believe me, I was thinking about it."

She chuckled and nodded to me, and then to Valka. "My name's Angela Cape. Pleased to meet you."

"You're with Madden's Marauders," said Valka.

"A fan?" asked Angela, raising an eyebrow.

Valka shrugged. "No. I just do my homework."

Angela gave her a nod of respect. "Fair enough. So what do you think of us?"

Valka glanced ahead. "I think your captain's a bit too high-strung."

"Helen? Oh, she's okay. Anyone she smacks around deserves what they get for messing with her. Really, she doesn't get rough with anyone who doesn't deserve it." She winked. "Or else folks who like it."

"If you'll excuse us," said Valka with exaggerated politeness, "we'd like to make our entrance together, just the two of us. I'm sure you understand?"

"Oh, of course," said Angela. "You go ahead."

"Thank you."

A sign over the door of the Lonely Asteroid read, "Closed for private party." But the doors opened as soon as we approached.

The Lonely Asteroid was a friendly, well-lit place with high ceilings and a long bar running down one side of the room. The other three walls were broken into conversation nooks big enough to seat six to eight people, all surrounding an open area with a few small tables. Music played in the background, but the primary sound was conversation.

The place was full of people. Most of them dressed in the standard Worthy garb, but there were a few folks there without the uniform as well. As soon as the doors closed behind us, everyone turned our way. I couldn't believe how many there were, all there to see us.

A round, lumpy man about the shape of your average asteroid walked up with a pair of tall, narrow glasses filled with red liquid and handed them to us.

"Worthy Challers Dizen and Worthy Valka Parl!" He put special emphasis on the word *Worthy*. "I am your host, Kensington Book." He took a third glass from a robot following closely behind him and raised it in our direction. "Welcome to the Lonely Asteroid!"

A cheer went up and he tipped the glass back to drain half its contents. Most of the crowd did the same. Valka and I looked at each other, raised our glasses, and drank. The drink wasn't much like the one taste of wine I'd had at Scout Headquarters, but it was sweet and went down easily.

"I like this," said Valka, holding up her half-empty glass. "What is it?"

"Ah," said Kensington, his broad smile growing even broader. "This is what we call Brandywine. We brew it right here on the premises. Not synthesized, no! Actual fermentation, actual distillation." He had a loud, dramatic way of speaking, as if he were on a stage. Given the number of people still watching us, I had to admit that he was.

"Now, if you'll permit me, I think the first order of business will be to introduce you around."

Valka glanced around the room. "I'm pretty sure they all know who we are by now, and I think I recognize most everyone here."

"I don't," I said quietly, starting to feel like a dunce for not studying the Worthies more before we started.

"Yes, well, let's honor the formalities anyways, shall we?" Kensington slipped in between us, taking our elbows in his meaty hands and guiding us towards the nearest alcove, a half-circle bench covered with pillows and cushions. Names and faces ran past me as we did a slow orbit of the room, moving from booth to booth. I struggled to keep them matched up in my head, memorizing them in case it became important later. Valka, on the other hand, seemed to know most of the Worthies in the room by sight, and even managed to ask a few meaningful questions as we went along.

The Worthies were very pleased to have us join them. There was a constant need for crew and anyone volunteering to be a Worthy was welcome. Some of them made very up-front requests for us to sign on with their raiding parties, but Valka made sure to demur in every case.

I noticed badges clipped to people's shirts. They didn't appear to denote membership in a crew because some badges were just about everywhere, and some were quite rare. There wasn't time or opportunity to ask about them, however, so rather than look like a goof, I kept my mouth shut.

And then we came to the table for David's Destroyers. David lounged back in the deepest arc of the booth. He had his arms up behind his head and his feet stretched out under the table with Krinna nestled up under his shoulder. I had watched the two of them having sex just a couple days previous! It felt very strange to be meeting them face to face after that, and I found myself even more tongue-tied than I had been with the other crews.

Luckily, Valka covered for me. She was bouncing with excitement, very pleased to meet them. "Is Rendika coming today?" she asked.

"Delayed," said David. "Handling something. She'll be along."

"Oh, excellent," said Valka, and we moved along to the next table.

When we were finally done with the introductions, Kensington took his leave of us and wished us luck.

Valka took another glass of Brandywine from a serving robot and glanced over at the table where David and Krinna sat. "Did you see how confident he was? Definitely not trying to sell anything."

"Has he got reason to be confident? It seems to me that a successful captain wouldn't have much trouble keeping a crew together." I glanced around the room, taking another sip from the glass I had been nursing since we arrived.

"His second-in-command got enough credits together to get his own ship. David won't have the opening in his crew for long."

"It sounds like you want to sign up with him right away."

"Well, we can't both sign up. A crew has to have four members, and he's only got one slot free. But I wouldn't mind hanging out with them for a while."

"Then let's go on over."

Valka led me straight over and gave David a big smile. "Mind if we join you?"

David made a welcoming gesture, but said nothing.

We slid into the booth, Valka arranging to be next to David.

I noticed a black badge clipped to his shirt and nodded to it. "I see a lot of people wearing badges. Do they mean something, or are they just decoration?"

"Lots of things," said a fifth Worthy who sat down opposite me. She had bright orange-red hair and a slight frame, and had a black badge clipped to her shirt just like David's, along with a string of others of various colors.

I nodded to her. "You're Rendika, then?"

"Yep. Pleased to meet you...?"

"Challers Dizen. What's the black one for? I don't see too many of those around."

"Shouting at the void." She tugged at it briefly.

"What's that?" I asked.

David shook his head. "You wouldn't be interested. It's a pretty heavy deal."

Rendika gave me an appraising look. "Oh, I don't know. He might surprise you."

"You're a Scout, right?" asked David.

"Used to be," I said, feeling my pulse starting to thud. "We stole a couple of ships and destroyed a research station on our way out."

"Yeah. Heard about that," said David, glancing over my head. "Pity there weren't any recordings."

"What are you saying?"

He leaned back in his chair and looked up at the ceiling. "Oh, Challers..." He sighed. "We see a lot of people pay a lot of money to become Worthies without really knowing what they're getting into. They see the glamour and the luxury, but in the long run, they really don't have the spine for it."

Rendika reached across the table and squeezed my arm. "Don't listen to him. He's just trying to get you worked up."

"So tell me about this *shouting at the void*," I said.

"It's an amazing experience. I've done it four times. You know that the Boulevard is the topmost deck of the ship, right? Well, the Lonely Asteroid has a special airlock. Two worthies go in. We gradually lower the pressure to about thirty percent and adjust the mix to pure oxygen. It's low, but not a problem for people in good physical shape, plus we give you an injection that helps protect your body. The two Worthies have sex, and when one of them has passed the point of no return and is about to come, we open the airlock the rest of the way."

"What?" Valka nearly jumped out of her seat. "That's insane!"

Rendika chuckled and shrugged. "Maybe so. But it's an incredible rush. The airlock stays open for about five seconds. Usually, nobody even passes out. Contrary to what you might think, the internal pressure of your body keeps you from getting bubbles in your blood. The airlock is pressurized again to thirty percent, then gradually the atmosphere is returned to normal."

I felt the blood drain from my face. The very concept was terrifying.

David took one look at me and said, "See? Don't tease him, Rendika. He's not ready for that."

Krinna sat up and waved at the rest of the bar. "There's a reason you don't see too many black badges, Worthy. There's no shame in being sensible and turning it down. It's not instant death, but it's not without risk, either. Personally, I think you'd be better off just leaving it. It is crazy." She winked. "Who cares that the rooters love it?"

I looked at Valka. Her eyes pleaded and she shook her head slowly. "Challers, no."

I glanced around the table. "Do you mind if we have a moment?"

"Go ahead," said David with a slight twitch in the corner of his mouth.

Valka followed me to one of the tables toward the center of the room. A couple of Worthies approached us, but I waved them off. "Give us a minute, please."

As soon as we were something close to alone, Valka leaned close and hissed in my ear. "You want to do this, don't you!"

"I was thinking about it."

"No, Challers. This is vacuum. The void. Who knows what could happen to you!" She clutched my arm so hard it felt like she'd crush me. "I can't lose you. Not now. Not after all we've been through to be together."

"You're not going to lose me. You want to impress David, don't you? Look, we got into this to take risks. It's not like I'm getting into a duel or going off on a raiding cruise. They've got it all figured out. It can't be that risky for real. It's just a matter of facing down your fears. Come on, do it with me." I pulled her close. "It'll be great."

"I can't imagine how."

"You heard Rendika. The Wards love it. I bet it pulls in lots of credits."

She sniffed and looked up into my face. "You think so?"

"It would have to. Danger, sex, drama? I bet there's orgone all over the place when one of these things goes on. Orgone is money, and money is what we need to get—" I stopped abruptly when Valka's eyes suddenly widened. *That was close*, I thought, remembering that we weren't supposed to talk about the gentank.

She shook her head at my near-mistake. "I'm going to watch you. I'm going to be right there watching you, and if anything even looks like it's going wrong, I'm going to call the whole thing off. You tell them. You tell them that if I say it stops, then it has to stop."

"I will."

She kissed me so hard I thought she might smother me. "I love you, Challers Dizen. Don't you ever forget that."

chapter seven

Challers, Port

WE WENT BACK to David's table and sat down. Rendika took one look at my face and said, "You're going to do it."

"I am. Valka's not ready for it yet, but I think I'll have a go."

"Oh, terrific!" Her beaming smile turned a little flirtatious and she waggled her eyebrows. "If Valka isn't going, have you got anyone in mind to partner with you?"

"I was hoping you would. If you've done it four times, then I'd expect you'd know all the ins and outs."

David snorted derisively.

"So to speak," I added.

Rendika pretended to consider the idea for a moment, and then clapped her hands over her head, summoning a robot to the table. "Prepare the upper airlock, and bring Challers and me the gear for screaming at the void."

The robot beeped an acknowledgment and scurried away.

Within moments, Kensington's booming voice was catching the attention of everyone in the hall. "Worthies! Worthies! Worthies! I have just been informed that the airlock is being prepared for a ritual!"

*Ooh*s and *aah*s echoed back from the crowd. Evidently, this was something that caught the attention of even jaded Worthies.

Kensington walked over and threw his arm in my direction. "I give you Worthy Challers Dizen and Worthy Rendika Prelain!"

Rendika hauled me to my feet. I glanced around nervously as everyone in the room raised their glasses in my direction. "Smile and wave," she said, barely audible over the cheers. "You're the center of attention for the next half hour or so."

I smiled and waved. "Do me a favor," I said to Kensington. "If Valka says she wants to stop it, then it stops, okay?"

He nodded. "Of course."

When I glanced back at Valka, she was giving me a smile that looked more like a wince.

"Good luck," she said.

The robot returned with a pair of autoinjectors, one labeled for me and the other for Rendika. She took the one labeled for me and had me hold out my arm to receive the injection. I managed to keep my head enough to follow the program and do the same for her.

Underneath the injectors there were two sets of folded-up garments in a stretchy, flesh-tone fabric. The robot handed one to me and one to Rendika, rolled to one side, and snapped a salute with its tray.

"This way," said Rendika. She led me through a door and up a few steps of a narrow staircase, and then suddenly she shoved me against the wall and kissed me, worming her tongue between my lips. She tasted of Brandywine and mint.

"Well!" was all I could say when she pulled back and gave me an intense look.

"All right, Challers, this is it for real. Are you really in, or are you just playing a game?"

"Really in."

Her eyes shifted back and forth, searching my face. "All right," she said, turning back towards the stairs. "Let's go."

At the top of the stairs, there was a ladder leading up to a heavy hatch hanging open from the ceiling. Rendika immediately turned to me and pulled off my shirt. "Okay, Worthy, let's see what you got."

I was naked in seconds. She took a step back and assumed an exaggerated pose of consideration. "You'll do. You've put on a few milliLowells of mass since you arrived, you know."

"You saw me when I got here?"

"Sure. Everyone did." She held out her arms. "Now come on, I'm wearing too many clothes."

I pulled her shirt off, trying to be gentler than she had been with me. "I thought folks only watched the Worthies."

"Usually only the Worthies do anything interesting."

Her body was slimmer than Valka's, and after weeks of enjoying a bountiful double rack, Rendika's mere two seemed somehow insufficient. I reminded myself that two was quite enough for most folks and focused my attention.

The garment turned out to be a skintight elastic bodysuit, evidently made at some nearby fabricator, because they fit perfectly, almost too snug to get into at all. They had openings at the ankles, wrists, and neck, as well as the crotch and two more for Rendika's breasts. I had to suppress a laugh when I stopped to look at the two of us.

"Stop that," said Rendika, with a smile. "You're not helping."

"Sorry," I said. "But I feel more than a little silly with my cock and balls hanging out of a hole in my clothes. What's this for, anyways?"

"It helps keep the pressure on your internal organs. Keeps your blood from turning into foam when they open the door."

My amusement dissipated immediately. "Oh."

"You still want to do this?" She folded her arms and cocked her hip.

I took a deep breath and let it out. "Yeah. I still want to do this."

"Then let me help you get in the mood."

She knelt at my feet and took my cock in her mouth, sucking hard on the soft flesh. In between vigorously drawing my cock between her lips, she lifted it with her fingers and took long, fast licks along the underside. The whole time, she had my balls in one hand, squeezing them very gently and rubbing them together. Her technique wasn't at all like Valka's, but it had me good and hard in less than a minute.

She stood up and took my cock in her hand. "Feeling more focused?"

"Oh, yeah." I took her shoulders and bent down to give her a kiss. She nuzzled me a little, and then turned and climbed up the ladder.

The view as she preceded me was stunning, but more than a little surreal. The pressure of the suit caused her vulva to pop out a bit, making it more pronounced and noticeable. I was still hard when we got to the top of the ladder, where I found myself in a spherical chamber about three meters in diameter. The bottom half of the chamber was covered with matte-black padding. The upper half was constructed of curved triangles of armored glass, beyond which stars shimmered, their light twisted by the effect of the Port's warp field. My body shook with a sudden, violent shiver.

"Pretty amazing, huh?" She stood tall to tap on the transparent bubble. It made hardly any noise at all. She turned back to me, challenge still coloring her posture, but said nothing more.

"On the station, we shut out the outside as much as possible. Tried to ignore it, pretend it wasn't there. This…"

"Here is different." She moved in close, rubbing her body against mine. My cock, which had been flagging, revived in contact with her warmth.

I swallowed. "Yeah." My heart already beat faster and my breaths came sharper, as if it knew what was coming.

"Breath deep," she said, as she massaged my cock between her hands. "Fill your lungs. You want your blood to be as well oxygenated as possible."

I didn't need any encouragement. The fear I had been holding at bay was rising, and my lust was rising right along with it. My ears popped. "Are they lowering the pressure already?"

"Yes," she said. "But they won't go any further until it's time." She guided my hand to her breast. "Now touch me."

The flesh was tender under my hand, and somehow the feeling brought my mind back from the spiral it had fallen into. I stroked it and smiled when I felt the tiny nipple harden under my palm.

"You're doing very well," she said. "Most folks abort before getting this far."

"Thanks." I didn't need any reminders that there was anything to be afraid of. I bent down and kissed the upper slope of her breast, but found it receding in front of me as she slowly sank to the floor of the chamber. I followed her down and sat alongside her.

My ears popped again and I winced. Like anyone else, I had a strong sense of danger associated with the feeling. Losing air pressure was almost always a bad thing.

"Lick me," said Rendika, gently pushing me downwards. "Get me ready too."

She raised her knees and I took my position between her thighs. Her pussy filled my senses. As I licked and sucked at her intricate tissues, I ignored the popping in my ears. It seemed like it would never stop.

She kept her pubic hair shaped in a triangle high on her mound, so her lips were smooth—very pleasant to play with. Her body took a while to respond, but once it got started, the transformation was dramatic. Her inner lips turned a deep shade of purple and became drenched with fluid.

I was so engrossed in enjoying her that I failed to notice that my ears had stopped popping. There was only the sound of our breathing and the soft hum of the ship around us.

"Okay, Challers. It's time."

Without looking up, I crawled on top of her. She guided my cock as I pushed forward. To banish the creeping fear, I thrust hard right from the beginning, as deep and fast as I could manage. She pulled her legs up to wrap them around my waist.

Something wild and desperate thrashed in my brain. *Insane!* it said. *Valka hates you for this!* The sight of her pleading face flashed in my mind.

There wasn't anything to do but keep going. I needed to get my climax quickly or I wasn't going to get it at all. That wouldn't be good. I pushed on—seeking that state of mind devoid of all reason and impulse beyond sex, sex, sex—growling deep in my throat.

Then something clicked inside me, some internal switch, and I could finally feel the wave build. The Worthies, the ship, the airlock—it all melted away and there was only Rendika and me, our bodies entwined, our flesh commingled, striving for the transcendent event. The wave crested, and I threw my head back and groaned, grimacing.

I heard a sudden *whoosh* followed by complete and utter silence.

My body was a conflagration of conflicting sensations. My skin prickled. My ears stung. I could feel my saliva bubbling on my tongue, my tongue swelling, and the fabric wrapped around my body squeezing it tightly. At the same time, Rendika's cunt spasmed around my cock, wringing jolt after jolt of pleasure out of me.

I looked down. Rendika was smiling at me, blinking as bubbles formed, and then popped and disappeared, in the corners of her eyes. Her breasts swelled, turning slightly pinker, as was the flesh around her neck and cheeks as the fluids in her body moved to respond to the absent pressure.

The panic fought against the orgasm, dulling it, shortening it. I collapsed against her, clutching her body. Air. I needed air. I wanted to scream for it, beg for it, but there was nothing for my lungs to work against, nothing but silence.

Then, suddenly, it was over. Air hissed back into the chamber and I could breathe again. Laughing, crying, screaming, gasping, I lay where I had fallen, all coherent thought destroyed by the mad chaos I had just been through. After a minute or so, I was finally able to roll onto my back and stare blankly up at the stars.

"You did it." Rendika sat up and stretched her arms. "How do you feel?"

"Like I've been put through the recycler." My head was pounding and my joints felt stiff and achy.

"You need to get up and move around while they bring the pressure back up. It'll help later."

I managed to get to my feet without much difficulty. Given what I had just been through, I was surprised I didn't feel any worse. I scratched the back of my neck. My ears popped again, and I worked my jaw to try to keep them popping as the pressure came back.

"So tell me something," I said as I looked up and out, "you've already got your black badge. Why do this all over again?"

"It's why I'm a Worthy. I love the adrenaline. It makes me feel alive. I can't wait to find out what the next adventure is, what's orbiting the next star, what we'll find at the next station. Plus..." She moved alongside me. "Out there, that's where we live. The void is our playground. We go where we want, do what we like, and if anyone wants to stop us, they have to make us."

Behind us, the hatch unsealed itself and swung open. At the

bottom of the ladder, Rendika poked me in the ribs. "Get dressed quickly. They'll be waiting for us."

"Wow. I'm not sure I'm in shape to face them."

"You're a Worthy. It's your job to put on a good show."

I sighed. She was right. I pulled my clothes on as fast as my trembling limbs would allow, and then hurried down the stairs.

When we emerged into the main room again, the hall erupted with applause. There were lots more people now than there had been when we started. Kensington walked over, bowed to me, and presented me with a black badge just like Rendika's. The whole time, I searched the crowd for Valka's face, but I couldn't see her anywhere. I managed to spot David standing halfway to the alcove where we had been talking earlier. Once the presentation was done and I had accepted a few congratulations, I made my way through the crowd to him.

"David."

"Hmm?"

"Did Valka stick around?"

"Oh. Yeah. She's here." The corner of his mouth twitched, flashing that slight smile I'd seen before, and he gestured with his head toward his alcove. "She's with Krinna."

"Thanks."

I moved past him and maneuvered through the crowd. I could hear her voice, a soft murmur against the conversations going on all around me, and I followed it back to the corner alcove.

I couldn't see her at first. The floor of the circle was full of writhing, naked bodies, one of which I recognized as Krinna's. "Valka?"

"Challers?" Her voice was coming from underneath. It sounded slow, like she was taking extra care with each word. "Lemme up," she said. "Lemme up. Thash my boyfren'."

As the pile untangled, it became clear to me what had been happening. Buried amidst the pillows, Valka had been lying on her back while Krinna and three other people sucked on her breasts, and a fifth man fucked her cunt. He rolled back off of her with a stupid, vacant look on his face and cum dribbling from his cock. His dark hair and heavy eyebrows reminded me a little of Masters, a fact that only made me despise him even more.

My headache suddenly got much, much worse. The guy wasn't even wearing a vacking condom! I wanted to shout at her, to draw my weapon and kill, to punch and kick and scream, but people were watching. The rule we had made about who we would have sex with, how we would treat each other—it hadn't even lasted a single day before she broke it. I turned to walk out.

David stepped in front of me. "You're not mad at her, are you?"

"Get out of my way."

"Hey, Worthy, drain the circuits. I just want to help. Your girl there—she's had a lot to drink. Besides, you can't exactly get mad at her for having some fun while you were screaming at the void with Rendika."

I opened my mouth to speak, but Valka's voice stopped me. "Challers?"

I looked over my shoulder. Valka was standing, milk still dripping from her nipples, and leaning on a support beam while a line of semen ran down her thigh. Krinna stood behind her, expressionless, her gaze switching between me and David.

David put a strong hand on my shoulder. "She's going to need your help, Challers."

"Yeah? Looks like she does just fine without me."

chapter eight

Challers, Port

I OPENED the door of my pod and threw myself onto the chair, grinding my teeth to hold back tears of rage and betrayal. I told Portcon to shut off my lights and my terminal, and I lay there in the dark until merciful sleep ended my suffering.

When I awoke, Portcon was its usual slightly cheerful self. "Good morning, Worthy Challers Dizen. There has been significant financial activity in your account in the past day. Would you like to review the summary?"

"Sure. Why not." The emptiness outside the ship had invaded my heart. Any distraction was welcome.

"Ward orgone generation totaling 8,543 credits have been deposited in your account. Shares of winnings from wagers placed on your success totaling 2,603 credits have been deposited in your account. Life support and consumption fees totaling 648 credits have been deducted from your account. Purchases amounting to 10,940 credits have been deducted from your account. End of summary."

"Wow. Is that an unusual amount to make in one day?"

"Most Worthies do not earn that much in one day. You earned more today than any other Worthy except Worthy Valka Parl. However, there have been larger single-day totals. The record is held by Worthy Mildred Cady, who earned 23,542 credits in a single twenty-four hour period."

I pushed the button to raise the back of my chair to a sitting position and did the math. At that rate, it wouldn't take long at all to make the money to get Valka into a gentank. Even if I only netted a couple thousand a day, it would only take fifty days—half that if Valka and I shared our credits.

And then the previous night's events came back to me, and I covered my face with my hands. I was a Worthy. People would be watching me. I couldn't cry—they would see, they would lose all respect for me, but why did it matter? Valka and I were finished. I knew it and my life was suddenly coming apart at the seams. Tears streamed down my face and I screamed.

Portcon waited until I quieted down. "Worthy, there are four messages waiting for you from fellow Worthies, one of which is in video format, and one from Cue Kensington Book. You also have 561 messages from Wards in a mix of audio and video formats."

"Play them."

Kensington's voice filled the pod. "Ah, Challers my boy, I just wanted to thank you for having your little coming out party down my way. You come back around and the drinks are on me, son."

I growled and shook my head. "Vack you."

Portcon asked, "Do you wish to send a response?"

"No. Play the next one."

This one came in David's voice. "Just wanted to let you know that Krinna and I got Valka back to her pod safe last night. Got some water in her and made sure she was sleeping safely. She's probably going to be pretty sick in the morning, but it might be a good idea to go talk to her. She was asking about you and—"

"Stop," I said, cutting off the playback. "Who are the rest of the messages from?"

"Your remaining messages are from Worthy Hinchley Friss and Worthy Rendika Prelain."

"Okay, play the next one."

A new voice, a deep baritone I didn't recognize, said, "Hey. Worthy Dizen...Hinchley Friss here. Just wanted to call you up, make sure there weren't any hard feelings. I saw you run out of the Lonely Asteroid and I, well...you can't blame a guy for taking opportunities when they come along, right? I mean, she was practically crawling into my lap. I wasn't going to say—"

"Next."

The face of my red-haired lover appeared in the air, replacing Portcon's head. The smile she had been wearing most of last night was gone, replaced with a look of concern. "Challers, this is Rendika. We need to talk. Come meet me at Heaven's Haven. I'll wait for you there."

Portcon's head reappeared. "You have five hundred sixty-three messages from Wards. They total over sixty-seven hours in audio-only form. Do you wish me to analyze and summarize?"

"What do most Worthies do with messages like that?"

"Faced with more messages than they can possibly review in a day, most Worthies trust me to send courteous responses, and make note of any with especially meaningful content."

"Then do that. I'll review the results later." I did not feel like talking to anyone, but I knew it made no sense at all to stay cooped up in my pod. I showered, cleaned my uniform, strapped on my pistol, and went up to the Boulevard.

Heaven's Haven was a bright little cafe a hundred meters aft from the Lonely Asteroid. A fenced-off area surrounded by trees and shrubs grown in planters sheltered a few tables. Rendika sat at one of them with an empty cup and saucer, wearing her dueling goggles. She waved her hand vaguely in the air in front of her.

I moved to stand in front of her. "Rendika? Are you all right?"

She pushed her goggles up. "Challers? Oh, please, sit down." She slipped the goggles off and put them into her holster.

I sat. "What were you doing?"

"These goggles have an interface to Portcon built in. Local holographic projectors, gestural interface."

"Nice. They didn't have those at the armory."

"Yeah, they're something of a find. We can only make them when we get certain rare components, so they aren't usually for sale in the shops. But that's not what I asked to see you about."

"No, I guess not."

"You want some coffee? This isn't the real stuff you get at Scout HQ, but it's not bad."

"Sure."

Rendika waved two fingers in the direction of the attendant lurking behind the counter and pointed to the table. "Challers, I did a little research into your background, I hope you don't mind. Correct me if I'm wrong. You've never had alcohol, have you?"

"You're wrong. I have."

"How much?"

We paused for a moment as the coffee arrived. "I've had a couple glasses of wine."

She shook her head, and then sipped her coffee. "Not enough to count."

"So?"

"When someone has as much to drink as Valka had, they get intoxicated. Drunk. Challers, her judgment was impaired." She reached across the table and took my hand. "Don't blame her for what happened last night."

I put my cup down. "We had made promises to each other just a few hours before. How could she forget? I don't care how 'intoxicated' she was. That was a promise."

"You're angry. I understand that. But the people you should be angry with are the Worthies who took advantage of her condition."

"Like Krinna."

She sighed. "Yeah. Like Krinna—though I bet if you talked to her, she'd have an explanation for why she was there."

"Tell me this...what is the name of the man who was fucking her?"

"His name's Hinchley Friss."

"He's a Worthy, right?"

She nodded.

I stood up. "Then I guess I know who I need to challenge to a duel."

"Now, hold on, Challers. Are you ready for that?"

"I've seen how the duels work."

"Yeah, and have you been in one?"

"I'm doing this. He needs to be taught not to mess with Valka."

"And I'm not saying you shouldn't, but Friss has been in a few duels. He might give you some trouble. It would be pretty humiliating to lose over this, and the Wards are always watching."

"I have to try."

"Do you have to try right this minute?"

"What are you saying?"

"I'm saying you should get some training with someone who knows how to win."

"Who? You?"

"I've been in two duels in my entire career and lost both of them. The one you want to talk to is Krinna."

"Krinna? I want nothing from her."

"She's the best duelist I've ever met. She can teach you. And I think maybe you can convince her that she owes you something for last night."

"All right."

"But right now you have something else to take care of."

"And that is?"

"Valka. There's this little thing called a 'hangover' that she's probably deep in the middle of right now. She's really sick, and if you're there to nurse her through it, it'll make up a lot for last night. Make sure she drinks plenty of water. Food, too, if she can stomach it, and some painkillers. She's going to have a nasty headache."

I stepped away from the table, and then turned back. "Thanks."

"Don't mention it."

VALKA'S DOOR opened even before I pushed the button. She lay on her chair, curled up on her side with a blanket clutched around her body. There was a faint odor of vomit in the air. She looked up at me with bloodshot eyes and a haggard, greenish face. "Oh, Challers. I'm sorry.

I don't know how that happened..."

I took my place at her side and gently touched her cheek. "Don't apologize. I talked with Rendika this morning. She said that you were acting that way last night because you had been drinking too much of that Brandywine."

"Even so. I can't believe I did that." She moaned and clutched the blanket around her. "I'm never drinking that stuff again. Ever."

"Neither am I."

"They said it would help me relax."

"I guess it worked," I said, trying to be nonchalant.

She laughed, and then winced, and it turned into a moan. "We were all watching you and Rendika up on this big screen they pulled down. I was so afraid for you, but at the same time, I was getting really hot watching you and her together. They kept putting glasses in front of me and I just drank them. It did help—it was a lot easier to get into the mood everyone else was in, cheering you on. And then...I guess..." She scowled.

"What?"

"I don't remember much else."

"Can you remember who was giving you the drinks?"

"I don't know. They were just there."

"Were you still in David's alcove?"

"No. We'd gone out to get a better point of view of the screen. We were sitting at one of the tables."

"Was it David or Krinna?"

"I don't think so."

"Good."

She looked up at me. "Challers, what are you thinking?"

"I'm going to challenge a Worthy named Hinchley Friss to a duel. But first I need to get some pointers. Rendika said I should talk to Krinna."

Valka nodded. "Yeah, Krinna's a good person. But why do you want to challenge Hinchley Friss to a duel?"

The question stopped me cold. Should I tell her what had happened? She'd probably know soon enough, anyways. But I didn't want to grind it in any deeper. She was in enough pain.

"I've just got a score to settle. Don't worry about it. Can you sit up? Rendika said I should make sure you get plenty of water."

She groaned and rose to a half-sitting position, taking the cup from my hand. I didn't know whether she had noticed my clumsy conversational sleight of hand, but she didn't say anything.

chapter nine

Renedy, Stakroya Station

"STAKROYA STATION, acknowledge. This is Scout six-four-five-nine, Captain Shauna Grant commanding. Acknowledge our key."

I tapped furiously at my keyboard, setting the last few tags on the report files, kicking myself for having been distracted by Star and his discovery. It could have waited.

"Stakroya Station, acknowledge!"

I glanced up to see a panicked look on Star's face as he stared at the main holoscreen. The round face of a dark-haired woman with a stern expression filled the space.

"I'm not quite ready," I said. "Answer them, Star. Give me a few more minutes."

"But I don't know the protocols!"

"Fake it. Better to answer them wrong than not to answer them at all."

Star toggled a control and turned his chair to face the screen. "Uh...acknowledged, Scout six-four-five-nine. Go ahead."

"We're ready to receive your transmission, Stakroya. We've been ready."

"I'm sorry, ma'am. We've had a bit of a...um...personnel shake-up here lately. Can you give us a few more minutes?"

"What kind of personnel shake-up?"

"Our communications specialist has been...uh...removed from his position. Renedy was an apprentice just a few days ago and I only just started."

"I see. Standby, kid. We're going to come aboard and give you a hand."

Star gave me a worried look. I stepped up next to him. "That won't be necessary, ma'am, we're almost done."

"That wasn't a request, citizen. We are coming aboard. Please notify docking control."

"Yes, ma'am."

The connection cut and Star let out a shuddering breath. "Vack!"

"Do as she says, Star."

"Right. Right." He fumbled at his console, finally remembering how to open a line with docking control just as I was about to do it for him. I went back to tagging and assembling the files, and tried not to think about having Scouts in my communications cluster. I yawned. How long had I been awake? Too long.

I went back to my console, back to work. If I finished the work before the Scouts actually arrived, I might still come out in decent shape. The last time the Scouts came aboard the station was when they picked up Challers and Valka. Before that? Nobody could remember. At least, nobody I talked to. There might have been something in the captain's logs, but I didn't have access to those records. In any case, when the Scouts came on board a station, something big was up and I didn't feel like being at the center of it.

Too soon, the elevator doors opened. Captain Grant was taller than I expected. When we stood up to show respect, she still towered over both of us. She wore a tight, long-sleeved shirt and fitted pants that flattered her generously endowed body. There was something with little straps and buckles under the shirt that wrapped around her breasts and seemed to give them shape. The sight stunned me. Everyone wore baggy coveralls and work aprons on Stakroya, and to see someone dressed like her was a complete novelty.

"Renedy Jawmet?" she said.

"Yes, ma'am."

"Your posted duty roster says that you are currently in charge of the communications cluster."

"Yes, ma'am."

"And you've held this post for six days."

"Yes, ma'am."

"And before that, you had been apprentice communications tech for how long?"

"Ever since I finished school. About sixty days."

"Does that seem irregular to you?"

"Yes, ma'am."

"Good. I'm not the only one. Explain, please."

"I'm sure Captain Shaunson can explain it better."

"So am I, but you're going to explain it too."

"The guy who was here before was reassigned."

"Why?"

"Uhm...he attacked me."

She cocked her head to the side. "He did? That must be an interesting story."

"I don't know. I guess."

"Tell it to me."

I took a deep breath and tried to stop my hands from shaking. The question of how much of a fuss to make didn't have a good answer. "He was making trouble for me. Trying to get me to...well...I think he wanted to have sex with me or something. Anyways, when I tried to record what he was doing to show Captain Shaunson, he flipped out and attacked me."

"Attacked you?"

"Tried to strangle me. Choke me. Gave me a concussion. I was in the infirmary for a week."

"I see. And where is he now?"

"I think he's down in the docking bay. They put him on a cargo loader."

"A serious assault like that and Captain Shaunson didn't put him out the airlock?"

"No, ma'am."

"Why not?"

I swallowed hard and glanced at Star. He looked away. "I don't know. Maybe they were...friends or something."

"I see."

Please believe me, I thought. I didn't want to admit that I hadn't immediately reported the file I found. Lying in a report was enough to get someone sent off to the Fleet or the Merchants. Lying to her face? It had to be even worse. I'd heard stories that sometimes they would take away half the population of a station, bring them to some other station that was all shot up, and put them in as the new crew. *Would they do that to us, all because of me?* I suddenly felt very cold.

I had kind of implicated the captain, but what else could I do? He had been in collusion with...well, he looked like a Pirate anyways.

She nodded and turned to Star. "And you're the new apprentice, I take it."

"Yes, ma'am," he said.

"All right...it looks like the problems with your reports are warranted. How much more time will you need?"

I swallowed hard. "Half an hour, ma'am. No more."

"Very well. I'll go talk to your captain. That should give you enough time to finish up. If not, I'll help you put it away."

"Thank you, ma'am."

"I expect all the details in your report."

"Yes, ma'am."

When the elevator doors finally closed behind her, I relaxed and collapsed into my chair. "Thanks for not saying anything about that file."

"Yeah," said Star. He looked a little sick.

"It's for the best. Believe me."

"I hope you're right. Let's get those reports and log files finished up. "

I blinked and turned back to my console. "Right." I scanned the text in front of me, but nothing made sense. "What was I doing again?"

Star stood behind me and put his hands on my shoulders. "Relax, Renedy. It's going to be all right." He squeezed, gently at first, then more firmly as I let out a half-groan. His fingers were strong, his grip sure and confident.

I didn't want him to stop. It felt too good. But even as he worked the tension out of my muscles, I knew my reprieve was rapidly running out. I patted his hand and took a deep breath. "Thank you. I think I'm okay now." I looked up at him and returned a warm smile.

As he returned to his seat, it occurred to me that his little massage was the first time anyone my age had ever touched me. It wasn't that bad. Maybe, if I thought about it a while, I would want him to touch me again. It wasn't a need really, but...it would be nice.

I wondered if this was what love felt like.

THINGS CHANGED after that Scout's visit. The next day, Captain Shaunson held a meeting. There were regulations that had been overlooked. Rules that had been lax in enforcement. They weren't new rules, they had been there all the time, he said, but there were a lot of shaking heads in the crowd. Nobody believed it, and from the look on Shaunson's face, neither did he.

The worst of these rules was that there would be no more single apartments. Anyone who wasn't married had to live with their parents. We had two days to move out. Not only that, a marriage would only be considered valid after the woman was pregnant. The rooms currently used for single apartments would become "privacy" chambers where engaged couples could get started on that little project. In addition, they would be available for parents to get time away from their children. It wasn't lost on any of us what they'd be doing: making more children.

I was nearly in tears by the time the address was over. I would have raced out to go cry in my apartment, but I had gotten a message just before that I was to report to the communications cluster immediately after, so I just stood to one side and moped while the crowd took their turns at the elevator.

"This is vack-yack," said Star, taking a spot next to me.

"No kidding."

"What are you going to do?"

"I guess I'm going to have to move back with my dad," I said.

"You could...get pregnant."

I looked over at him. He wasn't kidding. "With you?"

He shrugged, and looked away. "You got a better choice?"

"A real charmer, you are."

"I'm under pressure too, you know."

"Well excuse me if I don't sympathize! I'm being told that I have to carry a creature in my belly for almost a year, raise the kid for half my life, then watch it get dragged away by the Fleet or the Merchants. That's what's going to happen, you know. Lots more kids. Lots more overpop."

"Yeah. I know."

The line for the elevator finally came to the end, and Star and I wandered in. Shaunson was in the communications cluster already, standing by one of the consoles. "You took your time getting up here," he said with a frown.

"Big line for the elevators," I said.

"I needed to talk to you because some of the rules we're bringing back have to do with the communications cluster." He picked up a small box from behind him and handed it to me.

It was full of tiny circles of plastic, no thicker than a fingernail. I took one out and examined it. The plastic was embedded with swirls and lines of gray, with a thick dot in the center. It looked like the camera. It looked like Scout tech.

"You will install these in the privacy chambers as they're cleared out."

"What are they?"

"Sensors. You will be taking recordings to confirm proper behavior."

"And...what is proper behavior?"

"The birthrate has been falling recently. These measures are necessary to ensure that our population doesn't drop too low."

I rattled the box. "So how does this help?"

"The Scouts believe that some couples have been...taking measures. I argued that our cramped living conditions made private time difficult. That's when it was pointed out to me that there are already regulations pertaining to this situation."

"Right. So how do we install them?"

"Just press them to a clean surface. One on each wall, one on the ceiling. The network architecture is already in place. Work orders will be coming to you as the rooms are vacated. I'm sure I don't need to tell you that this project is not for public knowledge, just like most of your other duties. Now, I'm sure you have plenty of work to do, so I'll leave you to it. Carry on, citizens."

He left without another word.

"Taking measures?" asked Star. "What did he mean by that?"

"He means to keep from getting pregnant. Like using a piece of isolation film to keep the stuff from getting in." Star gave me a puzzled look. "You do know how babies get there, right?"

"Oh. That. Well, sure."

I rolled my eyes. "Come on. Like the captain said, we have work to do."

chapter ten

Challers, Port

KRINNA STOOD in the center of a huge chamber, easily forty meters across. The floor was vaguely bowl shaped and there was a huge dome overhead. A triple row of seats ran around the top of the ten-meter wall surrounding the bowl.

"Welcome to the dueling ring," said Krinna. "I heard you were looking for some help."

I walked out to the edge of a red circle marked three meters in from the wall. "I got something to talk about first."

"Okay, so talk."

"I want to know why you were part of the orgy clustered around Valka when she was drunk yesterday."

"I was curious. Seemed like a good idea at the time. I didn't know she had some special thing going with you."

"Well, we do have a special thing going. And I don't think it's right to take advantage of someone who's intoxicated."

"Challers, sometimes people get intoxicated in order to lower their inhibitions. They *want* to get drunk. Valka never said no, never told anyone to stop until you showed up."

"Valka had never gotten drunk before. She didn't know what it was going to do to her. I left her with you. I expected you to take care of her."

Krinna shook her head. "Valka's a Worthy, just like you. Responsible for herself. If anyone should be out here making this argument, it's her."

"She doesn't remember it."

"Oh really? Well, then no harm, no foul. Challers, I did take care of her. When you *abandoned* her, it was David and me that brought her back to her pod and made sure she didn't choke on her own puke and *die.*"

Her words stung all the worse for being true, but I had a mission and an image to maintain. "Worthy Krinna Lawson, I challenge you to a duel, to first tag. If you lose, you admit that you took advantage of Valka and that you failed to protect her from the other people who were taking advantage of her."

"Learn by doing, eh? All right, Challers. I accept. If you lose, you admit that you let your anger get the better of you, that you have no moral standing in this argument, and that from now on, there is no grudge between you and I." She pulled out her dueling goggles, flipped them open, and slid them into place.

I did the same. "Agreed. Portcon, have you registered this duel?"

Portcon's face appeared in the air over the arena. "The duel is registered. The green light will come on in one minute."

Red lights appeared around the edge of the arena. I walked about ten meters past the edge of the circle and stood there, my arms loose at my sides.

"Your weapon's set on tag, right?" said Krinna.

I nodded.

"Good. Wouldn't want you to get in trouble for a stupid beginner mistake."

"I won't."

My heartbeat intensified as I waited for the signal to start. Sixty seconds suddenly seemed like a very, very long time. I kept my eyes on Krinna.

The whole logic for calling this duel ran through my head all over again as I waited. The events of last night would remain between us until we got them sorted out. I knew I didn't have much of a chance. I had only watched duels, not fought them, and the hours of practice I had put in at the range would be no match for Krinna's skill and experience. But I had to try, if only to clear the air.

Green. I drew my pistol as quickly as I could, aimed, and fired. Somehow, I got my shot off before Krinna did, but the tiny explosion hit the wall behind her. A clean miss.

Krinna's shot didn't go wild. It struck my shoulder with a loud bang that rattled my senses and stung my skin. I looked down, and saw that my shirt had a hole of shredded cloth about three centimeters wide, right over the joint of my shoulder.

I holstered my weapon and shook my hand. It tingled. "I yield."

"Are you ready to fulfill the terms of the duel?"

"Yes. I admit I let my anger get the better of me. There is no grudge between us."

She put her weapon away. "Very well. Then I expect to hear no more about it. Do you still want to learn from me?"

"Yes."

"Good. Let's start with what was wrong with your stance."

Krinna didn't waste any time with preliminaries. Right there in the dueling ring, she started showing me what I was doing wrong and how to fix it, from the ground up. Everything, she said, started with the feet. As soon as I had the basics, we took a lunch break. I checked in on Valka while Krinna retrieved a meter-and-a-half pole, a ball, and a net. She balanced the ball on top of the pole and challenged me to draw my weapon and fire, making the ball go into the net. That was the exercise. We repeated it, again and again. It was a lot harder than it looked. We kept going until my arm was too sore to continue.

Krinna walked over and gave me a friendly hand on the shoulder. "How's Valka doing?"

"She's feeling better, but she doesn't think she'll be out of her pod today."

"Yeah, that sounds about right." She moved around behind me and started massaging the muscles in my shoulder and back, the exact ones that were sore from the hours of practice. "Take off your shirt. Your muscles are really tight."

I looked over my shoulder.

Her expression was unreadable. "Take it off."

I pulled the shirt over my head, careful to keep my goggles on, and held it bundled in front of me while she worked on the tight, sore muscles. While the shooting range we used was empty, I knew there was a strong chance that at least a few Wards were watching us.

"You're coming along quickly. You've got a knack for this."

"I don't know..."

"Don't contradict me." She squeezed hard, putting pressure on a particularly sore muscle.

"Ow!"

"I think we're done with the quick-draw drills for today. Time for a demonstration. Put your shirt back on, then go down by the targets."

My muscles complained as I wrapped the shirt around my body again, but they weren't as tight as before. I jogged the thirty meters or so down to the target ball and turned to face her.

"Hold still." She drew her weapon and shot me right in the belly.

"Vack!" I flinched too late, and then held out my shirt to look at the second ragged hole.

"How did that feel?" she asked.

"What?"

"How did it feel? Did you feel the impact?"

"Uh...no, not really."

"That's the reason we wear these loose-fitting shirts and pants. The fabric vaporizes easily and absorbs the hits, holding the explosion away from the body. They don't hurt unless they actually strike the skin."

"Inverse square law," I said.

"Exactly."

She turned a control on her pistol. "I've turned it up to 'stun.' Any serious duel is fought using this setting, and you need to know what it feels like. Hold still."

"Now hold on," I said, holding my hands out.

BANG!

My hand felt like it had been hit by a hammer. A blinding jolt of pain ran up my arm. "Vack!" I cradled the injured limb and dropped to my knees. I could feel bones grinding. The room spun and I fought to stay upright.

Krinna rushed to my side. "Challers!"

"I think it's broken," I managed to get out.

"Portcon!" Krinna shouted. "Medical attention!"

"Medical team is en route. Arrival in one minute."

"I'm sorry, Challers. I should have made sure you were prepared."

"No, no." I could feel sweat breaking out and the dizziness wouldn't go away. "You told me to hold still. I should have held still." The palm of my hand had a red mark that was rapidly turning the purple of a deep bruise.

"Fine." She put an arm around me, supporting my weight. "Lean back."

She helped me lay down, pulling off my goggles and sat under my legs to hold them up. The dizziness passed, and I didn't feel like I was about to vomit.

The medical team arrived quickly, loaded me onto a gurney, and carted me to the medical station. It turned out that the break wasn't severe. After a local painkiller and a half hour of surgery, they sent me to my pod to recuperate. I was officially "off the list" for forty-eight hours. That meant I had to hang up my orgone belt and take it easy; my status as a Worthy was suspended. At least I wouldn't suffer the fine and lose half my credits for going off the list voluntarily.

I stripped down to nothing, dropping everything on the floor, and climbed onto my chair with a blanket wrapped around myself. The whole lower half of my arm ached, on top of the lingering discomfort from the training session with Krinna and exposure to hard vacuum with Rendika. I was glad for the opportunity to get some rest.

Dinner arrived with some pills that made me very sleepy. I didn't resist them.

In the morning, Valka arrived in her Worthy outfit and, without a word, shuttled my breakfast from the delivery door to my lap. I didn't really need the help, but I saw no reason to get in her way.

She made sure I ate the entire meal, took my medicine, and then leaned back against the wall and crossed her arms. "I'm a little angry with you, you know."

"Um, what?"

"It's not your job to go challenging duels on my behalf. At least, not without talking to me first. I'm a Worthy too, you know."

"But you didn't remember anything. I was the only one—"

"And how long did you think it would be until I found out? It was all over the Morning Summary. Every Ward on the ship was watching."

"Watching you get..." I didn't want to say the word "raped."

"Watching what? Watching me get raped? Is that what you think? Don't I get a say in how the event is defined? I've been raped, Challers. At the Ovor Maternity School, and before that on Stakroya Station? You think I don't know what rape is?"

"The alternative is that you chose it." I waved my hand in the direction of the blank holoscreens. "I'd rather believe they took advantage of you than that you deliberately broke our promise."

"It's not that simple, Challers. I've tried to tell you that I'm sorry I broke our promise. It's my fault. *I* was the one who was drinking. I knew something was happening, I knew I was getting flirty and silly, and I stayed there. If I felt I was the victim, then I would have called the duel, or asked you to call it on my behalf if I thought that was best. But no. You had to go off and try to 'protect' me, and look where it's got you."

"But I didn't get this in the duel. I got it in training—"

"Training for a duel you want to call on Hinchley Friss."

"You saw that?"

"Vack, Challers, what do you think I was doing all day yesterday? I was sitting in the dark, watching your holofeed. Well, I had it on. Mostly, I was listening."

"You were?"

"It made me feel better to know you were okay. I nearly fell off the bed when you got hurt."

She had a point. No matter how I squirmed, she had me. "I guess it's my turn to apologize."

"Tell you what," she said. "You accept my apology, and I'll accept yours."

I smiled back. "Deal."

She leaned down and gave me a warm, loving kiss that stopped short of being passionate. "Now, you rest up." She nodded at the holoscreen. "I'm going out to do some shopping. Maybe you'd like to watch me?"

"Okay, but no sex, please, okay?"

"I promise not to have sex with anyone today. Even if I get drunk."

"Thank you."

She gave me two good-bye kisses—one on my forehead and one, very lightly, on the back of my injured hand—and then smiled, waved, and slipped out the door.

"Portcon, please display the holofeed for Worthy Valka Parl."

The screens lit up and I settled back to watch.

chapter eleven

Challers, Port

"SO HERE'S THE PROBLEM," Valka said as she entered the elevator. She turned and gazed up at the camera. She seemed to be talking only to me. "The problem is right here." She grabbed her upper pair of breasts through her shirt. "They're fine like this when I'm just lying in the pod, but walking around, doing things..." She winced dramatically. "They start to hurt."

The elevator doors opened. "So I heard about this thing they have here to help keep things from bouncing so much. It's called a brassiere." She strode out of the elevator and the screen flipped to another view, and then another, as she walked out onto the Boulevard.

"Now, as it turns out, I'm not the only Ovor at the Port, and I'm not the only one who needs this kind of thing," she continued. As she walked, the screen shifted viewpoints, showing the front of her and focusing on her face and chest. I figured that image was coming from one of the hovering camera-bots we had seen while walking to the Lonely Asteroid.

She looked straight at the camera. "So there are a few shops that can make what I'm looking for. And that's where I'm going."

With an abrupt turn, she descended a set of stairs in the middle of the Boulevard and jumped onto the slidewalk. The two-meter wide conveyor belt with a moving handrail on the left side whisked her along at a brisk jogging pace. She turned her head and talked over her shoulder at the camera that was now behind her, her voice rising a little against the noise of the machinery. "Now, I'm not necessarily looking for anything in particular. I'm going to see what there is and see what I like."

A numbered sign reading "600" flew by overhead and, a few seconds later, a platform with a stairway passed on the right.

"And if I come across something that Challers might like too, that'll be a bonus."

I smiled and watched her hop gracefully off of the slidewalk and onto the next platform. She climbed the stairs briskly while the camera swung around to focus on her face again.

"The first is right here." As she entered the shop, the camera zoomed back to encompass the whole storefront. Next to a three-dimensional moving image of a woman wearing a few pieces of frill and decoration on strategic parts of her body, the holographic sign over the door read, *Delicacies*.

The view shifted to a high-angle point of view of the shop interior and Valka walking in through one side. There were racks along the walls with colorful bits of string and fabric hanging from clips and hooks set at strange angles.

A shopkeeper stood up from a console in one corner of the small room. "Worthy Valka Parl, welcome to Delicacies." The clerk was a tall woman, easily a head taller than Valka, with a long braid that ran down her back. "I'm Kimbrel Chrysalis."

"Thank you. I understand you have items designed for Ovors?"

"Indeed. We have a nice selection of ready-to-wear here in the shop, plus we have access to a fabricator where we can order up any modifications you wish to make. I take pride in giving customers a perfect fit, no matter what their preferred body style. Now, I've got your measurements from the public portion of your vital statistics, but I find that those can be somewhat inaccurate for my purposes. Would you mind if we did it the old-fashioned way? I've got my own specially calibrated scanner."

Valka nodded politely. "Of course. Scan away."

Kimbrel took a device from under her console and fiddled with it until a red beam began playing over Valka's clothes. She frowned.

"Are my clothes in the way?"

"Well, they do complicate things a little..."

"I don't mind." Valka dropped her gun belt, pulled off her shirt, and skinned out of her pants, leaving her in nothing but her orgone belt and a pair of calf-high boots.

"Ah, much better," said the clerk.

I had seen Valka naked many times before, and in person rather than on a screen. This time, however, the sight had a much bigger impact on me. I couldn't tell whether it was because Valka was sort of in public, the matter-of-fact way she went about it, or that there could have been hundreds or even thousands of other Wards watching her alongside me that made it so arousing, and I didn't care. All I knew was that it got me.

"There," said Kimbrel, shutting off the device. "Got it. As a Worthy, no doubt you have high standards. You're looking for support and comfort, but you also need a stunning look and no lack of sex appeal. This ought to do nicely." She stepped over to one of the racks and took down a small garment made out of a shimmering black fabric. It was somewhat larger than the other garments on display, but I still couldn't see that more than a half a square meter of fabric had gone into its construction.

Valka took it from Kimbrel's hands and looked it over. "I think I'm going to need some help with this." I didn't blame her. There were openings everywhere, and what part went where wasn't obvious.

"Of course," said Kimbrel. "Allow me." She took the whatever-it-was back from Valka and knelt down, holding it for her to step into. As the fabric was pulled up her body, it gradually took shape, slipping over her curves and over her shoulders, finally coming to rest, skintight, around her.

It was magnificent. The whole thing hung from a pair of very short sleeves over her shoulders and a thin collar around her neck. Strips of fabric crisscrossed her upper chest, supporting two cups under her upper breasts. The supports for her lower breasts came from another set of strips that ran under her arms to hang from the back of her neck and shoulders. Then, the whole thing ended in a pair of straps that ran down over her crotch. Back on Stakroya Station, such a thing would have been unheard of. The sheer outfits we had worn for cadet uniforms with the Scouts had been nearly see-through, so this thing could have been considered more modest, but from where I sat, it was the sexiest thing Valka had ever worn.

It looked great, but after a few seconds, I realized it didn't really fit Valka or her personality very well. And when she looked at a holographic projection of herself, she agreed. "No, I don't think so. It's a bit too stark. Have you got something a bit less, mmm, swoopy?"

"Ah, perhaps something more advanced is more on your wavelength. Try this."

Kimbrel took the first item from Valka as she slipped it off, and then took out some discs of flat plastic. She placed a disc on one of Valka's nipples and the disc immediately clung in place, conforming to the shape of her breast and spreading along her skin like a self-animated fluid. When Kimbrel placed a second one on the opposite side, the two pieces reached out to each other in both directions, meeting at Valka's breastbone and spine, leaving only a barely visible seam. A third and fourth disc did the same thing on Valka's lower pair of breasts, and then a fifth spread over her groin. Valka watched curiously as the plastic settled on its final shape. The bright red color worked better than the black did, for some reason, though I was at a loss to figure out why.

"In spite of the appearance, the material is breathable to sweat, and stays flexible indefinitely," said the clerk.

Valka turned and stretched, and the shiny plastic moved along with her. When she tapped it, however, it seemed rigid. "That's weird," she said.

"They brought these back from a Merchant ship raid a while back. I'm not sure what they're really for, but they make quite unusual and serviceable undergarments. The disc will conform to wherever you place it and connects to its neighbors. Would you care to, ah...bounce a bit?"

Valka rolled up onto the balls of her feet and shook from side to side and up and down. There was a strong dampening in the motions of her breasts; they hardly swayed at all. "So how do I take them off?"

"Just get a fingernail under them, lift them up, and they'll return to their original shape."

Valka tried it. The plastic flowed back into a red disc between her fingers.

"You know, I don't care how that looks, that's cool." She turned the red plastic over, looking at it. "How does it know not to cover my hand? How do they know what shape to take?"

"Ah, well...that took a good deal of experimentation and research." Kimbrel smiled. "I hope you don't mind if I keep my trade secrets to myself. Suffice it to say, you won't see another garment like that on the Boulevard."

"All right, I'll take them. How much?"

"Each disc is a mere thousand credits."

Valka's eyebrows shot up.

"For such a unique item, that's rather a bargain, don't you think?"

"How unique?"

"I have a total of eight discs left. I sold one set of three already, so if I sell you this set here, plus the three others to someone else, you'll be one of only three Worthies who own them."

Valka smiled. "I'll take all eight."

Kimbrel chuckled. "Ah, now this is a woman I can do business with." She held out a small tablet. "If you would validate the transaction?" On the tablet, the outline of a handprint was overlaid over some text that was unreadable on my screen.

Valka placed her hand on the tablet, causing it to emit a beep of acknowledgement. Kimbrel put the eight discs into a box while Valka dressed. She accepted the box with a smile, said her goodbyes, and went out the door.

I tore my eyes from the screen to find my palms sweaty and my cock making its presence undeniably known.

The other shops she went to that day had nothing so exotic, but she bought one or two pieces at each of them, making sure to put each of them on display before having them packaged up. The long waits as she walked or rode the slidewalk between destinations turned the whole affair into an erotic ordeal, but I couldn't stop watching. I found myself hungry for her, missing her terribly, and uncomfortably aroused.

And then came lunchtime. I thought that when she stopped to eat, I would get something of a respite.

The little kiosk she found sold a tubular meat product called "sausage," which was about two centimeters thick and fourteen long and served on the end of a skewer. I expected her to eat it in her usual straightforward way, but instead, she sat at a table, held the thing up in front of her, and licked the underside with a little growl of appreciation that ended in a giggle.

The analogy was not lost on me. I could almost feel her tongue on my cock. When she slipped the sausage between her lips and slid it inside her mouth, I had to choke back a moan of frustrated desire. Vack, I wanted her. My cock twitched, and I slid my hand under the blanket to stroke myself with the same light touch she was giving the meat. When my wrist twinged, I switched to my left.

The tension that had been building for hours sang through my nerves. It was a strange sensation, knowing that she was putting on this performance for me, from hundreds of meters away. I wanted her there with me. She was, sort of, but also wasn't, and the confusion of need and desire made my head spin.

Then she bit off the end, releasing a spurt of grease from inside that dribbled down her chin. It was too much. I arched my back and came, hard, soaking the blanket, filling the pod with groans of frustrated pleasure. When I could focus on the screen again, she was wiping her mouth with a napkin and dropping the skewer in a recycling receptacle.

I hadn't masturbated in months. The art of the solitary orgasm had been my only outlet back on Stakroya Station, but once I was a member of the Scouts, that was a thing of the past. Shirley, my mentor, had also been my steady sexual partner. While we almost never had sexual intercourse, as that act was reserved for fully trained Scouts, I had never lacked for an orgasm if I felt like it. When I had been discovered spying against the Scouts, the imprisonment and interrogations left me with little in the way of sex drive. And after our escape from Scout Headquarters, Valka had always been there for me.

I rose from the chair and cleaned myself off, stuffed my blanket into the cleaner, pulled out a replacement, and climbed back into the chair. I looked up at the screen to see Valka standing and chatting with David and Krinna.

"Let us make it up to you, both of you," said David. "No pressure. Just dinner, conversation."

Valka shook her head. "I don't know. Challers isn't feeling too well—at least not when I looked in on him this morning. Tonight might be too soon."

Krinna reached out to touch Valka's shoulder. "Then tomorrow night. Please. I feel just terrible about everything that happened."

She did? The shift from her attitude in the dueling ring made me frown. Why was she telling Valka a different story from what she had told me? Wouldn't she know that I'd be watching, or that someone would get back to me with the information?

"I'll ask him," said Valka.

"Please do, and send him our regards, and wishes for a speedy recovery." David flashed a smile. "Good to see you again."

Valka nodded and passed them by, returning to the slidewalk.

I ate some lunch, and between my masturbatory exertions, the food, and the pill that came with it, a nap seemed like a very good idea. Valka had finished her shopping trip, so I shut off the screens and allowed myself to slide into unconsciousness.

CHAPTER TWELVE

Renedy, Stakroya Station

STAR MADE UP in diligence what he lacked in intelligence and, on the whole, he was a passable student. The fact that I didn't know the material all that well myself didn't help any. Many times we just went through the data management lessons together on the big holoscreen. If the material was something I was already familiar with, I'd focus on the work queue, keeping half an ear out for the little "Unh?" sound he would make when he didn't understand something.

The work shift generally passed smoothly, and as was becoming usual, I finished the work queue well before the shift was complete—all except one. "Install network disks, Room 5-78b."

Star had just finished a lesson, so I tapped him on the shoulder and grabbed a few disks out of the box. "Come on, I'm going to need your help with these."

"Hmm? Yeah, okay."

At the door to Room 5-78b, we met Tenno Parl coming out. He shot us a sour look. "Just couldn't wait to get in there, could you?"

"Actually, we weren't—" Star began but I elbowed him before he could say anything stupid.

"Better than moving back in with my folks," I said. "Are you and Lor going to take the big step?"

"Yeah, I guess. No choice about it now. Dad recycled my hammock, so I'm going to be sleeping on the floor."

"It's good to know that being on the security detail doesn't get you out of following the rules," I said.

"Just the opposite. Dad says that security has to follow them even more than anyone else, or we won't get any respect. That's the best tool when we have to deal with folks who think the rules don't apply to them."

I nodded and slipped past him into the room. "Nice talking with you, Tenno."

"Have fun," he growled without the slightest bit of sincerity. He hefted a crate with a few personal items in it and stalked down the hall.

After the door closed, I took a look at one of the disks. "You need to be more careful, Star. If you had told him we weren't here to use the room...uh, for what he expected, he might have gotten curious and asked what the reason was. Then what would you have told him?"

"Hmm, I didn't think of that."

"No, you didn't. If you're going to work in the communications cluster, you're going to have to get better at keeping secrets." I looked up at the walls, scanning the room.

"What are you looking for?"

"Trying to figure out the best place to put these. I have no idea what their field of view is."

"They'll tell us if there's a problem, won't they?"

"Yeah, but I'd like to avoid that if I can."

"I guess the center of the wall would be best."

"Maybe, but if it's a holographic system, then they can't be too far apart from each other. Not only that, it'll be easier to notice at eye level. Here, hold me steady. I'm going to put this one on the ceiling." I pulled the chair over from the plate of metal welded in the corner that served as a desk and climbed up on it.

Star's hands circled my waist while I stretched up to stick the disk to a crossbar between two light panels. I hoped the glare would help disguise its presence.

"So, do we have to record people actually...doing it?"

"Yeah, but chances are, we won't have to review the recordings. They'd have to tell us what to look for, and they won't do that."

"Why not?"

"It's pretty standard for these things. If they told us, we would be able to tell people what not to do to avoid their scrutiny. They don't like doing that." I stepped down and found myself face-to-face with Star. He gave me a sheepish smile and looked away.

I sighed and shoved the chair against the wall. "What is it, Star?"

"Well, I was thinking..."

"Good start for the day."

"I was thinking we really should use the room. For like...what it's for. So we don't have to move back."

I reached up and put the second disk on the wall a few centimeters below the ceiling. "Purely as a practical matter."

"Well, yeah. I mean..."

"Oh, vack." My shoulders sagged, and I turned around and sat heavily on the chair. "Yeah. I guess. I mean, there really isn't any getting out of it, so I guess we might as well, right?"

"Is it so bad?"

I looked up. Star was looking at me like I had just stolen his lunch and thrown it in the recycler. "Oh, Star, I'm sorry." I stood up and put my arms around him. "I just feel so pushed into this. I'm so sorry."

"I'll make it special for you," he said quietly. "You'll see."

IT WAS THREE DAYS until Star was ready. In the meantime, I had moved back in with Mom and Dad, got my little bunk-shelf and my little storage cubbyhole back, and had six arguments with my stupid younger brothers. I was an adult, with a job and everything, and yet I didn't merit any more space or privacy than a child.

Except in one place.

The whole work shift, Star was as nervous as a schoolboy on his first trip out under the stars in an airsuit. When the hour finally came, he practically dragged me to the elevator.

"I can't wait to show you," he said. "I've had the room reserved all day. I got everything ready before the shift. You're going to love it."

"All right, Star." I was worried that he was getting his hopes pumped up too far and I would have to fake my reaction. I was never very good at that.

I didn't have to fake it.

The walls had meter-wide swatches of white film stuck to them, with elaborate drawings done in red markers. Each one had a big circle, inside which was a couple holding hands, or embracing, or kissing. On the desk, there was a plate with a pile of sugar cookies that had our initials written on top, and a bottle, an actual bottle made out of glass and everything, right next to a pair of goblets that looked like they were real glass too. The room was spotlessly clean, including sheets so bright-white they almost glowed. A half-dozen pillows were artfully arranged on the bed to make it look like they were carelessly tossed there.

"Star...this is...this is amazing." I walked over to the wall and examined one of the pictures. "Where did you get the ink?"

"It's from one of the markers the inspection crews use to mark the hull for repairs. It'll stick to anything. The film is from the infirmary. They use it to seal up wounds and stuff."

I picked up the bottle. "What's this?"

"It's something called 'Firebelly.' One of the guys down in the docking bay won it off a Merchant. He said it was just the thing to calm down first-time nerves."

"How much did that cost you?"

"It doesn't matter. If it makes this special for you, then I'm glad I spent it." He moved in close and took my hand in his. "There's no need to rush. We've got an entire sleep shift to ourselves. Let's just take it easy and enjoy it. Okay?"

"Okay."

He led me over to the bed and sat me down, then retrieved the bottle, glasses, and the cookies. While he filled the glasses, I took one of the little pastries and examined the writing on top. "You did this too?"

"My mom did. She has a trick where she takes a little sugar, some soy, and water, then stuffs it in a plastic bag and writes with it."

"Did she make the cookies too?"

"Yeah."

"She must have used up her discretionary allowance for a month for all that."

"I didn't have any left after buying this," he said, handing me one of the glasses and sitting down next to me.

I sniffed the beverage. It smelled sharp and vaguely medicinal. I took a drink, and immediately understood why it was called "Firebelly." The stuff burned all the way down. Coughs and wheezes racked my body.

"Whoa there," said Star.

"You could have warned me."

"Sorry, I...actually, I didn't know. This is the first time I've tasted it myself."

The stuff tasted terrible. I kept the goblet in my hand and took a bite of the cookie. "These are good, at least."

He smiled. "Thanks. Hey, listen. I got some holos. Maybe it would help us get in the mood? They're sexy."

"Uh, you know that Greel used to try to show me stuff like that, right?"

"Yeah, but this is different. Those were things he had recorded off the private pickups. Big no-good stuff. These were made for people like us. They know they're being recorded. You'll see."

I gave him a doubtful look and took a smaller sip of Firebelly. It was a little easier in small amounts, and I could feel some warmth spreading through me. If it would help make the whole ordeal go smoother, I was fine with that.

"If you don't like it, we'll stop." He slotted a memory chip in the desk and tapped a few keys. The holoscreen lit up, and he turned and sat down next to me. He was close, our hips touching—closer than we had ever been. Even so, I couldn't imagine how we would get from where we were to where we needed to be. It just boggled my mind.

The holoscreen lit up with a rotating logo. Underneath, the words "One Void Too Far" spun by. Once they passed, the viewpoint shifted. The room was some kind of cockpit with wide control couches surrounded by clean, brightly lit consoles. A man and a woman reclined side by side on a couch, dressed in the trim, pure-white outfits of Scouts. She had short blonde hair and big breasts, and he had dark hair and a muscular chest.

"John, you know this delivery has to be made in one jump. We won't have time for two. Lives are depending on us," she said.

"I know, Karen. I will make a particularly special effort."

I had to chuckle at the stilted dialogue. I had watched holos before, but the acting in this one was atrocious, not to mention the screenwriting.

"I have every confidence you can do the job," said Karen, leaning over to pull his face to hers.

While they kissed, John's hand pushed her shirt up over one heavy breast, exposing it to the camera. He squeezed and kneaded her for a few seconds while they kissed, before breaking free. When he licked her nipple, he took a strange pose, head tilted to one side, clearly making sure that we could see the action as he ran his firm tongue up and down over her flesh.

In fact, the point of view had shifted subtly as I was watching, making his head and her breast nearly fill the available space. Karen made soft, agreeable noises as he worked, bringing her nipple to an erect peak.

Star shifted his weight and I felt his arm move closer behind me. I looked at him. He saw me, smiled, and looked back at the screen.

When I turned my own attention back, the two "Scouts" were naked. John was kneeling astride Karen's body, holding her breasts in his hands, squeezing and groping and licking and biting. While he did that, Karen took his cock in her hands, stroking and massaging it as well.

"Is this okay?" asked Star. "Because I have other kinds of holos if this isn't helping you."

"This is good for now," I said.

I was beginning to doubt that the people on the screen were really Scouts. After all, the woman who had interrogated me in the communications cluster was a strong, capable woman. The creature on the screen in front of me just didn't have the same kind of charisma. They had to be actors.

The scene being played out was interesting, though. I had never been inside a Scout ship, so I didn't have much idea of what one looked like. It puzzled me a bit—what they had been saying about deliveries and jumps and all that—but I decided to just watch and maybe I would figure it out.

At some point, the contoured control couch had flattened out into an oval cushion just big enough to hold the two of them. Karen shifted her legs apart, and John nestled down between them to bring his mouth down to her crotch. He licked and sucked, drawing her inner labia between his lips and darting his tongue out to prod at her button.

"Now that looks interesting," I said.

"Want to try it?" asked Star.

"Maybe later," I said and took another sip of Firebelly. There was definitely a nice warm feeling growing inside me. "Right now, I want to keep watching."

Star sighed, but didn't press the issue.

With growing urgency, Karen's moans shifted to cries and shouts as she writhed under John's mouth like she was being tortured. Only, she wasn't being tortured; she was transported with ecstasy, driven to a state I had never felt, never seen, never even heard of before. I wanted that. I wanted that for real.

Before she could reach a climax, however, John climbed up higher, kissing her breast as he arranged himself between her legs. The point of view shifted again, angling down between their bodies so I could see his cock moving slowly inside her. She gasped as his body meshed with hers, and when he moved his hips, her grunts came in syncopation with his.

A strange sort of disappointment settled over me, as if it wasn't supposed to happen this way. I knew, in my mind, that this was the act Star and I were expected to perform, but it felt dry and lifeless. There wasn't a flaw in the performance that I could point to as the trigger for that feeling—except that Karen and her pleasure were no longer the focus of the scene. He seemed brutish. Crude.

"You want to try something else?" asked Star. He had sensed my unease.

"Yeah, what else have you got?"

He stood up, stopped the holo, and selected a different file. "Maybe this one."

This one didn't bother with a title, didn't bother with the scraps of plot that the first one had. It also put the action in front of the holoscreen, more visible and with more room to choose a point of view.

The woman in the holo was wearing a Merchant uniform, but she didn't look like the Merchants I had seen. She wasn't a lumpy, round pile of flesh barely able to stand under full gravity. Instead, she had a fairly normal body except for a massive pair of breasts. She lay on a circular, vaguely bowl-shaped platform that looked like it was upholstered with some soft fabric. Her hips and thighs were generously padded, but not what you would call fat; most of the excess weight that Merchants normally carried over their whole bodies was gathered in that tremendous chest. Waves of brown hair spilled out in a lustrous halo, surrounding a serene face of pale, perfect skin.

I felt Star shift again, and when I looked at him, I realized my jaw was hanging open. He had a hopeful look on his face, watching my reaction closely.

A sound from the console drew my attention back to the screen, and I saw another Merchant enter the scene. She had red hair and was built similarly to the first—perhaps slightly smaller, but still immensely endowed by any measure. I felt a momentary sinking feeling, comparing those bosoms to my own, but the envy turned to hunger as the newcomer reached down and unzipped the long seam on the front of the reclining Merchant's jacket. Two flaps of fabric fell away, revealing the breasts beneath. Her aureoles were a light pink that faded gradually into the pale flesh around it, poking up only slightly from the smooth wide curve.

The brunette opened her eyes and smiled, then shifted her arms under her breasts to lift them up toward the newcomer. Without a word, the redhead took a squeeze-bottle from her pocket and drizzled a clear liquid over the globes before her, then laid it aside and rubbed the slick fluid over them in sweeping strokes of her hands. The huge nipples tightened into stiff peaks rising several centimeters from their resting places and the creamy skin glistened.

Part of me said that I should find the size and shape of those breasts disgusting, but I could not deny the awe that filled me, watching them there. After a few minutes, the redhead climbed onto the platform, removed her own jacket, and let her breasts fall onto her partner's, sliding them over each other. I took another drink of Firebelly and shifted on the bed to get a better view of their faces. Calm, languorous smiles made them look so pleased, so serene it was hard to believe there was anything wrong with the scene I was witnessing.

Star climbed onto the bed behind me, putting one leg on either side of me, and gently laid his hands around my stomach. I wondered if he could feel the heat growing inside me, if he could tell that my toes were tingling. He had to sense something. There was just too much going on inside me for none of it to have gotten out.

I took down the zipper of my own coverall and raised Star's hands to my breasts. He followed the motions on the screen, making lazy circles as wide as he could on my limited chest, circling in to my nipples when the women in the holo did the same. I had a sick, perverse thought, imagining it was me up there, taken away by the Merchants when Stakroya was overpop, taken away and transformed into one of those huge-bosomed women.

The women brought their bodies closer, as close as their bizarre anatomies would allow, and stretched their necks to kiss each other across that expanse of flesh. Until that moment, I could fool myself that I was watching a strange physical ritual, but that kiss was so tender and loving that I could no longer fool myself about the feelings that were being portrayed. Whether the actresses were actually in love or not, that's what it looked like and the thought felt just as wrong, and yet just as familiar, as the idea that they were having sex.

My mind flashed to a memory of Valka stripping out of her airsuit and discarding the sweat-stained liner underneath while I was getting into my own. The flush I had felt confused me at the time, because I had not recognized what it was. Now, I understood.

chapter thirteen

Renedy, Stakroya Station

I WANTED to have sex with a woman. The flash of understanding was full of promise and also despair. I knew what was wrong with me, why I didn't find Star or Tenno or any of the other eligible men on Stakroya Station attractive, and that understanding was powerfully liberating. At the same time, I despaired of explaining to Star, or of ever finding that kind of relationship on the station. I was sure I was the only one, sure that I would never find anyone with the same sickness I had, sure that I would never know true love. I choked back a sob.

"Renedy? What's wrong?" Star stopped his manipulations and hugged me close.

"Nothing. I'm...I'm sorry, Star. I don't know if I can do this."

There was a long pause. The action continued on the screen, but I was no longer watching. My eyes were filling with tears and my mind swirled with confused emotions. I desperately wanted someone to hold me, someone I could confide in, someone who would comfort and soothe me.

"Hush," he said and kissed my neck, holding me tighter.

Somehow, I pulled myself together and downed the rest of the Firebelly in my glass. Through the coughing fit that came after, I managed to wipe away the threatening tears, and scrape together the mask of bravado I needed to put on.

"We don't have to do this now," said Star.

"No," I said. "Just give me a little time, okay? I'm just...this is all very new for me. I'm a little afraid."

"We've got all night."

I stood up to put the glass on the desk and felt the deck roll beneath me. "Is there something wrong with the gravity?"

"I think it's the Firebelly," said Star. "Come and lie down." He pushed some pillows aside and patted the bed next to him.

I lay down on my side, and he rolled me onto my stomach and

started running his hand over my back. It was a soothing gesture and I could feel a bit of my anxiety being worn away with each stroke.

"I don't know what's wrong with me," I said. "There's somma wrong wimma mouth."

Star shushed me and just kept rubbing my back. Slowly, he undid my boots and took them off. Then, after a few minutes, I felt his hand on my collar. I let him slide my coverall down off my back, down off my arms, and down off my legs. My flimsies went with it, leaving me completely naked.

"Star? You think imma be a good mom?"

"The best," he said.

"I don' really like babies. Too mush noise."

"I know. But my mother says it's different when they're your own kids."

"Wudna be so bad, goin' 'way to be a Mershan'. Getta have big gian' boobs."

"I don't know if you get that choice when they take you."

I rolled over on my back. "Would I look pretty with big gian' boobs?"

"You could afford to gain a few milliLowells. We all could."

"You know wha' I mean."

He stroked my breast with the same light, soothing touch he had used on my back. There was a strange look on his face, like the coldness of a Marine in one of the adventure holos, grimly facing battle. He stood, kicked off his boots, and stripped out of his coverall and flimsies.

"Wass wrong?" I asked, squinting. It was hard to focus.

"Nothing," he lied. His cock was small and limp, and I wondered how he was going to manage that way.

He sat down again and bent to bring his mouth to mine. I hiccupped in the middle of the kiss and couldn't help giggling. That broke through his stern focus and he laughed a bit. "I'm going to need your help," he said.

"Whasha need me do?"

He changed position, kneeling next to me, offering me his cock. "Could you use your mouth?"

I narrowed my eyes. "I thought you knew how folks make babies."

"Yeah, but I need to be hard."

"Alrigh'." I got up on one elbow and took it between my lips, then kissed and licked it, holding it away from his body with my other hand. I looked up. He had his eyes closed, with a look of intense concentration on his face.

"Am I doin' it righ'?"

"Yes," he said quietly. "That's good."

It swelled in my hand and in my mouth, quickly growing bigger than I could comfortably fit between my teeth. Without a word, he moved down, fitting his knees between my legs, and lowered himself on top of me. Eyes still closed, he bumped around until he found the right place, then slowly pushed his way inside. There was some resistance, a sharp stick of pain, and he was through. It was done. I should have been a woman. That should have been enough, but it wasn't. We had to finish this, and then hope it worked. Then, maybe, we would be treated like adults.

The pain faded to something more like a dull ache as Star pumped slowly in and out of me. The metallic smell of blood mingled with the medicinal aroma of the Firebelly and the sugary taste of cookies on my tongue.

"Come on, Star," I said, softly. "Let it go."

"I'm trying," he said. "Please, just...let me do this. My way." He squeezed his eyes tighter. Pumped harder. It wasn't doing the ache in my belly any good, and it wasn't really making me any hotter, but I told myself it was what needed to be done, so I endured. His tempo sped up gradually, until his body slapped against mine. At last, with his face contorted in a frightening grimace, he let out a long, loud groan and collapsed on top of me. He pulled out, rolled over, and I felt something warm and sticky trail along my leg.

All I wanted to do was curl up and go to sleep. It hadn't felt good. It hadn't felt right. I felt dirty and cheated and compromised. I rolled away, turning my face toward the wall, and silently choked down my tears.

It was several minutes before I realized that he, too, was crying. It was so soft I could barely hear it under the sounds of passion coming from the forgotten holo running on the console.

I rolled over and laid my hand on his elbow. "Star?"

"I'm sorry," he said, his voice cracking with pain. "I wanted to make this special for you."

"'S not your fault," I said, snuggling in close to him. "We just...we just don' know wha' we're doin' yet."

"It's not supposed to be like this," he said.

"Let's rest a while. Maybe try again later, okay?" I kissed him on the cheek.

"Okay. Practice."

He shut off the console screen on his way to the corner lav station and splashed a little water on his face. He came back to the bed with the tray of cookies, set it down in front of me, and sat down.

I bit into one of the cookies. The sweet taste comforted me and I felt my despair drain away a bit. We ate the cookies in silence, taking them from the pile in turns until they were all gone. The static in my head cleared a bit and I felt ready to stand up again.

"I feel like I need to clean up," I said, feeling doubt and hesitation creep into my voice. "Would you help?"

He smiled and brushed crumbs from his hands. "Sure."

At the corner lav station, he took out a rag, ran it under some water, and squirted a dot of soap on it. When it was as lathered up as it would get, he brought it to my face and began the job of scrubbing the day's grime from my body. He worked efficiently and quickly, and before long, I was washed and rinsed, my skin glowing and clean. I turned around and did the same for him with a fresh rag, then turned on the hot-air vent to dry.

I had hoped that such an intimate thing, getting so close to each other's bodies, would help make us more comfortable together. It worked—at least, somewhat. There was a bit less mystery about his anatomy than there had been before, but it didn't do much for me. And from Star's lack of reaction, it seemed it hadn't done much for him, either. I had to admit it; there was nothing between us, nothing we could base a marriage on. We were doomed.

Star put the cap back on the bottle and popped his memory chip out of the console. He turned, saw the look on my face, and made a sad smile. "I really am sorry. I tried the best I know."

"I know. It's not your fault. I guess we're just not meant for each other."

"It is...kind of. I think." He sat on the bed and ran his hands through his hair. "I need to tell you something. You deserve to know." His eyes were full of pain and I was afraid he would start crying again. "But I can't do it now. Tomorrow, okay?"

I sat down next to him and took his hand. "Okay."

It wasn't until we got to the communications cluster the next day that we could talk about what had happened the night before. The privacy chambers had no privacy; our workplace, however, was clear. The irony wasn't lost on either of us.

After we got the morning diagnostics and utilities started, and had the encryption utility loaded up, I called Star over to my desk. I put a training holo on, in case anyone came in, and took his hand. "There was something more you wanted to tell me, last night."

"I don't...feel anything...when I touch you. I'm not like other guys. The only way I could finish was by thinking of..." He swallowed and stared down at his feet. "Thinking of someone else. A man."

"Well then, I guess we're even," I said. "I have the same problem."

"But...it's okay for you to be attracted to men." The pain and shame in his voice was gone, replaced by confusion.

"No, no...ugh. I mean, I'm attracted to women. I saw Valka Parl naked, just for a moment, when she was changing out of an airsuit after emergency training, and I think of that sometimes." I squeezed his hand and looked around the room. "My mom says I might not get pregnant the first time. We might have to try again."

He grunted.

"Maybe if we agree that it's okay to think about whatever we need to think about to get through it, just for the two of us, it might be a little better?"

"Yeah. That would make it better."

I looked over at the console, realizing I had missed something important. "Where did you get that Merchant holo, anyways?"

He blushed, stammered, and just shook his head.

I gave him a hard look.

"There are ways. Merchants who will carry data chips that aren't on the manifest. They get passed around, copied...There's code on there that isolates the console when you play them. It makes it look like the console is just idle from the outside, but it can run the holo."

I threw my arms around him and hugged him. He had taken a big risk for me. I kissed him, hard and fast. Star might not be someone I could love, but he was someone I could respect, and someone who respected me. And that made him unique on Stakroya Station.

Maybe we had a future after all.

chapter fourteen

Challers, Port

VALKA RANG my bell a few minutes after I woke up. I felt good enough to take a shower, so I told her to give me ten minutes while I cleaned up. It wasn't that I didn't want her to see me—we had done that together a number of times—but I smelled a little foul and I didn't want to subject her to it. Portcon was just making the announcement that dinner was available when she came in.

"So, did you like my little show?"

I used my good hand to scoop her in close and nuzzled her neck. "Does that tell you anything?"

She giggled and nuzzled back, and then adjusted to give me a solid kiss on the lips. "I did it all for you."

"And the thousands of credits you got as a result."

"That's a bonus. I'd have done it anyways, just to see the look on your face when I got back."

"So show me what you bought."

"I thought you already saw it all."

"Oh, the screen is nowhere near as good as seeing it in person. Come on."

She pulled away slightly and waggled a finger at me. "Oh, no. For one thing, you're still recuperating. For another, I'm saving them. I was thinking of wearing the green one to our dinner with Krinna and David tomorrow."

"What have you got on now?" I rubbed her back, feeling for straps, and caught a strip of hard plastic. "Aha!"

"Now, hold on there, that's cheating. It's not polite to ask a girl what kind of underwear she's got on."

"It's not like you're going to have them on for long, anyways."

"Oh?"

"After that performance you put on, I could have my arm broken in sixteen places and draped over my back, and I'd still want to have you."

"Oh, that's too bad." She smiled and shook her head with fake regret. "But I did make a promise, and I'm determined to keep all my promises to you from now on."

"Valka..."

"Do you remember that quaint little tradition among the Scouts, where the mentor and student would abstain from all sexual activity for two weeks before their first cruise?"

"Yeah, it was supposed to make their first session aboard ship more intense. Release more orgone."

"Well, I'm not going to make you wait two weeks."

"You're serious. You're really going to make me wait until tomorrow?"

"Completely. Now, if you'll excuse me, I have some business to take care of. There's the little matter of a few hundred messages from my fans that I need to answer. Have a good night!"

I frowned and shook my head, and then frowned a little deeper. "Portcon?"

"How can I assist, Ward Challers Dizen?"

"Wait, wait...Ward? I'm a Ward again?"

"You are not wearing your orgone belt, so therefore you are a Ward. Do you wish to pause this conversation until you can put on your orgone belt?"

"No, no, that's fine. How many messages have come in today?"

"There are 687 messages. I am prepared to respond on your behalf."

"No...I don't think I want to do that today. Please classify and summarize."

"498 are expressions of support, compliment, or encouragement, of which a significant fraction are wishes for a speedy recovery. Another significant fraction are compliments on your relationship with Worthy Valka Parl. 122 are expressions of condemnation. Sixty-six are offers of advice or information."

"Do I know any of the people offering advice?"

"None of them match members of your preferred sender list."

"Wait a minute...preferred sender list? What's that?"

"Your preferred sender list contains those senders you have designated to be specially brought to your attention."

"And who do I have on my preferred sender list?"

"Your preferred sender list is currently empty."

I groaned. "All right. Put the following people on my preferred sender list: Valka Parl, Shirley Smith, Robert...um..." I searched my mind for Robert's last name. What was it? "Halko. Robert Halko. And, um...Grecca..."

"There are currently four people in Port who use the first name of 'Grecca,'" Portcon suggested after a few seconds.

"Have any of them sent me any messages?"

"One of them has sent you a message."

"Add her to the list too."

"Worthy Valka Parl, Ward Shirley Smith, Ward Robert Halko, and Ward Grecca Hamaza have been added to your preferred sender list."

"Good. Please play me any messages from those people, including the ones you responded to yesterday."

Robert's voice came first. "Well, kid, you certainly know how to get the game started. If that was what you intended, then my congratulations to both of you. I'm sure you got some great numbers. If not..." He chuckled. "Then my condolences. Either way, looks like you're off. Good luck."

The next message came from Shirley. She chose to send a full-body holographic projection. In the message, she wore black, baggy, comfortable-looking pants and a shirt, and a pair of fuzzy blue slippers. She looked a lot less sexy than she had in the tight-fitting Scout uniform, but she had ditched that—as we all had—as soon as we arrived at Port. The message had been recorded in her pod while she sat back in a chair identical to mine.

"I'm sorry I haven't sent anything before this. The Port says that they take care of everything a Ward needs, but it takes a lot out of me to keep Robert comfortable, and I guess that focus has kept me away from staying in touch with you." A faint smile crossed her lips. "But then I guess you and Valka have had plenty to keep you distracted too, eh? But that's not why I'm recording this.

"I heard you and Valka signed up to be Worthies. I guess I should wish you congratulations or good luck or something, but I like to think I can be honest with you. I wish you had checked with me before going into this. I don't think it's right. Just look at that 'screaming at the void' ritual—does that sound like the kind of thing people looking at the long term would do? The Worthies don't have the kind of committed relationships I believe in—the kind I hope you believe in too. I've been watching those shows and that's a real corrosive environment. If things look like they're getting rough, I want you to keep in mind that you can always quit. Please don't wait until things are beyond repair to do it, okay?"

When the message ended, I told Portcon to stop, and just sat there, thinking. Was I taking that kind of risk? I only had to look at my first night as a Worthy to know she was right. That had nearly broken us, right there. Were we stronger for it, or weaker? I had put the feelings of that night in containment, but they were still there. I still felt betrayed and anxious; I just hadn't admitted it.

I wasn't sure what to do about it. I couldn't just tell her. The Wards would hear and, through them, other Worthies. I wasn't a Worthy, but Valka was, and if I recorded an audio or video message, she'd have to play it where the cameras could catch it. I could try a text message, but even then it was likely the cameras could pick it up. If we were going to have a private conversation, we would both have to be Wards, and in order to do that we'd have to give up a huge chunk of credits—credits we couldn't afford to lose if we were going to get that trip to the gentank.

And then it occurred to me that anything Valka had said since putting on the belt could have been just a performance. She wanted access to that gentank, she wanted it bad. I tried to bury the thought, but it just wouldn't go away. I wanted to believe Valka loved me. After everything we had gone through to be together, how could I have any doubt? And yet, there it was.

"Next message," I said, desperate for anything to distract me from that line of thinking.

"Hi, Challers." The voice was definitely the Grecca I knew. "Looks like you had some real fun last night! And by that I mean not fun. If you need someone to talk to, just bip me. Or even if you don't. I'm feeling a bit isolated, you know? That airlock ritual looked like fun. Do you have to be a Worthy to get in on that? I want you to tell me all about it. Bye!"

"Next message."

"Oh, so that's how it is?" The sudden change from Grecca's friendly tone in the first message to the hurt, angry tone in the second was so abrupt that, for a moment, I thought it was the wrong person. "A polite brush-off from Portcon? Don't have time to answer all your messages yourself? I don't care if you're the vacking emperor himself, Challers Dizen, I saved your vacking life and I deserve more respect from you than this!"

I winced, covering my face with my hands. "Next," I said, dreading what new sabotage I had done to my relationships.

"There are no more messages from preferred senders. You have 685 messages from Wards not on your preferred sender list."

"Portcon, begin recording a holographic message for reply to those messages."

"Recording." A red sphere appeared in the air just to the right of Portcon's head.

"Hi, folks. I don't like giving Portcon the job of replying to your messages, so I'm recording this instead. I'd love to respond to each of you, but I just don't have time—not with hundreds of messages coming in every day. So here's the short version: if you're offering support and encouragement, thank you. If you're telling me I'm making mistakes...thanks for that too." I rolled my eyes. "I know I've really farted in the airlock these first couple days. And if you have advice and opinions, well, I just wish I had time to listen to everything, but be assured I'm just doing the best I can. Again, thanks for everything. End recording."

"Recording stopped. Do you wish to send this recording as is?"

"Let me review it." I watched the message, made sure that it was starting and ending in the right place, and told Portcon to send it to everyone who had sent messages that I hadn't answered personally, except for Grecca.

That one I would have to fix personally, and the sooner the better. I got myself dressed, leaving the orgone belt on its hook.

"GO AWAY, Challers. Go play with your new friends. You know, the ones who are Worthy?" Grecca's voice was muffled by the door of her pod, but her words could be understood, especially since she seemed to be shouting at the top of her voice.

"Do you want my apology or not?!" I shouted back.

The door opened. Grecca stood in the doorway, arms crossed over her chest. "Well?" Her slender frame was wrapped in a dark-green jumpsuit that made her skin look sallow and her blonde hair look plain.

"I'm sorry. I didn't realize your message was in there with the rest."

"Oh, so you didn't think that someone who saved your life would want to send you a message when you take a big step like becoming a Worthy?"

"I didn't even know the preferred sender list even existed."

"What list? You couldn't say, 'Portcon, are there any messages in there from Grecca Hamaza?'"

"No, I couldn't! I never even knew your last name! Shirley only ever introduced you as 'Grecca.' And I did manage to get your message eventually, or I wouldn't be here. Grecca, I'm sorry. Listen, can we talk somewhere else?"

Her lips made a hard line. "I missed you, Challers."

"Come on. Let's go. Have you been up to the Boulevard? There are some great places to eat up there."

"I look a mess. And if I go with you, there are going to be cameras."

"None of that matters. I just want to talk."

"It matters to me, Challers. Can you give me a few minutes to clean up?"

"All right. I'll meet you by these elevators up on the Boulevard." I pointed down the hallway.

She nodded. "Don't worry. I'll be there."

I went straight to the elevators, took them up to the Boulevard, and found a place to wait that faced them.

Sometime after I sat down, a stranger walked up and sat down next to me. He was slightly overweight, about my father's age, and wore a bright-red tunic with green pants underneath. He looked ridiculous.

"Hi, Challers? I'm Jor Kledman." I put up a finger to interrupt, but he just kept talking. "I just wanted to tell you that I'm really glad you came to Port. It's a real pleasure to meet you, and I wonder if you would like a little advice? It's really nice that you're attached to Valka and all, but there are some incredible women out there that you're just not—"

I finally cut him off with an abrupt, "Thank you," my hand held up in the air between us.

"How rude," said a woman coming up from the other side. She was even bigger than Jor Kledman and she wore a muumuu with centimeter-wide stripes of red, yellow, and blue. "Don't you know he's waiting for someone? You don't just walk up and start talking that way."

I tried to get a word in while she took a breath. "Actually, I—"

It was no use. She and Jor started arguing over me until a third person, a Chevalier newgen by the look, joined the discussion. The volume increased, attracting attention from passersby who quickly joined the crowd. Raised voices quickly became shouts.

In frustration, I stood up on the bench, drew my pistol, and fired it at a point between my feet. The sharp crack as the beam struck the heavy deck plate silenced all of them. "I am waiting for someone. I would like to be able to actually see the elevators when she comes up. Is that too much to ask?"

"Vacking Worthies," grumbled the first one, turning on his heel. "All alike."

When the little crowd dispersed, I noticed Rendika standing a little ways off, leaning against a potted tree.

"Nicely handled," she said in a tone that clearly indicated it was not so nicely handled. She ambled over. "Want some company that'll let you get a word in once in a while?"

"Sure, why not."

She sat next to me and slumped down with her ankles crossed out in front of her. "So. How's it been?"

"You probably heard about the practice session with Krinna."

"Yeah, she told me about it right after it happened."

I held up my hand and flexed my wrist. "Medics did a good job. It's hardly even sore now. How about you? Any more trips to the airlock?"

She laughed. "Oh, Challers...I don't scream at the void with just anyone."

"Really? So...how did you decide to do it with me then?"

"You know how often we get decent Worthies around here? I mean, folks worth three farts in a closed airlock? Doesn't happen often. I could see you were going to make a name for yourself as soon as I saw you walk in."

"So you saw potential."

"Yep. And what made you want to try something so crazy as to throw yourself into the void without a suit?"

"Well, I told Valka that the Wards would love it, that it would earn lots of credits."

"That is quite true. Speaking of which, thanks for that...I got a nice take for that part too."

"You're welcome."

"So was that it, then? You did it for the money?"

"Well, no. That wasn't all of it. It's also..." I looked up at the transparent ceiling, out at the stars that wavered and danced beyond the warp field. "Back on the station, everyone treats the outside like it's a terrible monster waiting to devour them, waiting to snatch away their life. The worst punishment anyone can think of on a station is to get thrown out an airlock—even though, when you come right down to it, it's a pretty quick death."

Rendika nodded.

"I guess it was a way for me to say, 'I'm not that person anymore. I've been through it, I did it, and I'm not going to let my fears define me.'"

"Yep. You get it. You going to take Valka out there?"

"I'm not going to force her into it, or try to cajole her. That doesn't work anyways. She's her own person."

Rendika patted my thigh affectionately. "You're a good guy, Challers. Don't let them take that from you."

I chuckled and scratched the back of my neck.

She leaned over and kissed me on the cheek. "Hold on to Valka," she whispered, almost too softly to hear. "Hold on tight." Then she shifted to bring her lips to mine.

The kiss took me completely by surprise. Her mouth was soft but insistent, her tongue tender but probing. I found my arm snaking behind her back, feeling the soft fabric of her shirt under my fingers. The kiss lasted a long, long time.

Too long.

"Hmm." The voice came from nearby. Grecca's voice. I opened my eyes. She stood about two meters in front of me with her lips pursed. "I thought you wanted to talk," she said.

Rendika disentangled herself. "Sorry," she murmured. "Couldn't help myself. I guess I'll, um...yeah." She stood and gave Grecca a nod. "Nice to meet you."

"Oh, don't run away on my account," said Grecca. "After all, I'm just a lowly Ward. I don't really matter, now do I?"

"No, I think it's probably best if I go." Rendika hurried away, leaving me with a sick feeling in the pit of my stomach.

I got to my feet, holding my hands out. "Grecca. I—"

"Look, why don't you just say what you were going to say and get this over with."

My stomach churned. "When we first got here, I was so glad to finally be with Valka, without any stress or expectations, that I was just completely absorbed with it. I never meant to neglect you. It's just that...well...Valka and I have known each other a long time."

"Oh? And how long have you known her?" Grecca tossed her head in the direction Rendika had gone.

I reached out for Grecca, but she stepped back. "I understand that you're not my boyfriend, Challers. I understand that I'm not the only woman you know, or the only woman you have sex with. But I did think we had a relationship of some kind. At the very least, a close friendship. But I guess I was wrong, wasn't I?"

"No, Grecca!"

"Goodbye, Challers. Good luck as a Worthy. I hope it makes you endlessly happy." She turned and walked into an open elevator. As the doors closed, the first of many tears stained my cheeks.

chapter fifteen

Renedy, Stakroya Station

"SO HOW IS your little project coming along?" asked Mrs. Shaunson, pouring tea—real tea from actual leaves—into a cup in front of me. Tea with the captain and his wife wasn't a normal event in most stationers' lives. Every other time I had met him personally, I had been in trouble. I couldn't imagine why we were here.

"Project?"

She glanced over at Star, who just shook his head.

"Getting a place of your own," said the captain.

"Oh!" I blushed. "That. Um...no success yet. But we've only tried twice." At least now I knew what they were after: a status report.

"Well, I'm sure it won't take long. Both of you are healthy young folks."

"The sooner, the better," said Star. "I can't wait to move out. My family is great, of course, but...it's really hard."

Mrs. Shaunson nodded primly. "I know. Just keep trying, things will come together."

Maybe I was being paranoid, but everyone seemed to know the trouble Star and I had been having. Was there some kind of conspiracy going on? I looked at Star.

He wouldn't meet my eyes. "We'll do that."

I took a sip of the tea. It was sweet and warm. "This tastes a little like some kind of fruit," I said.

"Oh, that's strawberry," said Mrs. Shaunson. "We get them in from time to time, and I like to dry them out and use them this way. It makes them last a lot longer."

The conversation turned back to safer topics and I breathed an inward sigh of relief. The second try at sex hadn't gone any better than the first, even with the help of the rest of the Firebelly and a determined effort to find a fantasy image that would make it tolerable. I was almost relieved when my cycle started up, making further attempts pointless, at least for a few days. But it was only a temporary respite. We would have to try again soon.

When the tea was all drunk and the biscuits eaten, Captain Shaunson stood up and we followed suit. "Thank you for coming by," he said. "Good luck to both of you. I sincerely hope that this arrangement works for you."

"You're welcome, sir. It was a pleasure," said Star.

He escorted us to the door and followed us out into the hallway. "Is everything set up now in the privacy chambers?"

"Yes, sir," I said. "Data is coming in, categorized and stored according to the procedures."

"Good." He glanced around, scanning the high corners of the passage. "It does seem somewhat ironic, doesn't it? With the name and all."

"Well, folks don't like having sex where just anyone can see," I said. "But yeah, it is a bit odd calling them 'privacy chambers.'"

"Cameras can't be everywhere, though, can they?"

"No, sir. There's always someplace that's been forgotten," said Star.

"Mmm. You probably ought to find out where those places are, what with all the repositioning that's gone on lately."

"Yes, sir."

He slapped us both on our shoulders. "Carry on, citizens."

When we got up to the communications cluster, I sat down and thumbed my console.

"What was that all about?" Star asked. "If the captain wants some work done, why doesn't he just put in a work order?"

"Oh, that wasn't a work order. That was just a suggestion," I said. "You should probably look in the work order queue, though."

He brought it up on his screen. The last item on the list for the previous day was INSTALL NETWORK DISKS, ROOM C-1C. It was marked completed by Captain Shaunson himself.

Star made an inarticulate sound of understanding, then gave me a dramatic wink and went back to his console.

So there were cameras in the communications cluster now too. I resisted the urge to look around the room to see where he had placed them. Now Captain Shaunson's question made sense. If we wanted a place to talk privately, we'd have to find it somewhere else.

In between encrypting files and validating them for the next Scout ship arrival, I started poking through the various holo feeds coming into our data stores and tracing where they were coming from. I wasn't supposed to actually look at the content of those feeds, but it was our responsibility to make sure they were transferring properly.

Most of the cameras seemed to focus on places away from the

public areas—like the classroom and the mess hall. They seemed to be coming mostly from apartments and small workplaces. If I wanted to have a private conversation away from those little eavesdroppers, and away from folks like Greel who would gladly file a report with the Scouts for a small consideration, I would have to find a place we could go to have it.

Mentally, I made a list of all the places someone could go to get away from people. It wasn't hard; I had made lists like that before. There were plenty of maintenance tubes and access corridors, but those needed special clearance to get access to them, and entry and exit were logged. They didn't have cameras, but I'd get in trouble if I went in there without a good reason. Those wouldn't work, and neither would anyplace that had a regular staff associated with it. The closest I could come up with was the recovery room in the infirmary, but even that was supervised by Dr. Klane and I wasn't sure how much I could trust him either.

I made a grunt of frustration and got back to my work. The new feeds coming in had quadrupled the amount of data we had to wrangle every day, and Star still hadn't finished all his lessons, so it fell to me to get the job done as best I could. I really didn't need to be working on Shaunson's cryptic little suggestion.

It just wouldn't go away, though.

Shaunson wouldn't have said anything if he didn't think there was a place to get away from the cameras reliably, someplace where Star and I could go to talk, and have a reasonable chance of not being overheard. We had enjoyed having the communications cluster to ourselves, where we could talk freely, and now that had been taken away. Just when I had someone to talk to, someone who understood, suddenly I was cut off again. I felt like someone had turned the gravity off. I felt floaty and sick, and couldn't feel my feet under me.

"You all right, Ren?"

"I'm all right."

"Maybe you should go down to the infirmary."

"I gotta get these files secured. I'll be all right."

"You sure?"

"Yeah." I swallowed my anxiety and focused on my screen and my work. By sheer effort of will, I was able to put my anxieties out of my mind.

I really hadn't realized how much time had passed when the elevator doors opened and a cheery voice called out, "Lunchtime!"

I looked up. Nella Kindailie was holding a couple of trays from the mess hall, and a small white plastic case I recognized as a medical kit. She had on a brand new white coverall.

As she set one tray down in front of me, I asked, "Nella, what are you doing wearing medical white?"

"I'm apprenticing with Dr. Klane now." Her smile was broad and toothy.

"Things didn't work out in hydroponics?"

"Oh, no, everything was fine. But Captain Shaunson decided we needed someone else in medical. After all, the doctor's over fifty. Who knows how much longer he'll be around."

I nodded and started eating. "So, how does that leave you bringing us lunch?"

"I got a report that you weren't feeling well, and Dr. Klane sent me up to take some readings."

I scowled at Star. "You didn't."

He shrugged. "You were looking pretty green."

"All right, fine. Let me finish this and you can take your readings." I ate quickly, intending to get the operation over with as soon as possible. Nella and I had never been what you would call friends, even though we were about the same age and had taken many classes together growing up. She was always one of the friendly girls, part of that exclusive clique that spent more time talking about boys than on their schoolwork. Most of them had gotten married right after completing their training and had disappeared off my scanners for the most part.

"Are you still with Spiran?" I asked from behind a mouthful of squash.

"Oh, yes," she said. "Had my first with him. Named him Nalow after his grandfather."

"Well, congratulations. I guess that means you and Spiran have your own place?"

"Yes, we just moved in. It's nice."

"That also means we're back to full population."

"Overpop, I'm afraid. Shensa and Jiffer had one last week."

"Oh, wow..." The memory of the Merchant holo flashed across my mind, and a feeling of longing coursed through me once again.

"Are you done eating? I'd like to get those readings."

"Oh, right." I quickly gobbled down the rest of the meal and turned my chair around. "Ready."

"I'm going to need skin contact for this," she said, taking a standard medical scanner out of the case. "I'm going to need you to strip to the waist." She glanced at Star meaningfully.

"Nothing he hasn't seen before," I said. "And we've got lots of work to do. He'll be fine here."

Star nodded, chewing, watching a training holo.

"Hmm. Then I suppose that's okay," said Nella.

I unzipped my coverall and pulled my arms out of the sleeves, pushing the tough material back behind me. Nella turned on the device and studied the screen on the back while she pressed it to my neck.

"So how are you feeling today?"

"It's just stress," I said. "I'm not sick or anything."

"Dr. Klane will judge that. What are your symptoms?" She moved the scanner to my chest, and then to my armpits. I could see a slight pink tone coming to her skin, and I watched her eyes go back and forth between the scanner, my face, and my breasts. She was looking at me...looking at me the way I looked at those women in the holo. The thought of it brought some heat to my own face and my heart jumped in my chest.

"A little sick to my stomach, a headache, I guess. It's really..." How had I never noticed her before? How had I missed it? The look on Nella's face was one I had seen before. I couldn't believe it.

She brought the scanner up, shut it off, and stowed it back in the case. "These look okay, but I'll have Dr. Klane take a look just in case. If you start feeling bad, you just come down, okay? We don't want your health getting in the way of things." She smiled and winked at me, then scooped up her case and hit the button for the elevator.

I pulled my coverall back on and watched as the doors opened and took her away again. I shook my head. No. I couldn't have seen what I just saw. It had to be wishful thinking. I looked over at Star, then up at the ceiling. I couldn't just ask him about it. Not with who-knows-who listening.

"Stakroya Station, this is Cruiser six-five-one-two-stroke-two, acknowledge."

Star reached out and opened the signal. "Acknowledge, Cruiser six-five-one-two-stroke-two, what can we do for you?"

There was a pause. "We are en route to your location. Please coordinate with docking control. We need an exterior hatch for docking."

I punched up docking control on my screen and sent a quick message, then flashed the response over to Star.

"Hatch Four is available, Cruiser six-five-one-two-stroke-two. Shall I notify Captain Shaunson of your arrival?"

Another pause. They must have been a fair ways out, a light-second or so away, for the response to be that slow. "Affirmative, Stakroya. Cruiser six-five-one-two-stroke-two out."

While Star made the call to Captain Shaunson, I sat back in my chair. The Fleet was coming.

And we were overpop.

What business did I have trying to get pregnant while we were already overpop? How selfish could I be? If I did get pregnant, that would almost certainly mean someone would get taken away by the Fleet or the Merchants, probably someone I knew. It might even be Star. They always took young people just out of training. I wanted to cry again and felt the tension coming back to my shoulders and neck.

A minute or so later, a message came in from Captain Shaunson. "You might want to come down to the Promenade."

chapter sixteen

Renedy, Stakroya Station

SO THE FLEET was coming to take someone away. I debated going. It hadn't been an order, exactly. Did I want to see one of my classmates dragged off by a press team? It might be someone I would want to say goodbye to. I didn't have many good friends, but it seemed like the right thing to do. Star and I secured our consoles and headed for the elevator.

We weren't the only ones who had been told about the event. The Promenade was crowded like I hadn't seen it since Challers and Valka left. Security had cordoned off one of the bridges connecting the upper level of shops to the docking ring. We stood waiting for a few minutes, and then Captain Shaunson walked out onto the bridge.

"Citizens of Stakroya Station," he said, his amplified voice echoing throughout the huge space, "we are about to witness a change in the way justice is served in this great community. I know the great majority of you are honest, hardworking men and women with nothing but the best intentions for your family, friends, and neighbors. We all make mistakes from time to time and we have means in place to deal with those small mistakes. Once in a great while, however, one of us will stoop so low as to recklessly—or worse, intentionally—put lives in danger."

A hatch opened opposite Shaunson and two huge Marines emerged, holding a struggling, shouting man between them. They had no trouble at all maintaining their grip.

"Nasten Greel, you have been found guilty of the attempted murder of a citizen of Stakroya Station. We will no longer tolerate your matter among us. Your meat is not fit for our recyclers. Under ordinary circumstances, you would be consigned to the void. In this case, however, there is still one service you can do for your station. As the station is currently over its population limit by exactly one, you have been chosen to go in the place of a young person who would ordinarily have fulfilled that obligation."

Greel shouted even louder, but it was impossible to hear him over Shaunson's amplified voice.

"Go now, and serve mankind in a manner more in keeping with your nature."

The Marines dragged the kicking, screaming Greel down the stairs and through a hatch leading to the docking ring, while Star and I and everyone there cheered and clapped. He had made more than a few enemies, it seemed.

As the cheering began to die down, Shaunson spoke again. "Citizens of Stakroya Station! As you have seen today, so shall it be from this day forward. Due to our loyal and productive service, authority has been granted to us to choose who shall be taken when our population grows beyond our means to sustain it. No more shall the best and brightest be taken from us just as their potential is ready to emerge. Instead, we shall purge those who drag us down, those who corrupt us, those who endanger us. My fellow citizens, let us celebrate!"

More hatches opened and cargo containers were pulled out by more of the muscular soldiers. One by one, they began handing out packages to the crowd, one for everyone present. The white ones were for adults, the gray ones for children, and the red ones for in-betweens. Star and I got white packages after a few minutes and sat down to open them alongside everyone else. They both had packets of sweets and snacks, a couple of lagerbulbs, memory chips that looked like they might have holos on them, and a large canister of protein powder. After toasting each other with the lagerbulbs and singing a few rounds of "Our Shining Station," Star and I packed up the remains of our packages and went back to the communications cluster. There was still plenty of work to do.

"So what do you think of that?" asked Star.

"Better Greel than some kid who doesn't deserve it," I said, feeling a lot better about my life and about the idea of getting pregnant. If having a baby meant that some burner like Greel got carried off to the Fleet, I was all for it.

"Who do you think they'll take next time?"

"I don't know, maybe Mrs. Blanchak?"

"She's a nosy old roller, but I don't know if she deserves it as much as Greel."

"Mmm. Well. I'm sure Captain Shaunson can find the right people."

"Maybe." Star shrugged. "It's a big job for just one guy, though."

"What are you saying?"

"I'm saying, maybe we should look at some of those holo feeds and see whether we can't make some suggestions. Dads who beat up their kids. Stuff like that."

"I barely have enough time to package them up! Besides, that's against the rules. That's one of the things Greel got in trouble for."

"Greel got handed over to the Fleet for trying to kill you, Ren. Nobody ever said anything about what he was doing with the holo-recordings. I'm just about done with my training. I could take some of the work preparing files for the Scouts."

I shook my head. "No, Star. I'm not like him."

"You know Mrs. Blanchak won't be quiet about who she would like to see going."

"I'll think about it."

The thought occupied my mind for the rest of the shift. Who would I throw to the Fleet to save one of my classmates? I couldn't think of anyone I knew who deserved it, but I also knew that some of the worst crimes were things that you could keep quiet.

As the shift came to a close, Star poked his screen. "There's a privacy chamber free. After dinner, do you want to have another try?"

"No, I think I'm going to give it a rest tonight. Maybe I'll just go out to the oxygen deck and think."

"Want some company?"

"Thanks, Star, but no. We've been together for something like fifty hours straight, and I could use some time alone. Okay?"

"Okay." Star frowned, shrugged, and turned back to his station. "I guess I'll get a head start on tomorrow, then." He didn't seem too disappointed.

I wasn't the only one who decided to visit the oxygen deck, but it wasn't crowded either. I was able to find a bench where I could eat and think without too much interruption. Once I was there, though, I had a hard time bringing my thoughts to any focus. Who was I to judge my fellow citizens? Who was I to invade their homes and businesses the way Star suggested? On the other hand, if I didn't, someone with less scruples would be sure to take that role, and probably with less information available.

And then, in the midst of that chaos, the face of Nella Kindailie sprang to mind, flushed with arousal, and I almost jumped off the bench with surprise. Where had that come from? I ran my hand through my hair and tried to calm down. I gathered up the remains of my meal and made my way toward the recycler slot near the main hatch. As if Star's suggestion wasn't disturbing enough, the idea that Nella might be interested in me sent thrills up my spine and tantalizing fantasies spinning through my head.

The Promenade was where the real party was. All the pubs were packed tight, loud music and laughter spilling out of every door. Everyone seemed very happy with the way things had worked out and they were celebrating. There would be a lot of discretionary spending accounts depleted by the end of the dark shift. I didn't feel like joining those celebrations, though. Instead, I walked along the upper balcony, looking down at the revelers, with an odd, dispassionate separation hanging over me. I wasn't part of the party. It had nothing to do with sex, but I still felt that the community being enjoyed wasn't my community.

This was a good day and I couldn't enjoy it.

I drifted along until I came to the elevator. I selected the level where my family lived without thinking. I stared at the indicator as it showed my progress from level to level. My family didn't feel much like my community either. I loved them, but my secret was so dire and so dangerous that I couldn't burden them with it—even though I was certain they would keep my secret.

The elevator opened and I walked slowly down the curving passageway, past one family dwelling unit after another. Almost everyone lived in apartments like these. Some of the doors were open, giving me glimpses of clusters of children watching holos or working on lessons, or playing games marked out on the floor or walls. Was that really me?

My family's door was closed. I thumbed the lock and stepped inside. My younger brothers sat in front of the holoscreen, playing a game I hadn't seen before. No doubt it was something that came in one of the gift packages. Focused on their game, they didn't see me slip inside and up into my sleeping cubby, kicking off my boots as I went. Even with the soft beeping of their game in the other room, I still felt desperately alone.

Once again, the memory of Nella holding her scanner to my chest returned to me, but I did my best to forget it. I had only just discovered that there were people like Star, and the Captain, and me; how lucky would I have to be to meet another one so soon? It had to have been wishful thinking and my libido making me see things that weren't there. Besides, how was I supposed to approach her? Just walk up and ask, "Excuse me, but when you were looking at my boobs, was that professional curiosity, or do you maybe want to touch them?"

I rolled over and put my face to the wall. It didn't make any sense to feel so much despair, but the more it sank over me, the more isolated I felt, and the more isolated I felt, the deeper the darkness became. Before long, there was nothing but a long dark hole in front of me, a wordless throat of emptiness. I did not fall asleep so much as surrender to it.

"COME ON, time to get up!" A yank on my foot half-pulled me from the sleeping cubby.

I blinked and squinted, half-formed nightmares of a station entirely empty of people slowly fading from my brain. "Unh?"

"You forgot to set your alarm. Come on, work shift is starting." Star held out my boots with a stern look on his face.

I climbed down and pulled them on. "What are you doing here?"

"Looks like your parents decided to use one of the privacy chambers last night. From what I've heard, they weren't the only ones."

Out in the main room, my brothers were sprawled about, fast asleep, their game still playing multicolored light on the walls.

"Do I have time to clean up?"

"No, sorry. Light shift starts in about three minutes. You missed the early meal too. Don't want to be late logging in. Not now."

"I guess not." I grabbed a couple of the snack packets from my gift box. They would have to do.

On the elevator, Star asked, "Did you think about what I said yesterday? About looking at the holo feeds?"

"I thought about a lot of things. Didn't come to many conclusions, though. Let me ask you this: what do the Scouts want with those feeds, if not to catch people doing what they aren't supposed to be doing?"

"What the Scouts think is wrong and what we think is wrong probably aren't the same thing."

"Yeah."

"If it's okay with you, I'd like to start reviewing those feeds."

"I don't know. I guess. What are you going to do if you find something?"

"Send it to Captain Shaunson. He's the one who's going to make the decisions about who gets sent away, right?"

"Yeah, okay. Just don't put them up on the big viewer, okay? That would just be too creepy."

"Okay."

The elevator opened and we stepped out into the communications cluster. We thumbed into our consoles just a minute or so late. I cleared the automatic "Renedy Jawmet, you are late to your post" message without much anxiety. After all, a lot of people would be late to their posts that morning.

I slipped into the daily routine of morning maintenance—checking on various critical databases, clearing messages, and assembling the day's tasks. It was easy to forget yesterday's anxieties when today's mundanity occupied all of my attention. Star finished the last of his lessons and helped out, and before the day's meal break, we were done with all of the reports and file transfers. The Fleet cruiser had left shortly after the packages had been handed out, so there wasn't much business on my list for that. It looked like we'd be more than ready for the next Scout ship arrival. The files needed for the next Merchant ship, due to arrive near the end of the shift, were also ready and waiting.

I pulled up one of the training holos for the master communications officer test. Technically, I needed to pass it to even be considered for my position as communications chief, but Captain Shaunson had the authority to override that requirement. I could do all of the routine stuff, but there were plenty of emergencies that I wasn't equipped to handle. Getting qualified would put more credits in my discretionary account. That's what I told myself, anyways. The truth was, I desperately feared letting my mind go off on some idle speculation.

"I had an interesting conversation last night," said Star.

"Oh?"

"Well, not a conversation, really."

"What was it?"

"Actually, it was a conversation, but I wasn't in it so much as hearing it."

"Star!"

"Okay, okay. I heard some old guys from the docking bay talking about this whole thing with the privacy chambers, and the Fleet taking a criminal, and that kind of stuff. They had never heard of anything like it. Not themselves, not their folks, not anyone. The rules have been the same for as long as anyone can remember."

"Well, how long is that?"

"I don't know, but these guys have long memories, and they've heard the stories from their parents and grandparents. Like, you know the story of Pol Shiffer and the hull breach, right?"

"Well, yeah. My grandmom told that story to me when I was a kid."

"There are lots of stories like that. These guys knew them all. But the rules have always been the rules."

"So if they're changing the rules, then there's got to be a reason for it."

"Yeah. That's what these guys were saying. They said maybe they just need more kids to be born so there'll be more overpop and more folks to get taken away."

"That doesn't make any sense," I said. "You've heard the stories about how Stakroya was founded. A Merchant ship showed up at another station and they took half the people out here to staff it. The old station wasn't even overpop. So that means if they want more people, all they have to do is build a new station somewhere and do the same thing to put people in it. In a few years, you have enough population for twice as much surplus."

"Well, there is a war on," said Star. "Maybe they need more people right away."

"How long has the war been on? For as long as anyone can remember, so there's no difference there. And if they really need people that badly, then why bother following the rules at all? They could just take everyone they need. No, something has changed. Something big."

Star shrugged. "I guess you're right. But I don't suppose it matters much. There isn't a whole lot we can do about it."

I frowned and went back to my screen. I tried to study, but the qualification test somehow didn't offer as much promise as it had a minute ago. "No. Not much at all," I said, half to Star and half to myself. I paged through the material, skimming the headings on the lectures and exercises: Advanced Data Structures. Information Control and Security. Access Monitoring. "Not much. But not nothing, either."

chapter seventeen

Challers, Port

THE ROOM was small, I knew, but the holographic images on the wall were perfect. Instead of sitting on pillows around a low table, sipping sweet, hot tea in a booth just off the Boulevard in the star-faring fugitive city known as "Port," we were sitting under a glowing, golden dome, surrounded by a carefully tended garden with flowering vines hanging from trellises and iridescent shrubs at every corner. There was even a subtle floral perfume in the air behind the mingled scents of food.

It reminded me, for both good and ill, of the oxygen deck at Scout Headquarters.

To my right sat the woman who mattered more to me than anything in the universe, Valka Parl. Even though she was dressed in her ordinary Worthy's clothes, she still looked stunning. She had her long brown hair done up in an elaborate braid that looped down around the sides of her head, twined with chains of fine gold links. A single blue gem hung down over her forehead.

To my left knelt Krinna, the woman who had broken my wrist by shooting me with a high-powered infrared laser pulse. She had replaced her Worthy uniform with a tight green dress that came down to just above her knees. A simple circlet of gleaming metal ran through her close-cropped blonde hair.

And across the table sat David, the engineer behind the evening, still wearing the imperturbable expression that had been on his face when I first met him. "Go on," he said to Valka. "I can't wait to hear the rest."

She gave me a playful smile. "I think I'll let Challers tell the rest of the story."

I took a deep breath. "Well, we needed to infiltrate the Ovor Maternity School to get to talk to Suna. The only way we could do that was to become Ovors ourselves...female Ovors."

Krinna gasped. "You didn't."

"Yep. We did."

"What was it like, becoming female?" asked David.

A shadow passed in front of my eyes, a memory of Trace, and the things the Scouts had done to her in the name of efficiency. Even that memory, however, couldn't spoil the evening. I let it go, promising myself to think about Trace again later. "Actually, it happens from time to time among the Scouts. In my case..." I glanced over at Valka with my own version of a playful grin. "I rather liked it. At least, temporarily."

Krinna's eyebrows shot up even higher. "You didn't!"

Valka and I laughed. "We did! Right there in the shower, washing off the gel from the gentank."

David raised his cup for a sip. "You must have gained a lot of insight into pleasing a woman."

"I guess I learned a few things."

Krinna raised an eyebrow at Valka.

"Oh, yeah," she said. "He did. Believe me."

"I'm surprised," said Krinna. "It didn't look that way with Rendika. That wasn't exactly finesse."

"I'm sorry. I was under just a little bit of stress, there. Give me a break."

David leaned back on his pillow and stretched out his legs. "I don't think she's going to take your word for it."

I shrugged.

"You're not going to just take that, are you?" said Valka with a challenging smile.

"I'm not here to prove anything to anyone," I said. "They can believe us, or not."

Valka put one fist on her hip in mock outrage. "Oh, you're not, are you? Well I, for one, am not interested in being called a liar. This is clearly a challenge, Challers, and I am shocked that you aren't stepping up to it."

"I'm getting the feeling that I don't have much choice here."

"You always have a choice," said David. "You just have to weigh the consequences. Do you really feel coerced?"

I laughed, unable to keep up the charade any further. "No, not really. I suspected that you two had this in mind all along."

"Three," said Valka. Her eyes sparkled with amusement.

"Hmm?"

"I told you, Challers. I told you what I like." She blushed a little and glanced over at Krinna.

"So what do you say?" asked Krinna. "Care to show me that you really have forgiven me?"

I flexed my wrist. There was still a little stiffness in it, but the pain was gone and with it, most of my indignation. I cleared the space on the table in front of me. "You're sure you're ready for this?"

She stood up, stepped in front of me, and sat on the table, stretching her legs out on either side of my body. "Bring it."

The posture made her skirt ride up above mid-thigh. A furry triangle was just visible among the shadows beyond the hemline.

I ran my fingers up her thigh and wondered if pubic hair was a fashion among the Worthies as a reaction against the clean look favored by the Scouts. Her legs were clean of any hair, so it wasn't for a lack of shaving. Krinna had hair there because she wanted it. Her thighs under my hands were firm, even hard. There was little in the way of body fat between my fingers and her taut muscles. Even the usual padding running from the top of her labia up toward the navel was much thinner than usual.

She lifted her hips and drew her skirt up around her waist, exposing the lower edge of her orgone belt. "A little easier now?"

"Thank you," I said. Her pubic hair was short and straight, just like the hair on her head, and I had to smile to myself at the similarity. I imagined her carefully trimming it before going out. I slipped down off my pillow to get a slightly better angle and bent down for a closer look. I slid one finger between her lips to gauge her warmth and lubrication and found something I hadn't been expecting.

Curious, I parted her with my fingers, revealing a clitoris that was easily an inch long and as thick around as my little finger, and it wasn't even fully erect yet. I couldn't help touching it.

"Pretty amazing, huh?" said David. He had shifted around to look over my shoulder. When I glanced up at him, he flashed a smile. "I hope you don't mind if I try to pick up a few tips."

"Ooh, what is it?" cooed Valka, peering around my other shoulder. I spread Krinna's lips wider to give her a better look before bending down to draw my tongue slowly up along the inside of one outer lip, tasting the muskiness that lay nestled in her folds. My tongue made a slow tour of her pussy, testing the sensitivity of each bit of skin, each fold and curve, and I catalogued each gasp and shudder.

In a few minutes, I learned that the best place to start was the upper portion of her inner lips, where a light vibration of the tongue tugged gently on her clit, eliciting a sharper edge to her breathing and a promising warmth. As the little organ poked out further and further from her body, her inner lips stretched taut.

When I switched to using my lips to stroke and tease her clit directly, she began moaning audibly, and lay back onto the table. "Oh, yes," she said with a voice already becoming hoarse. She squirmed slowly, pressing her body up into my face.

I pulled back, though, not letting her increase the pressure. I knew if I waited and teased, the result would be better. Every time she tensed her stomach, trying to grind herself into my face, I pulled away. Her moans turned into whimpers. Hitching my elbows up onto her legs helped me maintain the proper distance as her movements grew wilder.

When I judged that she was reaching a plateau, I pulled her clit between my lips, flicking the tip with my tongue. She gasped and grabbed my head. "Ohh! No, too much!"

"Sorry," I said, pulling back a bit. "I'll be more careful."

"Stop talking and get back in there!"

Instead of sucking her clit, I merely placed my lips around it and hummed as low a note as I could manage. I actually only ever tried that technique once; Shirley told me about it as part of my Scout training, but it hadn't done anything for her, so I hadn't done anything with it since then. Krinna was a bit more sensitive and it seemed like an appropriate thing to try.

I was right. The results were immediate. Her muscles tensed and she drew a short, hard breath. I drew one hand in to stroke her labia, slightly altering the geometry yet again. It was enough to push her over into climax. As she curled up tight, grunting, I held on as her body quivered with energy. Finally, the spasm released her and she relaxed back down onto the table.

Of course, there was no reason to stop there.

I started the whole cycle over again, beginning with her outer lips and gradually working my way in. This time, it took less than a minute to bring her to another gritted-teeth orgasm, and the result was even more powerful. "Challers, oh...it's true..."

"Mmm...see?" said Valka. I could hear a note of arousal in her voice too.

David made an appreciative sound of approval. "I should be taking notes."

Valka turned, slid her pants down around her ankles, and kicked them off. "Then perhaps a practical exercise is in order," she said, sitting on the table next to Krinna. Valka wore one of the more ordinary panties she had bought on her expedition, rather than the exotic red plastic. "After all, we're supposed to be your guests, not the other way around. I don't see why we should be doing all the work."

David licked his lips and dragged Valka's panties down off her legs, and I felt a twinge twist in my belly. It wasn't a bad one, but it definitely wasn't contributing to my fun. Even after everything that had happened at Scout Headquarters with Valka and I assigned to separate mentors, Masters and Shirley respectively, even knowing without a doubt that she loved me deeply, it still gave me a deep stab of jealousy to see anyone else with her in a sexual way.

I chided myself. I didn't own Valka, and I had just finished doing much the same thing to Krinna. I had no rational reason to deny her the pleasures of David's mouth.

Something inside me screamed, *But it's David's mouth, damn it!* I made a note that the voice was sounding like a spoiled child and tried not to let the acid in my stomach put a sour expression on my face.

Krinna took my hand and pulled me down on top of her, bringing my lips to hers for a well-lubricated kiss. "That was marvelous," she whispered, barely audible over Valka's detailed instructions to David.

"Mmm, thanks. It was a pleasure."

"Valka's right, though. I should pay you back."

"Do you have anything in particular in mind?"

"Well, I have my specialties, but none of the gear is here."

"Gear?" I lay down next to her on the table, leaning my head down against my arm so that Krinna's body and Valka's quivering breasts blocked my view of what was going on between my girlfriend's legs.

"I'll show you sometime. For now, why don't you get comfortable on the pillows? I don't know if I'm as good as a Scout would be, but I promise I'll do my best."

I lay down away from the table, trying to ignore the moans and cries of encouragement Valka was making. I kicked off my boots and Krinna helped me out of my clothes, leaving me in nothing but my orgone belt. She nestled in among the pillows alongside me. I expected her tight body to feel a lot different, but her skin was soft and when she wasn't using her muscles, she felt about the same as any other woman.

She ran her hand over my chest. "You feel kind of tense."

"This is our first time with four people," I said.

"Ah! I knew it had to be something." She glanced up at the table. "And you have a special relationship with Valka, don't you?"

"Yes."

"You're lucky. I only really got to know David ten days ago or so. We're not like that. We have sex. Not even really lovers, if the word means anything. I don't have anyone like that." Her hand drifted down to my cock, which had gone mostly soft, and caressed it lightly.

"I'm sure someone—"

She silenced me with a kiss, and then whispered. "Not as long as I'm a Worthy, no. There will be no someone special. Because everything is engineered. Because of orgone." She stroked my cock, taking it in her hand, coaxing it back to life. "But I'm not here to talk shop."

As my cock swelled, she shifted down to place a simple kiss on the very tip, followed by another and another, moving along the underside of my shaft until she touched the very base. She then retraced her path with a long, wide swipe of her tongue, and brought her mouth down around me.

Soon, all thoughts of what else was going on in the room were driven from my mind. Krinna had been too modest. Her energetic style, with rapid strokes and lots of intense stimulation with her tongue, were unfamiliar, but that made it even better. I arched my back, driving myself deeper into the pillows and pushing my cock deeper into her mouth. She accepted my thrust greedily. To block out all other sensations, I shut my eyes and concentrated on the marvelous feel of her mouth.

As if from a long distance, I heard the familiar sounds of Valka's orgasm, but they had no great significance. The only thing that mattered was my cock.

Then, there were lips on mine, lips that tasted of tea and spice and sweetness. I opened my eyes. Valka's face hung over mine with a broad smile and flashing eyes. "Enjoying yourself, lover?" she asked.

"Uh...yeah." With Krinna still working on my cock, it was hard to put words together.

"Good." She giggled, and then went back to kissing me. A breast brushed my hand and I turned it over to cup the soft curve. I squeezed it almost without thinking, just because it felt good to do so. A vibration moved through my cock and I heard a soft humming moan from Krinna's throat; she was doing the same to me as I had done to her.

The symphony being played on my skin drew my mind even deeper into the storm of ecstasy. I could barely control my movements. I held back, letting the orgasm build even higher, and the tension of it made my arms and legs twitch until I could hold back no more. My vision burst with colored stars as my climax roared in my ears. My groan grew to a shout and I felt hot splashes across my belly and chest.

Krinna's moans continued through and after, growing in intensity. When I could finally lift my head, I saw David was behind Krinna, driving into her with an intense rhythm. Both of their faces drawn with ecstasy, pulled tight, teeth bared on the ragged edge of orgasm. Valka and I watched as first Krinna, and then David tensed, moaned, and came. They collapsed around us, making a warm, sweaty, heaving tangle.

I looked over at Valka. She lay on her side, gazing at my face. "How do you feel?" she asked.

"Exhausted."

"I love you," she said and kissed me lightly on the cheek.

And all was right with the universe.

chapter eighteen

Renedy, Stakroya Station

THE MERCHANT SHIP slid into place and docked at the huge cargo hatch near the docking bays. Clamps engaged, magnets hummed to life, and the huge ship was secure.

"Wow," said Star, peering at his holoscreen. "That's gotta be the biggest ship that has ever docked here."

"Yeah, and it's new too. Look at the paint around the docking clamps. No scrapes." I selected an interior camera near the docking bay and turned the point of view towards the hatch they had connected to. Captain Shaunson was there, waiting patiently with a couple of security officers. The scene was a perfect symbol of the status of station folk in the galaxy. Even Captain Shaunson, leader of thousands of people on board Stakroya Station, was cooling his heels on the order of a Merchant ship captain.

Finally, the hatch opened. Five people stood in the revealed opening. I shouldn't have been surprised, given everything that had been happening, but I still found myself gaping at the sight. The Merchant who waited there for Captain Shaunson to step into the lock wasn't one of the lumbering, grossly obese figures we usually saw. Instead, she had the exaggerated curves of the women in Star's holo. After speaking with him for a moment, she turned and introduced two men standing behind her—a seven-foot Marine in gleaming blue space armor and a man in a bright, white Scout uniform. They were flanked by two Marine guards carrying heavy guns.

"And something else you never see," I said. "All three services working together like this? I wonder if your friends down in the docking bay ever heard of anything like this before."

"What? Oh, I was still looking at the outside." Star craned his neck to look over at my holoscreen. "That can't be good."

"We'll see." The figures turned and walked into the ship, and the hatch closed behind them. "Show's over," I said and turned off the camera.

"Has the ship requested any loading manifests yet?"

"Nope. Haven't sent anything over for unloading, either. This isn't a cargo run, that's certain."

"So what are they here for?"

"I don't know. Yet." I took a deep breath and slid a memory wafer into place. The program I had written on it took control and the holoscreen started scrolling through numerous walls of text. They were too small for the cameras in the room to follow, but leaning forward, I could read them fairly easily. I didn't have to watch this way, it certainly wouldn't affect the success or failure of my plan, but I couldn't resist watching my program in action.

There was no visual representation for it, but in my imagination, I saw the program I had written unfold itself into the console and unfurl tendrils of code along the data conduits leading to the Merchant ship. They encountered walls, access restrictions and security systems, but instead of trying to breach them, they simply gathered information about them and fed it back to the chip. This wasn't an attack; it was just a look around to see what sort of information could be gained. After only a few seconds, the screens went blank except for a tiny blinking light telling me it had completed its mission.

I started reviewing the logs. I didn't think my skills would be sharp enough to actually penetrate their systems. After all, the skills I was learning had been provided by the same people who had built the Merchant ship's data architecture. If they weren't able to keep me out, they would have to be incredibly stupid, and I knew they were anything but. At the same time, I was curious about what was happening on the Merchant ship and if I had the chance to work at it, I might be able to pry something loose. For now, I had data to analyze and code to write.

When the shift ended, Star took my hand and pulled me into the elevator. "Come on," he said. "You need to meet someone."

"Star, it's dinnertime. I'm hungry."

"It's handled. Come on." He pressed the button for the core systems level, which housed the life support, power, and ventilation systems—plus the infirmary.

"What's going on?"

"It's a surprise."

"This is about Nella, isn't it?"

"Aw, how did you know?"

"Star! I'm not an idiot. Why else would I be going down there? I'm not sick, so what else could it be?"

"So if you know, why didn't you go down there before?" he argued.

"I can't do that!"

"Why not?"

"What if she's not...you know. Like us."

Star just smiled. The doors opened onto a wide hallway with a big pair of double doors to the right, which were painted with a red dot on a white background signifying medical facilities.

Dr. Klane was just coming out. "Ah, greetings. Is there anything you need? I was about to go up and get some food."

"No," said Star. "You go ahead. Is Nella in?"

"Yes, she's covering." He winked and passed by us into the elevator. "Good evening to you both."

I watched him until the doors closed, and then turned back to Star. "What in the void?"

He smiled. "You'll see!" He took my hand again and practically dragged me into the infirmary. He marched me up to the desk where Nella was sitting and wrapped his arm around my shoulder. "You really ought to take a look at Ren, here. She's definitely looking pale. I think it might be some kind of deficiency."

Nella looked me over and frowned. "Yes, I think you're right. We better get you in for an examination right away." She got up from behind the desk and walked to the door of the recovery room. "This way, please?"

I looked back at Star. He had a huge goofy smile on his face. "I'll just wait out here."

Once Nella closed the door to the recovery room behind us, she turned down the lights and stepped close to me. She pitched her voice low, nearly a whisper. "To do a proper examination, we'll need to get you out of those clothes."

I stammered, feeling like I should say something but unable to come up with actual words.

Nella smiled wickedly, taking the zipper of my jumpsuit between her fingers and slowly drawing it down.

"You s-s-set this up with Star, didn't you?" I was too stunned to do anything but watch as she peeled the top of my coverall back from my shoulders and pushed it down my body.

"For people like us, getting what we need isn't always easy."

"But why? I mean..." She knelt at my feet, undoing my boots so she could get the coverall completely off of my body.

"Don't ask questions," she whispered, running her fingers up along the side of my thigh.

I shuddered at the touch. "But...I just can't believe..."

"Believe it." The backs of her fingers brushed against my sex, and even through my flimsies the sensation threw an incredible thrill down my spine. "Relax," she said, gently laying me down on one of the monitoring beds. "This won't hurt a bit."

So far, she hadn't touched me any differently than Star had, but somehow those touches electrified me in ways he never did.

Nella left my flimsies in place at first, drawing her fingers over my body instead, so lightly they felt like the air from a heavy ventilation duct. They drew up my belly, circled my breasts, then over my shoulders and down my arms. She bent down for a kiss, sweet and tender and soft, and when her tongue delicately found its way between my teeth, I couldn't help letting out a little moan. Of course. This was the infirmary recovery room; the only place we could be together that didn't have a camera.

She pulled back and laughed lightly. "My, you are in need, aren't you?"

"What about Dr. Klane?"

"Don't worry. He's one of us. He'll be away for a while."

"One of...us?"

"Ssh." She bent down again, putting her lips to my breast, and the conversation was over. My breath came sharply as her lips and tongue teased my tightening flesh.

"Wait. Stop." I tried to push her away gently, but she held my hand away, her mouth still working on my skin. I got a good grip and shoved. "No!"

She stumbled back with an unreadable expression on her face.

I sat up, scowling, arms crossed over my breasts. "I'm not a toy you can just drag off to a quiet corner and play with."

She cocked her head to one side. "That doesn't feel good to you?"

"Yes! It felt wonderful. But Nella, I hardly know you. We had a few classes together, but until recently, we haven't exchanged more than ten words!"

"I'm sorry," she said, ducking her head. "I didn't mean to scare you."

"What's going on here? I need to know."

She glanced at the door, then down at the floor, avoiding eye contact with me. "I was told you were like me. That you liked girls. I just thought we could have some fun together."

"Who? Who told you? Star?"

She took a deep breath, let it out, then raised her head to look me in the eye. "Captain Shaunson."

"Captain...of course. But how did he know? No, don't tell me. Star told him." I punched the bed next to me. "I'll kill him."

"No!" Nella grabbed my arm. "It's not his fault."

"Why not? He knew this had to stay a secret!"

"Listen, I can tell you about the whole thing, but you have to promise me something."

"What?"

"If Star or Captain Shaunson asks you...oh, vack...or...well, you just have to pretend that we've done it."

"It?"

"That I made you...that we had sex, and that you enjoyed it. All the way. Please. Promise me? I'll get in big trouble..."

"We could get in big trouble for doing what we were about to do!"

"I can explain. But you have to promise."

"Oh, all right. I promise. Can I get dressed now?"

Nella sighed. "Yeah, I suppose."

While I pulled my coverall back on, Nella pulled herself up onto the bed opposite mine. "So, there are people who like having sex with girls and people who like boys, and there are people who like both," she explained. "Only, sometimes the people who like girls are girls, and the people who like boys are boys. And those people don't really fit the way the Scouts and the Fleet and the Merchants like to run things because their families aren't all neat and tidy and they don't have as many children."

My jaw practically dropped into my lap. "There are people who like *both*?"

"Yes, and I guess some who don't like sex at all, but I've never met one of those. Anyways, folks like us who like the same sex don't have it very good, because there aren't that many of us and the Scouts don't like us. So we have to do what we can to protect ourselves. That's why Captain Shaunson got you and Star into the communications cluster. He thought maybe you were one of us, and started up the system."

"What? That doesn't make any sense. He tried to get me to resign!"

"If you had, then he would have known you weren't the kind of person he wanted there."

I looked around the room, as if there were answers written on the walls. "I guess that makes kind of sense."

"He's very careful only to bring in people he knows are our sort. He tries to arrange it so they're married to each other, if he can, and helps them find other folks for sex."

"Which is why he set me up with Star...and with you."

"Yes. And my husband. It's all a very careful balancing act." Nella glanced at the door and rubbed her hands on her knees. "He also tries to make sure we get posted to jobs where we can help protect each other. Me in the infirmary, you in the communications cluster, and other folks elsewhere."

"How many of you are there?"

"I don't know, but there can't be more than ten or twenty at most on the station."

"So what happens to the in-between people? The ones who like both, or the ones who don't like either?"

"I don't know. I don't think Captain Shaunson wants them in on things, which is why he insisted that I make sure you would like sex with a girl. To make sure you're not one of the ones who just don't like sex at all."

I paused for a moment, considering. I had my coverall almost back on, ready to zip it up. I was in on a big, black secret, something that would probably get all of us in big trouble if the Scouts found out. It scared me all the way down to my toes that this was all going on, especially with a Merchant ship docked to the station with the Scouts and Marines on board.

"And you need me," I said. "You need me in this group."

"Yes. Captain Shaunson made it clear. Star and I were to do whatever it took to get you in."

"Then I'm in," I said, stepping closer to lay a little kiss on the curve of Nella's ear. "All the way in," I whispered.

She pulled back and smiled at me. "Really?"

"I want you to trust me. But I'm not a ragdoll. I may not know a lot about sex, but I know one thing. If it isn't about both of us, it's not right." I remembered Greel, his scurrilous holos, and his sick insinuations.

"I'm sorry," she said. "I just—"

"Ssh." I put my finger to her lips. "No more apologies." I drew my hand down to the zipper of her white coverall, watching her eyes.

She nodded. "No more apologies." Her hand found its way between my suit and my skin, and I hurried to keep up, running her zipper down to caress her the same way she caressed me. We found each other's mouths and pulled ourselves together, finding symmetry in similarity.

It didn't seem possible, but kissing her on these renewed terms felt even better than before. Knowing what I was getting involved in, I had the confidence to let go of my anxieties and fully enjoy everything we were doing.

Somehow, we managed to get naked without taking our mouths and hands off of each other's bodies for more than a second. Her body wasn't that different from mine—slim and wiry compared to the voluptuous Merchant women who still inhabited my imagination— but I was so thrilled to have any partner at all that I didn't mind her lack of curves. She was a woman and she had given her body to me to enjoy, and that was enough for me.

I maneuvered her back against one of the beds and got her to hop up on the mattress. As I leaned down, the thought occurred to me that, from a certain point of view, one woman looks pretty much like another. I also wondered whether my body looked like this as well—this fur-crowned crease that concealed a treasure of beautiful, fragrant folds.

Nella sighed as my fingers delved between her tender lips, exposing her flesh to my curious eyes. I wanted to please her and I wanted to be pleased as well, but I also wanted to learn, and when would I get another chance?

"Go ahead," she said.

"Go ahead, what?"

"Lick it. Kiss it."

I shrugged, and gave a tentative pass with my tongue, and was surprised at her intense reaction. I licked her again, repeating the performance and getting an even stronger response. "Have you done this before?" I asked.

"Yes," she said.

I left a tender kiss at the root of the hairs that came closest to the top of her cleft.

"More. Faster!"

I couldn't help laughing a little, hearing the little gasps and cries and moans she made as I increased my pace. A euphoric sense of rightness filled me, bubbling up from someplace deep inside. Most anyone else, if they knew what I was doing, would find it scandalously wrong, but the smell and taste and feel of Nella's body meshed with my desires so completely that there was no way I could deny it was right.

Her hand brushed my ear, caressed my cheek, and then moved around behind my head. I pulled away a little, catching her eye. She smiled momentarily until a shudder ran through her and overwrote the smile with a look of pure ecstasy, and then she pushed me back down.

I was happy to oblige. Every gasp and groan was a feast for my starving psyche. I was glutting myself on her pleasure. As the shivers and trembles became more intense, she fell back against the bed, releasing her hold on my skull, but I didn't let up the pressure. She shouted, then shrieked, arching her back. I wrapped my arm around her leg to keep her steady enough to continue.

As her climax faded, she sat up, pulled her legs together, and put her hands on my cheeks. "Thank you," she said, bringing my face to hers for a kiss. "I wasn't expecting that. That was really good."

"You're so welcome," I said.

"You sure you haven't done this before?"

"Yep. Care to return the favor?"

"Gladly."

We switched positions. As I was laying down where she had been, she said, "It's your first time, so I'll go easy on you." There was a twinkle of laughter in her eye.

"Don't you dare," I said. "I expect the full treatment."

"You sure? Women have gone mad, you know." She opened her eyes wide in mock horror.

I laughed. "I'll risk it." I was already very aroused, just from being there with her, just from the thrill of it all, but I wanted to go as far as I could. I knew that with all the risks, we might never have another chance.

Kneeling between my spread thighs, she did something I didn't expect. Instead of using her fingers to part my lips, she stroked them a few times, then gripped my entire vulva, almost down to my thighs, and squeezed.

I sat up to look down at what she was doing. The maneuver pushed all of my sensitive parts together and fanned them out between her fingers. When she drew her tongue up along that cluster, it felt incredible. Nothing Star had ever done, nothing I had ever done for myself, felt as good as that.

Nella could have done nothing else but lick along that one place and I would have been ecstatic, but that wasn't the beginning and end of it. She sucked and nibbled and kissed, and when she had run through all the ways for a mouth to do things, she started moving her hand around. There was something about how that made the bits inside rub together that made it feel even better.

I couldn't have held back no matter what was at stake. "Oh, vack!" I groaned, falling back onto the bed. My hands, for some reason, went to my face. I was completely incapacitated by the pleasure she was giving me. "Vack, vack, vack!"

There was a little giggle from between my legs and the speed of her movements increased. Something crept up inside me, slowly, wriggling in between my squeezed-down labia; a finger, Nella's finger, tickling its way in. It seemed like a tiny thing, but when added to everything else, it brought me a whole new level of pleasure.

She took her face away from my body and said, "Pinch your nipples."

"Oh, vack, don't stop now!" I cried.

"Pinch your nipples or I will."

My hands leapt to my breasts. There was not even the slightest thought of disobeying her. As soon as I had the sensitive skin between my fingers, she was back, thrashing my cunt with her fingers and tongue. I gripped my breasts so hard they hurt, but somehow that pain only made the pleasure even stronger.

My toes tingled, my body trembled, I shouted out things I never thought I would ever say, and all through it, the only thought that ran through my head was *dirty, sick, perverted, WRONG!*

And my answer to that was an equally enthusiastic, *YES!*

The first orgasm blew my awareness open like explosive decompression. My vision dimmed, my limbs lost all control, and I screamed wordlessly at the void that surrounded me. Before I could even begin to collect my wits, it happened again, and again. Tears streamed down my cheeks, my muscles cramping with strain, and yet my body still kept going.

I couldn't take any more. I pushed Nella away, letting out a half-crying, half-gasping sound. My hands found a pillow and covered my privates with it, protecting me from another mind-destroying assault.

She stood and looked down into my wide-open eyes. "Wasn't that fun?"

All I could do was nod.

"I don't think there's any doubt you're one of us. Welcome to the club, Renedy."

It wasn't easy to leave the infirmary where Nella and I had shared my initiation. I hadn't realized how hungry I had been for what Nella offered until that hunger was sated, and I never wanted to leave the table again. There was a limit, however, to how long we could stay, and if someone came in who actually needed the infirmary, we would be discovered. It would be bad enough for me, but Nella was married. From what she had said, her husband probably wouldn't care, but everyone else would. We couldn't risk it.

I came out of the recovery room in a daze. My clothes were back in place and we had managed to clean up enough so I no longer smelled strongly of girl-sex, but nothing could wipe the goofy grin off my face.

Star was leaning back in a chair, arms folded behind his head, with a huge grin on his face. "Feeling better?"

I nodded. "Unh-huh."

He laughed and stood up. "Good. I'm glad for you." With an arm around my shoulder, he steered me out the door and into the elevator. "I was thinking that now might be a good time to use the privacy chamber."

At that point, I would have agreed to anything. "Sure," I said.

The sex was quick and businesslike. We took off our coveralls, I bent over the bed, and after a few minutes of getting himself worked up, we did it. I even kind of enjoyed it with the memories of Nella's fingers and tongue fresh in my mind.

And with that chore handled, I went back to my room and to bed.

chapter nineteen

Challers, Port

I TOOK a deep breath and let it out again. Walking up to the doors of the dueling arena, I told myself the clenching in my gut was nothing more than a response to the memory of my first time there. The doors parted and I went inside.

I was half relieved and half annoyed that Krinna wasn't there ahead of me, but I had come a few minutes before our appointment. I paced around the perimeter, checking my pistol and goggles for the eighth time that morning. Finally, the doors opened again.

"I'm glad you're here," she said, laying her duffel bag on the deck and pulling out her goggles.

"Well, I figure after the mistake last week, you'll be more careful."

"*I'll* be more careful?" She cocked an eyebrow.

"You're the instructor. The way I see it, you're responsible for what happens."

She nodded. "I suppose you're right. But let me make this clear: if I'm in charge, then that means you have to do what I say, when I say it. No hesitation. These are potentially lethal weapons. Deal?"

"Deal."

"All right. Let's start with some drills." She pulled her battered target out of the duffel bag and started setting it up.

I put on my goggles and moved to the opposite side of the arena, drew my pistol, and made sure it was set on "tag" and that the energy levels were topped up. Without hooking it up to my orgone belt, the power cell would be good for hundreds of shots at this setting—more than enough for a day's practice.

"All right, begin. Quarter speed. Get your form correct." Krinna stepped away from the target and put on her goggles.

I tried to find the proper stance, remembering the day of drills we had already been through. I drew and fired, trying to make the motion smooth and natural. It felt stiff and jerky, and my shot went wide. "Is Valka doing any better at this?" I asked.

"She's getting it. But don't worry about her. This afternoon we're here to drill you. Again."

I drew and fired. Another clean miss. It still wasn't right. One thing Valka and I had learned from talking to David and Krinna was that some Worthies challenged duels for just about anything. It was a dramatic way to settle differences, and the Wards always watched in large numbers.

"Again."

A glancing shot made the ball wobble, but not fall. Krinna stepped over to steady it, and then pulled away again. "Challers, concentrate. Nothing in your mind except your arm, your weapon, and the target. Again."

The shot hit the post, ringing it and making the ball fall off the front and roll out across the arena. I holstered the weapon and shook my head.

Krinna put the ball back in place, and then strode across the arena. She stood behind me, wrapped one arm around my chest, and took the back of my right hand in her firm grasp. "Just relax, and let me move you through the draw."

Slowly, she curled the fingers of my hand around the pistol butt, scooping it out of the holster. As we drew it up, she squeezed my hand around it, solidifying my grasp, and brought the weapon to bear. With her behind me, it felt right. A little burst of excitement filled my chest.

She stepped away. "No shooting this time. Just the draw. One-tenth speed, as slow as you can manage and stay smooth."

It felt better. The weapon moved. It felt a little like a dance.

"Again, just a little faster."

I did it again.

"Again. Faster."

A hitch, a grind—it was like gears slipping. I was losing it. I shook my head. "I'm sorry."

Krinna frowned. "Take off your shirt."

"What?"

"Take off your shirt. In that baggy sleeve, I can't see what your arm is doing wrong."

I had lost my modesty at the Scout Academy, so I took it off and threw it aside.

"Draw. Again. Slowly."

I drew. The air in the room was a little chilly on my naked skin, but it wasn't serious.

"Again."

Was I learning anything this way? We drilled the action twenty times or more without much change in the result.

"Take off your pants," said Krinna.

"Okay, now you're getting silly."

She fixed me with a no-nonsense glare. "Take 'em off."

"Whatever." I unbuckled my gun belt, dropped my trousers, and strapped the belt back on. The room was definitely a little chilly.

She drilled me again and again, walking around to watch me from every angle. Finally, after at least a half an hour's work, she snapped her fingers and pointed. "You've got your hip thrown out."

I looked down. "What?"

"You stick out your hip like you're bringing the gun to your hand."

"What does that have to do with anything?"

"It means the weapon doesn't come up on your midline. It throws your rhythm off. Here."

She came up behind me and put her hands on my hips, holding them firmly against hers. The touch brought a tingle to my skin. "Now try it."

When I put my hand in place, I could feel her hand press on my right hip, keeping it where it belonged. The whole motion suddenly felt much more natural.

I repeated the motion a dozen times with her standing behind me. The feeling of her there, fully clothed, while I was nearly naked had a strange erotic edge to it—one that felt familiar without really having a name.

She stood back. "All right. Do it again. Same way. Keep your hips solid."

Slap. Draw. Aim.

"Good. Again."

Slap. Draw. Aim. I could feel her eyes on me. I glanced over. She had her attention fixed on my ass.

"No. Concentrate, Challers. You threw your hip out again. Do it right."

Slap. Draw. Aim.

"No! No, no, no."

She crossed to her duffel bag and pulled out a long, slim strip of black plastic with a handle at one end. She swung it through the air a couple of times, making a swishing sound, and then she came back and stood behind me.

"Again. And keep that hip still."

Slap. Draw. WHACK. I spun around, rubbing the stinging spot on my hip.

She met me with a challenging look. "Keep that hip where it belongs." She gestured toward the target. "Again."

We went through a dozen more drills. Each mistake was punctuated with another stinging slap on my right buttock. To my surprise, I found it actually helped and, gradually, the motion became more and more natural, more and more practiced, more and more right.

"Good," she said. "Good. Now, this time, fire." There was a breathy edge to her voice that I recognized from our dinner together.

My ass still stinging from repeated blows, I drew, aimed, and fired.

I hit the target right in the center. The ball flew off its pedestal into the net. "Yes!" she shouted. "Perfect!" She ran across the arena to put the ball back in place. "Again!"

The drill continued. By the time I was done, my entire arm and shoulder was as sore as my ass. I rubbed the muscles with my good hand. "Can I get dressed now?"

"Oh." She chuckled. "Sure."

While I pulled my pants and shirt back on, she broke down the target and stowed it in her duffel bag. I didn't fail to notice that the instrument she had used to whack me when I made mistakes was still there in her belt.

"You enjoyed that," I said.

"Was it that obvious?" she asked as she moved away from the duffel to stand across the room from me.

"No, but I could tell."

"Does that bother you? That I...like it that way."

"No."

"Did it do anything for you?"

"Not really."

She frowned in disappointment. "Pity. All right, next exercise. Take out your weapon and make sure it's set on 'tag.'"

"All set."

"In this exercise, we're going for precision rather than speed. You may have noticed that our clothes are made to disintegrate when hit by these beams."

"Right. That's to carry the energy away from the skin and keep us from getting hurt."

"That's part of it. But there's another purpose. In a long duel, the clothes take a real beating. You'll knock holes in them. The Wards love it when that happens—that's why so many duels don't stop when the first hit is scored. We keep going until one person admits defeat."

"Sounds brutal."

"It is when the weapon is set on stun, but that's pretty rare. Most of us aren't willing to risk breaking a rib just to make a point. Set on tag, you really won't get much impact unless you're hitting naked skin."

"So you have to hit the same spot twice?"

"That, or hit places where the fabric is close to the skin, or hit the garment in such a way that it exposes a lot of skin for your next shot."

"Got it."

"So, for this exercise, your job is to expose as much as you can in thirty seconds. Your best shots will be the places where the garments come together. Shoulders, and the knots that hold things together at my waist."

I raised my pistol. "I'm ready."

"Portcon, please start a thirty-second countdown when I say 'go.'"

"Understood, Worthy Krinna Lawson."

She immediately dodged out of my line of fire, shouting, "Go!"

I swung to keep her in my sights, firing, and evaporating a chunk of her sleeve with a loud snap. Unlike the mass driver weapon I had trained with in the Scouts, this pistol had no recoil and it was easy to track her as I fired, in spite of her erratic movements. Each shot took away another few square centimeters of fabric. Some of the hits garnered a gasp or a grunt from her, but mostly she just kept evading, each movement precise. Even her breathing was controlled. Near the end of the thirty seconds, I managed to tag her hip where one of the flaps of her shirt was tied, and the end flew off, exposing one tit. I took a couple more shots, but I couldn't quite hit the other knot before Portcon sounded a klaxon and announced that time had run out.

Krinna stood, skin flushed, and surveyed the damage. "Wow! Nice shooting!" Her shirt was in tatters, holed many times, and hanging half open. "I was never very good at dodging."

"Didn't that hurt?"

"A little." She took off the ruined garment and shoved it into her duffel bag, leaving her half naked. She pulled out a replacement, but just hung it over her shoulder, displaying a comfortable confidence. "Care to take your turn at it?"

"I didn't bring a replacement shirt and I doubt I'll come off any better than you did."

"Fair enough," she said. "Bring one next time." She hefted the duffel bag and slung it over her shoulder. "One question, before we're done. Why did you only shoot at my shirt?"

"Well, for one thing, the white was easier to see. Second, I figured if I limited my shots to one area, I'd be more likely to reveal more skin in the limited time available. And last," I said with a wink, "I like breasts."

She let out one big "Ha!" and shook her head. "As good a reason as any. All right, time for the showers." She headed for the arena preparation room. She gave me a crosswise look. "Care to join me?"

"Sure."

The locker room next to the dueling arena wasn't terribly large, just a small dressing area next to a gang shower big enough for six people—eight if they didn't mind getting cozy. Krinna set aside her duffle and replacement shirt, kicked off her boots, dropped her pants, and walked under the nozzles.

By the time I had my outfit off, she had already lathered up her hair and had begun washing her body. When I turned on the water, I had half an erection and I knew it would get a lot harder if she kept touching herself that way.

"Face the wall," she said.

"What?"

"Turn and face the wall."

"I'm sorry if I've offended you somehow."

"It's not that at all. Just..." Her hand drifted down toward her pussy. "Do as I say."

I shrugged and turned to let the spray run over my face and chest. Over the hiss and splash of the water, I could hear Krinna gasping. Looking over my shoulder, I saw that she was looking down at my ass, squeezing her nipple and rubbing hard at her pussy. I bent back to get a look at it myself.

What she was watching were the bright-red streaks that crisscrossed the right side of my behind. "That really does get you going," I said.

Her gasps turned to moans and she sank slowly toward the floor. "I've...been holding off on this...oh...since I gave them to you."

I turned back and stood in the spray, unsure how to react. We'd had a lecture on pain play back at Scout Headquarters, but since it didn't really do much for Shirley or me, we never did much with it. I wondered whether Krinna had anyone to do that with. Judging from her reaction, I had to suspect that she didn't.

I listened to the strangled, choking sounds of Krinna's orgasm, and then stepped out of the shower to dry off. "See you tomorrow."

"Remember to bring spare clothes," she said.

chapter twenty

Renedy, Stakroya Station

I HAD TO BE very, very subtle. There would be someone on board the Merchant ship whose job it was to make sure their computer systems were secure. That person couldn't even become suspicious that anyone was trying to gain access.

I had to go slow. At the same time, things were happening and I had a feeling I didn't have much time to learn what was going on before it was done. My second reconnaissance mission went pretty much the same as the first—very little had changed. That was a good sign. It meant my first try hadn't been detected.

The third attempt used the information gleaned during the first two to push a little further, looking for open data structures and communications nodes. Most importantly, I was looking for a place I could set up a servitor process that could run my programs from inside their system. This was necessary to protect myself if my work was discovered.

You find out a lot about opening doors when you learn to lock them.

The Merchant ship's system wasn't terribly secure. I found several data structures with minimal security. In the one that looked the most disused, I set up a servitor process.

As soon as it was done, my curiosity got the better of me. I had a look at the data stored there. There were five self-playing holo-recordings—like the ones Star had brought to our first time together. I didn't have time to look at them, especially sitting in the communications cluster where anyone could walk in. I copied them to an empty data store in our own system and went back to work.

I put new programs on the servitor, more aggressive ones, and set them to their work, then closed down my link. The longer I stayed connected, the greater the chance I'd be detected.

An announcement came to the terminal from Captain Shaunson. There would be another address on the Promenade at the end of the light shift. All were strongly encouraged to attend. "You won't want to miss this!" he said.

Maybe, maybe not, I thought. I wasn't so naïve that I couldn't see what was happening—or, at least, what could be happening. The first address made us expect something nice to happen. There was no guarantee that would continue. There were Marines on that ship that only Captain Shaunson and I knew about. The last time they had come to Stakroya Station, they had been very visible. This time, it was a secret.

And the worst part was that I couldn't easily tell Nella or Star about it. They were part of Captain Shaunson's conspiracy—far enough into it that I doubted they could see anything that Captain Shaunson did as wrong. I knew from personal experience that he was perfectly willing to manipulate people to reach his goals.

Another message came up on my board a little while later, also from Captain Shaunson. He wanted us to check all the cameras starting at the end of light shift, and tell him about anyone who wasn't on their way to the assembly. Only a few people were exempt: Dr. Klane, some of the men who worked down in the life support plant, and a half dozen from the security detail. Star was on the list, but I wasn't. The message I got from this was that attendance would be mandatory.

That sealed it; there definitely was something odd going on.

I went back and checked my servitor process. Its job was merely to find weaknesses in the code locks protecting the Merchant ship's operations. There were a few little spots here and there where maintenance procedures hadn't been followed properly, where shortcuts had been taken to make someone's job easier.

One of the things it had managed to get into was the holocam feed system. There weren't as many of them on the ship as there were on the station, but there were a few—mostly in high-security areas like the main drive system, the bridge, and life support.

Mostly.

One camera stood out. It was labeled GENTANKS. What that meant, I couldn't tell, so I had the system run out and grab some still images from it. The result showed a room with row upon row of boxes with transparent tops. They were a meter high by two meters long and a meter and a half wide with some kind of liquid inside. Seeing it didn't really answer any questions.

Another thing the programs brought back was a back door into the life support systems. I couldn't really control anything, but I could see the settings on the oxygen generators. The normal complement was twenty-five crewmembers, according to the settings, but it was now putting out enough oxygen for a hundred and twelve. The same was true of the water recycler. The extra would be the Marines and Scouts. Why would they need so many? I wasn't learning much, but my sense of foreboding grew. I was desperately curious to learn more.

But then what would I do with the information? It wasn't like I had any power to change things. Whatever plans the people on the big freighter had, there wasn't much any of us could do about it—unless the message from Captain Shaunson had a hidden meaning. He did that a lot, it seemed. Clearly, anyone I reported as not going to the assembly would be strongly "invited" to attend. Anyone I didn't report had a good chance of avoiding whatever was going to happen. So maybe I did need that information. If I knew what they were going to do with those "gentanks," I might be able to figure out who might be hiding out to avoid them, and whether I should report them or not.

I sent some new commands to the servitor process and went back to my work, finishing off what absolutely had to be done, postponing anything that didn't, and skipping lunch in order to get it done as soon as possible. I tried to reconnect to the servitor process on the Merchant ship an hour before the end of the shift.

It wasn't there. Everything else was the same, but my servitor was gone. I disconnected immediately.

Someone had discovered it and deleted it. That made no sense. The manuals I had been studying said that the primary goal of any security force was to figure out who was intruding, so you could deal with them face to face. The proper response to discovering the servitor process would have been to watch it, see who accessed it, and trace it back. They couldn't do that if they deleted the process. It just tipped me off that my work had been discovered.

I quickly went through our own logs and deleted any record that I had been accessing the Merchant ship, then sat back and cursed. My chances of getting the information I wanted before the assembly started were pretty slim.

Then I remembered the holos I had copied out of the data store. It wasn't likely that anything really useful would be there, but it didn't hurt to look. I started scanning through them, looking at the metadata that would hopefully describe the contents of each file.

There wasn't much. A holo-recording would normally have an audio bit rate and format, recording depth, and a default stage size and stage rate, but since these were self-playing, they didn't even need that because they contained their own player software. Everything was blank—even the title. All I had to go on were the filenames and they made no sense. They were "Ovor Ed 1" through "Ovor Ed 5." There wasn't anything to do except start one up and see what it had to say.

A stage lit up, showing an older man in a clean white medical coverall, standing in a comfortable-looking office. There was even a potted plant in the corner.

"The Ovor body system is superior to the puregen human baseline in several important ways. Lifespan is extended by approximately twenty percent, food requirements per individual are reduced by fifteen percent, and in general, hormone balance facilitates a more agreeable outlook. In addition, the unique reproductive cycle of the Ovor makes pregnancy less dangerous, reducing both infant and maternal mortality rates."

While he spoke, a man walked into the frame. He was a head shorter than the first man and, in spite of being completely naked, he wore a friendly smile. He looked healthy and well fed with a trim waist and well-defined, if not particularly muscular, chest and arms.

Star stood behind me. "Nice. What's this?"

"I don't know. I found it."

"Where?"

"Shush."

The man in the holo continued, "As you can see, the male Ovor physiology is very similar. The only real difference is the presence of four aureoles instead of two." He nodded to the shorter man, who departed the stage and was replaced by an equally naked woman.

She was about the same height as the man had been, and likewise fit and well fed. The four round breasts on her chest shouldn't have been a surprise, given the appearance of the man, but the sight still brought my eyebrows up a notch.

"Ovor females look quite similar to the human puregen baseline on the exterior. However, there are significant differences on the inside." The scene was replaced by a strange anatomical diagram, similar to the pictures I had seen in motherhood class, but everything seemed out of proportion.

"The Ovor reproductive system does not have separate ovaries and fallopian tubes. Instead, they are embedded in the lining of the uterus. Every month, each ovary produces a large egg, which immediately implants on the uterine wall and begins growing. Without fertilization, the egg will grow to a few hundred milliLowells and wait in stasis."

The diagram changed again, showing a cutaway view of a bean-shaped object. Labels appeared with lines pointing to individual layers of the bean. "The egg is surrounded by a porous membrane, a layer of hard, protective connective tissue, and a food reserve of fat and protein." Tiny animated sperm started swimming around the egg, moving into the pores in its skin. "When the egg is fertilized, it begins to develop, and hormonal signals are sent to the mother's uterus to begin the birthing process."

The holo ended and the stage went dark.

"Okay, so where did you find that?" asked Star. "Or shouldn't you say?"

I just glared at him. With the cameras looking in on us, I didn't want to draw any more attention to what I was doing than I already had. "Go back to work, Star. Check on those cameras and see who might be skipping the assembly."

He shrugged and returned to his seat.

I was still missing a lot of pieces, but this appeared to link up with some of the other clues I had discovered. I had a chilling suspicion that the people on the ship docked with our station were planning on transforming us into this "Ovor" shape on the video. I knew that the Merchants and the Fleet had the ability to transform people—they did it to their own crews all the time—and those "gentanks" on the Merchant ship might just be the way they did it. If each woman on the station produced two eggs every month, we were going to have population problems like we had never had before.

Something had to be done and the only way that was going to happen was if I did it. I wanted to tell Star and Nella what I planned, but I knew that the more people I involved, the more likely it was that we'd be discovered.

"Star," I said. "I don't think I feel very good."

"Oh?"

"Yeah, I think it might be hormones or something. I'm going down to the infirmary."

"But what about the assembly?"

"I'm sure you can take care of it."

When I got there, Dr. Klane was sitting at his desk. "Something wrong, missy?"

"Just need to lie down a bit," I said, nodding towards the infirmary.

"What's wrong, then?"

"Just feeling a little sick to my stomach."

"We should run a few tests. See if you're pregnant."

"Oh, I'm pretty sure I'm not."

"Still." He followed me into the recovery room rather than the examination room, waited for the door to close, then bent down to whisper in my ear. "You know something."

I turned and hopped up onto one of the beds. He leaned against another. "I have some suspicions," I replied. "If we're lucky, it'll all blow over."

"I don't think it will."

"No, I don't think so either. Do you know how Merchants and Marines get to be the way they are?"

He narrowed his eyes. "How do you mean?"

"I mean, Merchants don't get fat from just eating a lot. Marines don't get huge by training hard."

"No."

"I didn't think so. Have you ever heard of something called a 'gentank?'"

"Yes. There's one on any ship. It's a kind of automatic medical treatment machine."

"I think it does more than that. There are hundreds of them on that ship. I think they plan on transforming all or most of us into something else. 'Ovors,' whatever that is."

He frowned and nodded once. "That fits with what I got in the mail. A whole set of medical textbooks on Ovor physiology. I've been studying them for weeks without knowing why."

"So you know how often Ovors have babies...or eggs or whatever. Why would anyone want to do that?" I asked, shaking my head.

"I don't know." He glanced at the door. "I take it you're not going to the assembly."

"No. I'm not. I'm going to hide out until they're done."

"I don't know if you're going to be able to hide here," he said, shaking his head. "Once the assembly is over, if there's any fighting..."

"I know. I know. I'll figure out somewhere else to go. I'm pretty sure Star will cover for me if he sees me wandering around."

"Good luck, missy."

"Thanks, Doc."

I SAW IT ALL.

Shaunson told them nothing—nothing that mattered. His speech was full of promises saying how Stakroya Station would be getting an overhaul with improved life support systems, better hydroponics, and more efficient water recyclers. While all that was being done, the crew would be held in "stasis tanks" aboard the freighter. He said that, as a result of the coming changes, we would live longer, happier lives, and it was all because of our loyal service.

My teeth ground together as I watched on the recovery room monitor. As far as I could tell, very little of it was a lie, and it was the biggest deception yet. When it came time for everyone to file into the Merchant ship and take their places in the so-called "stasis tanks," everyone complied. There may have been some grumbling or confusion, I couldn't hear the people very well over the holofeed, but nobody was making any trouble. They didn't even have to call out the Marines; our own station security handled crowd control.

When it was all over, I shut off the monitor and flopped onto one of the beds. What was I going to do? Staying back from the assembly had been a mistake. I would be discovered sooner or later. But what choice was there? Did I really want to become a walking baby factory? No. That wasn't going to happen.

Worse yet, Shaunson had exempted Star from the process, but not me, or Nella, or her husband. I ground my teeth in frustration. How could he do this to us? Wasn't he supposed to be protecting us?

The first thing I needed to do was figure out where I could hide out while the transformation of Stakroya Station was going on, and what I was going to do when it was done. If they were going to be rebuilding the life support systems, then I couldn't hide out there. Anything close to the docking bays was also out of the question; there would be too much traffic back and forth to the Merchant ship.

The infirmary wasn't the only place that didn't have cameras installed. There were plenty of access passages and maintenance bays that would be empty. It would be easy to find one with access to food and air. If my plan worked, the cameras weren't going to matter for very long.

And then what? Live as a parasite, hiding out in the corners for the rest of my life?

No. Vack, no!

I had to move quickly, before they got started on the work, changing the station architecture. I ran out, thanking Dr. Klane as I went. In one of the repair bays, I grabbed a spare diagnostic terminal and plugged its cable into the network. The little twenty-centimeter screen didn't even have a holographic interface, but it was portable and had enough computing power for what I needed. I grabbed some of the programs I had been working on out of my personal data store in the communications cluster before wiping anything even slightly incriminating.

In a back corner of the bay, someone had stashed a couple of the gift boxes from the previous assembly. Grinning at my good luck, I snatched one of them and took it and the terminal toward the nearest emergency airlock.

Ordinarily, opening one of these refuges would have triggered an alarm. They were only to be used in true emergencies. In the event of a major hull breach, the people inside the station could go there if they couldn't get to a secure compartment. Likewise, if there was an accident during an exterior inspection, there would be an emergency airlock within a few steps.

I opened the maintenance panel and hooked up my terminal. In a matter of seconds, I was inside. I stowed my little box of food, opened a panel to hook up my little terminal, and got down to some serious work. Being a fugitive had its advantages; I could devote my time exclusively to making sure I had control of the systems I needed to control.

I didn't know how long I had, but I was going to make the most of it.

chapter twenty-one

Challers, Port

NINA'S PLACE was small as restaurants went, but it was crowded enough that I didn't spot Valka until she waved to me. She sat in a small booth far in the back. I hurried past the seated patrons to join her. She had a drink in front of her, half finished, and a holographic menu floating in the air over the table.

"Hey, love." I gave her a kiss and slid into the seat across from her.

"How'd your session go with Krinna?"

"Pretty good. At least, she's not saying that I'm a total washout. Yours?"

"I think I'll be able to put up a good fight if someone challenges me, but at this point, I can't see making dueling a major part of my strategy."

"Strategy?" I puzzled over the menu. Everything had stylish names that had to be explained in the fine print. Why did a grilled-meat sandwich with onions and mushrooms have to be called a "Delight of the Ancients?"

"Yeah. Worthies who are in it for the credits—Worthies like us—have to specialize to really make things happen. Some of them go on a lot of raids, like David and Krinna. Some get into a lot of relationship drama. Some just dive into the sexual side. And some challenge duels over any little slight."

"David and Krinna go out on raids?"

"Sure they do. David's a ship captain. He wants you to join up."

"He hasn't said a word to me about it."

"I think that's because you don't really want to go."

"Smart man. I don't. It's dangerous. Ships go out and don't come back. Happens all the time."

She leaned across the table and kissed me. "Good."

I flicked a finger through the hologram to indicate my choices for drink and entree. Valka chose another dish, and then submitted the order. The hologram vanished.

"So what is your strategy?" I asked.

"Challers! You know I can't talk about that in front of the cameras."

"Hmm. Right."

I paused for a moment. It seemed like a good time to change the subject. "So it came up in training today that Krinna's got a thing for inflicting pain."

"Really! What happened?"

"She had this hunk of plastic she thwacked my ass with when I made a mistake."

Valka squirmed a little. "Ooh, I'm going to have to watch the recordings of that when I get back to my pod. Did you like it?"

"Not really. Kind of made me feel weird. Did you and Masters ever play that way?"

Valka made a small wince and shook her head. "We did, but he had a lot of rage issues, you know?"

"I was there when he snapped. I know."

"We decided it wasn't a good thing."

"It's a little sad that she doesn't have anyone to do it with. At least, not someone who enjoys being on the receiving end. I can't see David being that sort."

A robot rolled up with our food, deftly transferred it to the table, and then backed away.

"Mmm." Valka picked up the skewer her food was on, pulled off a piece of simulated meat with her teeth, and chewed. "Yeah, that would be sad."

Just as I was about to take a bite of my "Delight of the Ancients," I caught a gleam in her eye and cocked my head to one side. "Valka."

"Hmm?"

"You're not thinking what I think you're thinking."

She swallowed. "What? That maybe, under the right circumstances, I'd like to have Krinna's hunk of plastic thwacking me on the ass?"

"She's a woman."

"Yes, and? Challers, we're not at Scout Headquarters anymore, or on a station. Watch the holos once in a while, you know? All sorts of people have sex together here. It's a lot more open." She took another bite and shook her head. "Vack, you can be so dense sometimes."

I scowled and bit into my sandwich. The insult stung a little, but the concept of Krinna and Valka getting physical with each other—even if it was just Valka getting the treatment I had gotten during the day's dueling session—gave me a bit of a twitch in the crotch. Then my mind shifted course and I imagined David as a sex partner, and the twitch moved up into my gut.

"Does it bother you that much?" Valka twirled a skewer to attract my wandering attention.

"What?"

"I know that look in your eye, Challers. You're mulling something over. Does it bother you that much, that I might want to have sex with Krinna, and maybe let her smack my ass a few times? We did promise each other that we wouldn't have sex with anyone we hadn't talked about beforehand. So this is talking about it beforehand."

I nodded. It felt good that she was bringing it up, especially after the incident with Hinchley Friss. "Maybe we should try it between us. I mean, Krinna's not the only one who could do it, right?"

Valka shrugged. "I don't know. It's worth a try, I guess. I never really thought about you that way."

"Back at Scout Headquarters, Grecca and I used to have wrestling matches where the loser would get tickled. Shirley too. I liked that a lot. I especially liked winning."

She raised an eyebrow. She didn't look convinced. "Tickled?"

"Yeah. Not that much different, if you think about it."

We ate in silence for a few minutes. Then Valka asked, "So can I have sex with Krinna?"

"She's really got your attention, hasn't she?"

"Well, yeah. With those muscles, she hardly even counts as a woman. It would be almost like being with a man."

I blinked. "Really?"

"Well, for me, at least. You've been face-first in her pussy, so I guess you've got a little different perspective. I bet it's hard to consider her as anything but female after that. So, are you going to tell me not to?" She gave me a pleading look.

"Okay! Okay, I give. Go ahead and let Krinna slap you around."

"In a nice way."

I shook my head. "We have the weirdest conversations."

"Not weird when you're a Worthy."

"I suppose."

After dinner, we separated for what had become an early evening ritual of sending and receiving messages. Enough time had passed since the drama with Grecca that I thought it was time to try to patch things up, so I sent an apologetic message, and then pulled up the long list of messages. I scanned the incoming list myself just to make sure there weren't any names I wanted to respond to personally, so I didn't make the same mistake again.

I came across one name I recognized. "Play the message from Worthy Hinchley Friss."

Portcon's face disappeared, replaced by the smiling face of the man who'd had a pivotal role in the bad night at the Lonely Asteroid. He had a friendly smile on his face but I could see an edge of nervousness in his eyes, behind those bushy black eyebrows of his.

"Hey, Worthy. Listen, I know you're kind of gunning for me, and I guess I can understand that. If that's what you really want to do, I guess I'm not going to be able to change your mind. But I'm really not much of a duelist. I'm crew, through and through, and when I'm in Port, I just like to kick back and relax, you know? Just have fun. Which is what I was doing at the Lonely Asteroid. Just having fun. So maybe you and I could settle this over a few beers, maybe take a spin in the simulators and settle things in a way that won't get me covered in bruises. You know? Let me know. Thanks."

"Portcon," I said, "tell me about the simulators."

"Simulation facilities are available for Worthies to practice their skills while in Port. Stations can be put in standalone mode, or linked together to form teams to fill out the crew roster for a complete simulated ship. Worthies can battle each other or go up against opponents generated within the system. There are simulations and exercises for pilot, navigator, gunner, and command positions."

"Thank you, Portcon."

I sat back to think about Hinchley's message. Was he really that afraid of me? He must have been watching my progress, training with Krinna, but was I really performing that well? Maybe the target practice shooting at Krinna was what scared him. In any case, it didn't seem like a good idea to give folks the impression I was so bloodthirsty I couldn't compromise and had to settle things in a duel. My anger with him had cooled a good deal since Valka and I had patched things up, and I decided that his suggestion was a good one.

"Portcon, record a holographic reply to the most recently played message. Begin."

"Recording."

"All right, Hinchley, you've got a deal. I haven't used the simulators yet, so I'm going to go familiarize myself, and then we'll have a go. I'll let you know when I'm ready. End."

"Recording stopped. Do you wish to send this recording as is?"

"Yes."

"Recording sent."

"Portcon, show me the way to the simulators."

I HADN'T SEEN the controls on a Pirate raider before, but the format wasn't all that much different from what I knew—at least for piloting and navigation. There wasn't a gunnery position on a Scout ship, as they were unarmed, but it wasn't too hard to pick up.

Command was in charge of allocating energy from the ship's orgone collectors to the other three stations. Usually, the job was simple; piloting got access to any available basal orgone for warp maneuvers, navigation was given the transcendent orgone for long-distance jumps, and gunnery was given the crisis orgone for operating shields and weapons. Of course, there were situations where other configurations would be used.

From the tutorials and exercises I went through, it was pretty clear that space combat was a nail-biting experience, one that could leave you very dead in very short order. More than once, in the gunnery and piloting simulators, the controls went completely black except for the word FATALITY flashing across the main display. That being said, from the appreciative responses I got from some of the other Worthies, I wasn't half bad with any of them.

Once I had a solid understanding of how the controls worked, I went to the bar right outside. As soon as a serving robot came up to my booth, I asked it for a Portcon interface and sent a message to Hinchley.

I didn't have long to wait.

"That was fast," he said as he slid his stocky form into the seat.

"I don't want to drag this out, do you?"

"Nope." The robot returned to the table and he ordered a beer. "Since I was the one that delivered the challenge," he said, "I guess that means you get to pick which console we compete on."

"Navigation." My beer was sitting on the table, untouched.

His was delivered and he took a long draw on it. "If I win, then you drop your grudge over that night at the Lonely Asteroid. No calling a duel on me."

"Agreed. And if I win...hmm." I considered. What would I want out of this guy? I hardly knew him. "If I win, that means no sex for ten days."

"What?" He looked at me with disbelief.

"And if you do, then all the transcendent orgone you make gets credited to my account, and the ten days start over."

"Whoa...ten days. How about, ah...if I'm alone?"

"That counts too."

He looked away and shook his head. "Whoa."

"Would you rather take it to the arena?"

He held his hands up in a placating gesture. "No, no, Worthy, not a problem."

"Then it's a deal?"

"Yeah. Deal."

I called the robot over, we made the challenge official, and then headed back to the simulators. The conditions were the standard for navigator versus navigator; our virtual "ship" would be under fire from a simulated Fleet battle cruiser, with all the hyperspace distortions and shield fluctuations that entailed, trying to calculate a safe transcendent-orgone jump to safety. Whoever made the jump first won.

The whole affair gave me a new appreciation for what Robert had done for me when we escaped from Scout Headquarters. Our ship had been under heavy fire from weapons similar to what a Fleet battle cruiser carried and he had managed to get us away in a matter of minutes.

But thoughts like that weren't going to win me my challenge. There was a part of me that wanted to see Hinchley suffer for what he had done, but that wasn't my primary purpose in the challenge. I wanted to see how these challenges worked before doing anything serious. The thought that we'd be getting some attention from the Wards was also on my mind.

I sat down in the simulator. It recognized me and immediately displayed the navigator's console. A countdown timer appeared on the screen, and when it reached zero, the simulation began.

Astronavigation had been one of my favorite subjects at the Academy. Initially, the math had been troublesome, but Shirley found a way to teach it that made it all click. The secret was a visualization method that turned the entire room into a holographic display. The concepts sunk in really well and they never let go. After a while, I no longer needed the visualization; I could see the formulas and relationships in my head.

As the screens displayed the local space-time curves, tangled as they were with the ship's rapidly fluctuating warp field and the angry tunnels of scrambler beams, my mind raced along them, finding the contours that would lead to the solution. The rest of the world faded from my consciousness as the math sunk into my brain. There were lights and noise and shouts outside my console, but I had no time for them, no spare brainpower. They just were. I found the solution, laid it in, and punched the button.

The screen blanked, and then displayed my time. Four minutes, fifty-eight seconds.

I looked over to check Hinchley's. Four minutes, forty-two seconds.

I stepped out of the booth to see a small crowd of Wards and Worthies clustered around him. I walked up and clapped him on the back. "Congratulations," I said.

He glanced over at the big display showing my time just under his. His eyebrows shot up. "Worthy, did I catch it right? This was your first day in these simulators?"

"Yeah, why?"

"Because navigation is my best console. I didn't expect to see you out of there for at least another minute or two. That's one hot score. Are you sure you've never done this before?"

"Well, I learned the basics back at the Scout Academy. But yeah...never actually plotted a course before."

He shook his head. "You better get back to your pod, Worthy. I bet you have some messages to answer."

chapter twenty-two

Challers, Port

VALKA FACED ME across the bed, dressed in her red plastic underwear, in a combat crouch. "I can't believe we haven't done this already." She wore a huge smile.

"Now don't hold back," I said. "I want you to really try to stop me." I was wearing more of her red plastic, in the form of a jockstrap.

"I wouldn't dream of it. And who's to say I don't take you down instead?"

We were standing on the largest bed on the Boulevard—a monster four meters in diameter that must have been intended for orgies of a dozen or more—but this time, it was just for Valka and me. It cost a goodly number of credits to reserve the room, but it was worth it. The mattress under my feet had been adjusted to maximum firmness and stripped of linens to make it more like an actual wrestling mat. Around us, the hologram on the walls portrayed a crowd of cheering spectators. That was Valka's idea.

I shifted my stance and advanced toward the center of the circle. From there, no matter where Valka circled, she was within lunging distance.

She wasn't going to wait for me to make the first move, though. She ducked low and charged, aiming her shoulder at my midsection. I stepped aside to try to get behind her, but her outstretched arm caught my waist. I used the momentum to swing her around, trying to get her under me as we fell. But she swung further and when we hit the mattress, she wound up on top of me—one arm around my middle and one leg crooked around both of mine.

I tucked and turned, rolling onto my belly while she shifted her grip and tried to grab my arm to keep me from getting up onto my hands and knees. This was a classic wrestling position, one Shirley and I had practiced many times. I kicked one leg under, flipping my lower body out from under Valka, and then snapping my shoulders around to reverse the hold. Valka fell on her side and immediately tried to roll onto her belly. In a classic wrestling match, it was the standard defense.

It was exactly the wrong thing to do. I sat on her back, putting firm pressure on her upper back. I had a significant weight advantage, and if she couldn't get her arms or legs under her, she'd have a hard time throwing me off. She grunted and strained to pull one knee up, but that wasn't going to help her. I knew a lot more about this style of wrestling. I slid my arms up under her shoulders, scooping both of her arms up, and then gathered them into the crook of my elbow and gradually straightened up with her arms pressed securely to my shoulder. I made sure to hold them far enough above her head that I wasn't putting dangerous pressure on her neck. I sat on her ass with my knees tight around her abdomen to solidify the position.

"I win," I said. "Now you get your penalty for losing."

Valka growled in frustration.

As long as I didn't push too far, this hold wouldn't hurt her, but it did put her completely at my mercy. Part of me was disappointed that she hadn't been tougher to overpower, but I had the advantages of weight, strength, and skill. She never really had much of a chance.

And judging from the way her growls were fading, that was how she liked it. She relaxed some and stopped thrashing against my grip. I held firm, just in case she was trying to fake me out.

I trailed my fingers along her underarm, alert for the telltale twitch that would tell me I had found a ticklish spot. She was breathing hard, but the touch brought no reaction at all.

"Sorry," she said. "I told you. I'm really not ticklish."

"No?" I explored lower, moving down along her ribs.

"Nope."

I had to admit that she was right. She didn't seem to be ticklish in the usual places. I looked over my shoulder at her feet. Valka's legs stretched out, her toes pointed so the soles of her feet faced up. Shirley had only been ticklish there; but it seemed a bit of a bother to go after Valka's feet, given the hold I had on her. Besides, if I did that, I would be calling her a liar.

"Then I guess your penalty is going to have to be something else."

I reached behind me, took hold of the thin strip of plastic that held her panties in place, and pulled. The strange material detached from her skin and flowed up into my fingers, instantly reforming into a disc. I brought it up and pressed it to her neck. "Here. Hold this."

The plastic reformed again, turning into a ribbon around her neck with strips that ran down to the shoulder straps of her bra.

I was about to crack my open hand over her right butt cheek, but then stopped.

"Wait a second," I said. "We're forgetting something important." I remembered a similar time when Shirley and I were playing our tickling game and things had gone rather embarrassingly wrong. "You need something to say if it goes too far."

"What do you mean?"

"I mean some word you can say to get out of the game if it hurts too much, or if you feel like you're being injured, or if you just want to stop."

"Why don't I just tell you to stop, then?"

"It's part of the game for you to tell me to stop, or squirm or whimper, and I don't stop."

"Ah. So the word makes it clear when I really mean it. When it's not playing anymore."

"Right. So what do you want for your signal?"

"Uhmm, how about if I say, 'metaphor?'"

"That'll work." I brought my open hand down on her butt, making a satisfying whack. Valka, in turn, let out a satisfying yelp. What wasn't so satisfying was the stinging sensation in the palm of my hand. I understood why Krinna used her strip of plastic. There wasn't much to be done about it, not without interrupting things.

I took several more whacks, but the angle was bad and I could only reach a fairly small area. A red spot rose where my blows landed and I suddenly wanted to see her entire ass glowing. There was something very satisfying about the idea, something very right. And I could hear a change in Valka's breathing, as well; she was breathing deeper, almost panting with excitement.

I got an idea.

I leaned down to whisper in her ear. I wasn't worried about the Wards watching us as I was about the effect it would have on Valka. "I'm going to let go of you. But you're going to lie down quietly, not making a sound, nor moving a muscle. If you say anything or move from the position I put you in, there will be consequences. Do you understand?"

Her "yes" was breathy, full of excitement.

I laid her down with arms stretched up over her head, and slowly moved down her body until I was kneeling astride her legs with her round asscheeks right there in front of me, just begging to be slapped.

"I'm going to give you twenty strokes," I said, and then began.

"One. Two. Three." I alternated hands to keep them from hurting too much. Each stroke put a pink outline of my hand on her ass. Soon they overlapped so much that the individual outlines were no longer visible, just a bright-red tinge across her posterior.

As the count rose higher, I could hear her breathing becoming ragged. I listened close, paying attention to the reaction I was getting. That's how I heard it.

"Eleven. Twelve. Thirteen." She was counting the strokes along with me, so faintly that I could barely hear. I considered revealing that I heard her, but I waited instead.

She relaxed visibly when I left the last one. By that time, my hands were throbbing, so I knew her butt would have to be in similar shape. I rolled her over onto her back, and then knelt with my knees on either side of her ribs. Her chest and neck were flushed, and the look on her face was pure bliss. She wasn't smiling or laughing, but I could tell from the rhythm of her breathing that she was in an altered state of consciousness.

"Valka," I said. "Look at me."

She opened her eyes and lifted her head a bit.

"You were counting along with me, weren't you?"

"Yes," she breathed.

"I told you not to say anything, or there would be consequences."

"Yes."

I took one red cup from her bra and plucked it away from her skin. It reverted to its disc shape. "Give me your hand," I said.

She lowered her arm from above her head and I put the disc on her wrist. The plastic flowed into a wide wristband. I did the same with its mate, and then took the remaining two cups from her bra and made them into armbands just below her shoulders. Her cluster of four breasts quaked before me, freed from their restraints.

"Count to four," I said. "Slowly."

As she said, "One," I squeezed one nipple between my fingers. She winced, and then relaxed with a shuddering breath. "Two." I tweaked another, harder than the first. She paused a moment, and when she said, "Three," I squeezed a third, giving it a twist as well.

She lay beneath me, her breathing coming in quivering gasps.

"You can say the word," I said, "if you want me to stop."

"No."

"Is that no, you won't say the word? Or no, I should stop?"

"No." She winced in anticipation and grunted out, "Four."

I leaned down and bit her, taking a good meaty chunk of her breast into my mouth. She screamed and grabbed my head, but instead of pushing me away, she held me close. I could smell sweat coming up from her body and I tasted the sweetness of a few drops of her milk.

"Oh, vack, Challers," she said when I finally pulled away. Her eyes were wide. "Challers, please, fuck me right now!"

Watching Valka slowly become a quivering mass of desire had sparked my own arousal a good time before, and I was more than ready to get my own action. I yanked off the red plastic trapping my cock and nestled down between her legs. As soon as I had the right position, I thrust in to the hilt, no finesse or technique, just raw power. Our bodies slapped together as I took her with all the speed and force I could muster, and through it, she kept chanting my name, again and again.

When she came with her back arched and her hands tangled in her hair, she growled and groaned as spasm after spasm jerked her body. It was the most violent climax I'd ever seen her have.

The sight of her breasts quivering as my thrusts rocked her was mesmerizing. Even the bite mark, now showing a bit of blue where a bruise was coming up, was beautiful to me. I came quickly thereafter, filling her up to overflowing. I collapsed on the bed next to her, heaving great lungfuls of air as the echoes in my body died down.

"Wow," she said. "That was even better than I hoped."

I crawled up alongside her and kissed her cheek. "I'm glad you liked it."

She cradled one injured breast and looked down at the nipple, wiping a dribble of milk away with her thumb. "I think I'm going to have to take a little while off to heal up, though." She whimpered and lay back down on the bed. "Ow."

"Was it too much?" I asked.

She smiled, eyes glittering. "No, just...oh, Challers...I never knew you had it in you."

"You brought it out. I know what you mean now about getting excited because you're excited. How you can be aroused by a situation because you know it arouses me. Thank you."

"Anytime, lover. Anytime."

"Still want to do this with Krinna?"

She turned her head and nuzzled my nose. "You're so cute when you're jealous."

"And you're cute when you're evading my question."

"Yes, I want to see if she does things any different."

Her tone was a little challenging, but I let it go. "All right, all right. Go have fun with Krinna. When you're done, you can tell me what I can do to make it better."

She kissed me, and then settled back down. "Of course."

chapter twenty-three

Challers, Port

IT FELT FUNNY, going to practice with Krinna the next day, knowing that Valka planned on setting up a date with her. My feelings were muddled, to say the least. The idea that Valka would want to have sex with another woman in the first place was strange enough. On Stakroya Station such things simply didn't happen; in the Scouts, all interactions were strictly between men and women. Strictly.

As I walked along the Boulevard on my way to the dueling ring, however, I could see that my upbringing had given me a very limited viewpoint. I noticed for the first time that there were couples of the same gender, here and there, who were acting in ways I would expect lovers to act. Somehow I hadn't seen them before.

And then, of course, Port wasn't home only to men and women. There were also plenty of Chevalier newgens about, whose bodies had a mix of masculine and feminine features. One couldn't call them strictly male or female, and they didn't all have other Chevaliers as their mates. I remembered the occasion during my training when Shirley had coaxed me into a sexual encounter with one of them. It had been something of a challenge, to say the least.

I found myself wondering what it would be like to have sex with David. What would we do? How would it feel? The thought didn't arouse me very much, but then it occurred to me that it could be arousing to Valka. If it was, would that be enough for me to kiss him, or suck his cock? I hoped the question wouldn't come up.

One of the camera robots flitted up and projected Portcon's head in front of me. "Worthy Challers Dizen, there is an urgent direct message for you from Ward Shirley Smith. Will you accept the connection?"

I stopped walking. "Yes, of course."

Portcon's face was replaced with Shirley's, hanging in midair. "Challers, you need to come down to the medical center."

"What? Why? What's wrong?"

"Robert's dying."

I RUSHED out of the elevator as soon as the doors opened. Shirley sat in a corner of the waiting area, head cradled in her hands. I sat down next to her, put my arm around her, and she turned and buried her face in my neck.

"Is he...?"

"Not yet." Her voice was strained and ragged. "Grecca's in with him now."

"How did this happen?"

Shirley sniffed and sank back into her chair. "He's been deteriorating ever since we got here. There was damage to his thalamus in the escape from Headquarters."

"Why didn't you tell me?"

"I thought it would improve. Things were okay for a while, but then last night..." She sniffed again and swallowed, pressing her lips together. A tear fell down a cheek already well stained.

I couldn't think of anything to say. My own throat was closing and sympathetic tears welled up in my own eyes. "I'm sorry," I croaked.

Shirley took my hand in hers.

Valka came out of the elevator and immediately sat down next to Shirley on the other side. She said nothing.

"Thank you," said Shirley. "Thank you for coming."

Valka said nothing, she just nodded and took Shirley's other hand.

We sat in silence for a few minutes, just holding hands, saying with our presence what words could not.

Grecca came down a side hallway, stopping when she spotted me. "Challers."

I stood. "Hello, Grecca."

"He asked for you." She wrapped her arms around her body, as if warming herself, and stood near the passageway. "Third one down."

Valka and I went together. The room wasn't much bigger than a pod, crowded with monitoring equipment and medical gear. Valka stood at the door while I went to Robert's side.

He was pale and drawn with deep shadows under his eyes. With each precisely timed breath, a machine somewhere in the room clicked.

"I'm here, Robert."

His good eye flicked open and scanned my face. "Challers," he said, almost too faintly to hear. "I want you to promise me..."

"I know," I said. "I'll get the bastards who did this to you. I'll make sure they—"

"No," he croaked. "No. Don't do it on...on my account. Don't go out for vengeance. Do what you know is right. You're a good man, Challers."

"What? Why? I thought you hated the Scouts."

"I do. I hate them with every atom. They manipulate people, whole ships and stations full of people, like they were robots. Like human lives don't matter any more than...than rocks."

I narrowed my eyes. "So do I."

"And do you hate them for that too? Because it's no small thing. They run *everything*, Challers. Don't forget that."

"I won't." In the back of my mind, something told me that he was trying to tell me more than he was saying, but it was lost in the chaos of the moment.

"Fight for what you love. There's precious little else worth fighting for. You're a good man, Challers Dizen. Don't throw that away. Remember. *Everything*."

I tried to speak, but my throat wouldn't work. I nodded, choking back tears.

"Now please...go send Shirley back in. I want...my final moments with her."

Valka put her arm around me as we walked back to the waiting area. Shirley and Grecca were standing near the elevator, talking in hushed tones.

I nodded to Shirley, and she nodded back. There was no need for words. From a table nearby, she picked up a roll of material I recognized after a moment to be an orgone belt—Robert's orgone belt. She went down the corridor towards Robert's bed.

Grecca stood up tall and straight and looked me in the eye. "Shirley says I owe you an apology."

"No. It's me who owes you. You were right. I've been neglecting you ever since you got here. I was your only friend when we arrived, and I've left you alone. I'm sorry."

Grecca nodded. "Accepted. And I completely misinterpreted that kiss I caught you in up on the Boulevard. Shirley was watching the whole thing and told me I had gotten upset over nothing."

I held out my hands. "Friends again?"

She put her arms around me and hugged me close. "We never stopped."

When we pulled apart, Grecca gave me a thin smile.

"It's done," said Shirley from the hallway. "He's gone."

The three of us gathered her up in one huge hug and held her while she cried. It lasted only a minute or so before she sniffed and announced, "I don't know about the rest of you, but I'm ready for a drink."

We took the elevator up to the Boulevard and Shirley brought us to Robert's favorite place during his days as a Worthy: Ballantine's.

The bar wasn't particularly big, but what it lacked in size, it made up for in merriment. It turned out that we weren't the only mourners; six of Robert's friends from when he was a worthy were already there, drinking and telling stories about his adventures and misadventures in the days before he had gone undercover among the Scouts.

The four of us took a table nearby, not feeling entirely welcome in that circle, but at the same time, hungry for the camaraderie. Once introductions had been made, foaming mugs of beer arrived in front of us and we were invited to the party. More Worthies came in later, including all four of Madden's Marauders. The one who met me on the street my first day as a Worthy, Angela Cape, sat down next to me. It turned out she had known Robert before he left, and we shared a few stories about him.

Robert had been a steady, stalwart fellow right from the start. He had founded his reputation and image on playing straight with people and doing a good job, rather than on emotional gamesmanship and high drama. It cost him, many times, when a supposed friend played him for a fool, but he got a lot of sympathy from the Wards for it.

When he decided to use the gentank to give himself a much younger body and infiltrate the Scouts, everyone thought he was taking it too far. There was no way it could pay off. But Robert felt that the survival of the Pirate way of life was more important than his own personal wealth. He was fighting for something he believed in.

This wasn't the only topic of conversation. There was a lot of talk about missions that had gone out and not come back, about how things seemed to have gotten a lot more risky lately. I brought up the topic of egg missiles. They had heard it before, back when we had first arrived at Port, but this time they were nodding heads and grim expressions. Nobody could agree what to do about it, but at least they were listening.

After about an hour of celebration, Valka poked me in the ribs and nodded down the table. Grecca was leaning against the broad chest of a Worthy who had been introduced to us simply as Captain Wilsen. She'd had more than a few drinks and looked unusually affectionate.

"Do you think we ought to get her back to her pod?" I whispered.

Valka shook her head. "She needs to make friends."

"You aren't worried that he's going to take advantage of her?"

"She's not that drunk. Let her have her fun."

"I guess you're the expert."

She jabbed me again in the ribs. I smiled and rubbed the spot.

Shirley stood and raised a mug in the air. "To Worthy Robert Halko."

There was a chorus of agreement around the table, including a hearty "Aye!" from Captain Wilsen, and mugs were drained and slammed onto the table.

Shirley wiped her mouth on the back of her sleeve and glanced around the group. "Thank you all for coming. Robert would have appreciated it. I know I do. You all have made this much easier to bear."

"You may call on us for anything you need," said Wilsen.

"I'm going back to my pod," she said with a thin smile. "I'll sleep better having met you all."

That ended up being the signal for the end of the wake. We all went our separate ways, except for Grecca, who left with Captain Wilsen.

Valka snuggled in next to me, tucked under my arm as we walked. "I'm glad you made up with Grecca," she said.

"So am I. That was bothering me."

"We should invite her with us somewhere."

"Where? All we do is Worthy stuff. Practicing dueling and consoles, playing games with the other Worthies."

"And she wouldn't find that fun? She was a Scout too, as you may recall."

"It's not like we have piles of friends among the Worthies, either. Since we got involved, we've hardly talked to anyone but David, Krinna, and Rendika."

"It's better than she's got."

"Well, until tonight anyways. Let's see what happens with her and Captain Wilsen. If it doesn't work out, we'll do something with her."

She looked up at me with a mischievous grin. "I think you just want someone you can tickle."

I shrugged. "It's not the tickling, really. It's having someone I love at my mercy."

"You love Grecca?"

I paused. The word had just slipped out, but I realized it was true. "Yeah, it's funny, but I think I do, a little."

"Have you ever told her?"

"No."

"You should. You should tell everyone you love that you love them. They deserve to know."

I swallowed, feeling my throat tightening up once again. "You never know if that's the last opportunity you ever have."

She squeezed me tighter. "I love you, Challers Dizen."
"I love you too."

chapter twenty-four

Challers, Port

DAVID HIT the switch on the heavy bulkhead doors, turned to face me, and spread his arms in a broad, theatrical gesture. "Behold!"

Behind him, the opening doors gradually revealed the yawning expanse of one of Port's many docking bays. A ribbon of deck plate extended out into the abyss, alongside a blocky, menacing shape, its skin the black of deep space except for narrow armor-glass windows. It was three times as long as the Scout ship I had arrived on and looked like it would mass twenty times as much.

David walked backwards along the gangway. "This, my friend, is the *Destiny Achieved*—finest raiding ship in the fleet." He gestured toward a nasty-looking weapon mounted on the back of the ship. "The dorsal turret is a hypercannon that fires a two-microLowell slug at a rate of one hundred rounds per second. Each round carries enough energy to vaporize a small asteroid. The ventral turret is a scrambler beam with a collimation ratio of one to a million. I keep it tuned myself."

As he reached the airlock on the side of the vessel, he nodded toward the aft. "Engines are the standard design, capable of using all three orgone types. Orgone collectors can carry enough transcendent orgone for five kiloparsecs of travel before needing to be recharged."

I whistled in appreciation. "That's enough to get all the way out to the Norma arm."

"Not that we'd ever go so far in one jump. Not much there to see." David touched the handprint panel next to the hatch and it folded out on heavy hinges.

"Do you usually travel by jump, then?" I asked, ducking inside after him.

"Always. Warp travel is slow and hyperwarp leaves too much of a trail. That's why we almost never capture enemy ships; there's just too much risk that we would be followed back here to Port. The exception being Scout ships." He smiled. "We're always glad to take those whenever we get the chance."

Past the airlock, the interior of the ship was tight, but not cramped. The airlock opened onto a familiar-looking chamber. The floor had resilient, spongy material, the walls panels and storage areas were recognizable—there was even a ring of benches around the edge. The only differences were a few extra cables secured here and there.

David turned and gave me a wide smile. "Look familiar?"

"This is the drive chamber of a Scout ship!" I said.

"The first designs for raiding ships used parts from Scout ships. There are still a lot of similarities." He nodded toward the front of the ship. "Bridge is there. I'm sure you're familiar with all of that by now." Turning toward the aft, he gestured to both sides and entered a narrow passageway. "Galley is to the port and the bunks are to the right—though we often use that space for storage and sleep in the bridge chairs or the drive chamber."

I poked my head into both rooms as we passed. They were small but serviceable, reminding me of the rooms my family had occupied on Stakroya Station.

"And then, all the way aft, is the cargo bay." He opened a hatch at the end of the corridor leading to a space that took up about two-thirds of the ship's length, which was empty except for a few small pieces of equipment.

"You seem quite proud of her," I said, glancing around.

"Rightly so!" he said. "But I didn't invite you down here just to give you a tour."

"No, I didn't think you would."

"I want you to join my crew. I have the best pilot and the best gunner available. All I need is the best navigator."

I shook my head. "I'm sorry, David. I've heard the gossip. Ships are going out and not coming back. It's too dangerous."

He narrowed his eyes, taken aback. "You don't want to find out what's taking the ships? You don't want to stop it?"

"I know what's causing it."

David rolled his eyes. "Oh, that's right. I remember. That story about the new missiles the Scouts built, incorporating Ovor eggs in the design as a built-in orgone source."

I crossed my arms, determined to stand my ground. "It's not a story. It's the truth."

"It's an inference. You've never actually seen the missiles. You just strung together a bunch of guesses to explain what you were seeing. There are plenty of other explanations for what you saw. Trust me; the Scouts aren't warriors. They don't build missiles. They let the

Fleet do their dirty work. Besides; the Scouts haven't had a new idea in ages."

"And this is any different?" I walked into the drive chamber. "You're still using a design that incorporates scavenged Scout parts."

David stood at the edge of the room and shook his head. "This ship incorporates a thousand improvements over the original. They're vastly superior to anything the Scouts or the Fleet can produce."

I walked up to him and poked him in the chest. "Then why are your ships disappearing? I'm telling you, unless you figure out some way to deal with that threat, you'll all be at risk."

David put his hands up between us, surrendering the point. "All right, let's assume you're right. Let's assume those egg missiles really are out there. We can't figure anything out cowering here in Port while our supplies and spares slowly dwindle away. The only answer is to go out there and find it. Poke around. Make trouble. Get information we need to counter whatever it is."

I growled. "No! That's not going to work. The information isn't out there on the stations, or on Merchant ships. The secret is at Scout Headquarters! You need to get everyone together and hit there. All at once. That's where the missiles are manufactured." I pounded my fist into an open palm. "Take out the headquarters and the whole system falls apart."

"And replace it with what?" He tilted his head at a patronizing angle. "Challers, you really don't understand what you're talking about. Once you've been out there, earned enough to buy your own ship, and proven yourself in command, you can start talking about organizing larger expeditions."

"No, thank you. I'll stay right here in Port. If you people don't want to listen to me, that's fine, but don't tell me I'm lying and then ask for my support." I turned to go.

His voice rose, almost to a shout. "Worthy Challers Dizen, I call you a liar and coward. I challenge you to a duel. If you are defeated, you will admit that your tale about the Scouts' new weapon is a fantasy and speak of it no more. In addition, you will join my crew for our next raiding expedition."

I turned back, a snarl on my lips. I had had enough. "I accept. If I win, then you will find yourself a different astronavigator, and when a raid on Scout Headquarters is organized, your ship will be a part of it."

"Very well," he said. "Portcon, have you registered this duel?"

"Worthies David Cross and Challers Dizen, your duel has been registered. Worthy Challers Dizen, as the challenged party, you may schedule the duel up to twenty-four hours in the future. When do you choose?"

"Tomorrow," I said. "One hour after the beginning of the light shift."

"Registered. Worthies David Cross and Challers Dizen, your duel has been scheduled for Arena Four at plus one hours."

WHEN I TOLD her about the duel, Valka was livid.

"How could you let him do this to you? You call off that duel! Tell him whatever you have to! I can't let you go out there. Another ship went missing today. Challers, that's four since we've been here!"

"You sound like I've already lost."

"Are you sure you're going to win?"

I sighed and lay down on our little rented bed. "You're right. I shouldn't have accepted the challenge. It's just...I got angry. Lost my head."

"So take it back. Get out of the duel." She lay down with her head on my chest, one arm across my belly, and one leg across my knees.

"I can't. If I forfeit the duel, then it's the same as losing...and I would have to go on his mission. If I don't follow through on that, then I'd lose my status as a Worthy. Not only would I have to turn in my orgone belt, I'd also lose all my credits. I'd be a Ward for life, and then you'd have to earn the credits...you'd be by yourself."

She frowned. "And even then, you'd still be a virtual prisoner in your pod."

"There's no two ways about it. I have to win that duel. How dangerous is David, anyways?"

"I don't know. He hasn't been in that many duels. But he has been training pretty hard since he got back from his last raid."

"I need some kind of edge."

"Then you better think of something, because anything we talk about is going to get back to him. There's always a Ward or two watching, and some of them could be his allies."

"Why is it we never hear anything about his activities? We have to have some allies out there too. Someone rooting for the newcomer?"

Valka ran her hand over my chest. "We do. I look through my messages. But we also have people feeding false information. I get a lot of that kind of thing. Shirley tells me things sometimes, but she's just one person."

"And I haven't heard anything from Grecca since she met Captain Wilsen."

Valka giggled. "Can you blame her?"

"I guess I'm just going to have to figure something out for myself."

"Well, you're not going to do that lying here spinning your turbines." She picked at the knot holding my shirt together.

I looked over at her with an arched eyebrow. "And that's going to help?"

"If you're going to fight a duel to decide whether you go away on a raiding cruise, then I want every opportunity to be with you before you do." She pulled the knot out, slid her hand inside, and ran it up over the muscles of my chest. "I want to be close to you."

I put my arm around her and squeezed. Her hand explored slowly, rising and falling with my breathing, slightly cool against my skin. She pulled the knot on my other hip and spread my shirt open wide.

"Do you miss my old body?" she asked.

"Where did that come from?"

"Except for some muscles, you're pretty much exactly as I remember you from Stakroya Station." Her fingers toyed with my nipple, making it pucker into a tiny knob.

"If I weren't, would you love me any less?"

She looked up into my face, eyes shimmering. "I don't know...Challers, I don't know."

I kissed her. "I know that I love you just as much now as I ever have. More."

She laid her head on my chest and plucked at my chest hair. "I don't like this body. It reminds me of...too much. I thought that I would just get used to it. I thought buying the underwear would help. But I still hate it." A deep sigh blew across my body.

"I know. And..." I sighed and shook my head.

She nodded, understanding what I couldn't say.

"But you know, there is one pleasant memory I have of this body."

"There is?"

"I can remind you, if you want. You might remember."

"I don't want to remember. Challers, would you please make me forget? Just for a little while, please?"

"Gladly."

I laid her onto her back, pulled off her boots, unbuckled her belt, and slid her pants down onto the floor. I chuckled. "You're wearing the red plastic again."

"I like them. It's weird, but they're comfortable. They stay very close to the skin, but they don't get sweaty or nasty. I think they even regulate temperature. I noticed them getting cool when I got overheated during practice this morning."

"Well, right now, it's in the way." I pulled the plastic away from her pussy, and then regarded it closely for a minute. "Did the merchant ever say where these came from?"

"Only that they were taken in a raid."

"That means they were made somewhere. On a station, probably."

"Sure."

"Hmm." I put the disc against my wrist for safekeeping, where it turned into a tight armband.

"Well? Are you going to just sit there staring?"

I shook my head. "Sorry. Distracted." I gently pulled her pussy lips apart and gave her a long, slow lick followed by a kiss at the apex of her sex.

"Mmm, forgiven."

As her heady musk filled my senses, I remembered what had happened when I was first transformed into an Ovor female. In the shower, rinsing off the gentank gel, Valka had knelt down at my feet and gave me an incredible orgasm just by licking and nothing else. I decided to see what would happen if I tried that on her.

I opened my mouth wide and extended my tongue to a comfortable distance, finding my way through her delicate parts by touch. Once I found a good position, I stayed there, flicking her with my tongue, occasionally stopping to swallow.

Slowly, she started making noise—starting with heavy breathing, and then moving on to low moans and sighs. I remembered my training and slowed my efforts as she reached the plateau phase, using the tension in her thighs as a gauge. As she approached the edge of climax, I slacked off, but when she started to relax, I sped up. Only when she had her hands on my head, pushing my mouth closer to her body, only when she cried out my name in frustrated ecstasy, did I finally drive her over the edge into a screaming, grunting orgasm.

I climbed up onto the bed and lay next to her with my head propped up on one elbow. She lay in a panting, smiling puddle in front of me.

Idly, I reached into her shirt and tapped one of the cups of her bra. To my own touch, it was hard, though I knew from wearing them myself that the material bent and flowed with her body as she moved. It was also red, meaning it reflected red light. Would it also reflect infrared? That was the kind of light our laser weapons used.

There had to be Wards watching. There always were when we were having sex. I had an idea, but making it work in a way that wouldn't attract their attention and betray my edge to David wouldn't be easy. Worse, I wouldn't know whether it worked until the duel.

"Do you still have milk?" I asked.

"It's mostly gone. I get a few drops. I haven't been getting it out so much. I think that makes them dry up."

"Can I taste, before it's gone forever?"

She made a small frown.

"I know you don't like this body, but you have to admit it is kind of interesting."

"Sure, go ahead." She untied her shirt, and I plucked each cup from her breasts and transferred them to the pocket of my pants. Then, I paused at each breast to taste their sweet nectar. As I rose to kiss her, I gave her the quietest, subtlest "shh" I could manage.

I had my edge. I hoped it would be enough.

chapter twenty-five

Challers, Port

I GOT TO the dueling ring first and set up on the far side of the chamber. After all, he was the one challenging me, and I didn't want him getting a good look at me just in case his pet Wards hadn't told him. I made sure my pistol was fully charged, checked the setting, and holstered it again. I put on my goggles and waited.

David was on time, precisely on time, passing through the doors just as the chronometer clicked over. He walked to the edge of the circle and stood with his arms loose at his sides. He had his weapon in a cross-draw holster on his left hip, its muzzle lifted so high it looked like it was ready to just dump out onto the floor. He put his goggles on with his left hand. "You ready?"

"Just one thing before we start," I said. "I wanted to let you know, I've got my weapon set on stun."

"Kind of you to let me know. I hope you don't mind if I do the same."

"By all means," I said. "It's only fair."

He reached across and flicked the switch without moving his head. "Portcon, I'm ready to begin the duel."

"Worthy Challers Dizen, are you ready to begin the duel?"

"I am."

"Then the duel will begin in one minute when the green light comes on. You may signal submission by dropping your weapon." Red lights flashed around the perimeter of the ring.

I switched stance, turning my left side towards David, and raised my left arm, elbow bent, putting it between him and my chest, using it as a shield.

His head cocked slightly to the side. I couldn't see his eyes, so I couldn't tell for sure, but there seemed to be a quizzical slant there. I hoped that meant my edge hadn't gotten leaked to him. He bounced on his toes and flexed his hands, limbering himself up.

Around the edge of my goggles, on the interior, a strip of dim light gradually shrank as the time counted down. I had programmed it myself—something to give me a precise time when the lights would change to green. It hadn't been that long since Stakroya Station where we improvised materials and circuits to do jobs that needed to be done using components that weren't built for the job. I was moving before the lights changed, so my hand touched my pistol at the very instant the duel started.

I didn't rush. David dodged to the side, rolling as he drew his weapon, hoping to throw off my aim, but I wasn't fooled. I brought my weapon up just quickly enough to know my shot would be on target.

He came up in a crouch and shot first, hitting me square on my left shoulder. It was a classic spot to hit, full of vulnerable nerve endings and fragile bone. With a loud bang, my shirt shredded, sending a puff of smoke and fibers into the air in front of my face. The goggles shielded my eyes and ears, however, and a piece of hard red plastic shielded my flesh and bones.

My shot was true, hitting him on the kneecap, causing his leg to spasm and spoiling his aim. I heard a bang behind me from his clean miss. My second shot caught him in the belly, exposing his orgone belt. The third and fourth shot widened the opening in his shirt, leaving a huge, vulnerable rent.

He spun, favoring the right leg, bringing his weapon around and coming up in a profile stance to protect his chest. I fired again, catching him just below the armpit, but his shirt was well away from his body there and all I did was poke a hole in it. He fired at my hip, exposing another red plate of plastic.

"Cheat!" he shouted.

I fired again, trying to hit the hole I had made in his shirt, but he moved too fast and the shot skimmed across his back, ripping a wide, horizontal gash. He shifted his aim. The next shot would be aimed at my forehead.

As quickly as I could, I dropped to one knee and fired again, my left arm still protecting my body. There was a crackle and a hiss where his shot singed my hair. My shot hit him square on the right hip, blowing away the side knot of his shirt and causing a wide flap of fabric to fall away from his body. He grunted in pain and tried to spin away again, but fell onto the knee I had hit before. He grimaced and raised his weapon again. It was shaking. His shot went wide.

I fired again, hitting the knot on his other hip. His shirt fell open in rags. I aimed at his solar plexus. "Do you submit?"

He bent down, weapon aimed at the ground and clutched in front of him. The pain was getting to him. "Armor isn't allowed in the dueling ring! You should be disqualified!"

"If you're not man enough to beat a guy who's wearing women's underwear," I said, taking a step towards him, "then you're not man enough to be crying foul."

"Oh, that's low," he growled.

"Submit. Admit it. You've lost." I took another couple of steps, coming towards the center of the ring. I didn't want to crush him. I only had to defeat him.

Too late I noticed that he had hooked up his orgone tube to the butt of his weapon. I raised my weapon to fire, but he pulled the trigger first. The orgone-enhanced beam struck at my feet. The explosion threw me across the room. My pistol flew from my hand as I rolled to a stop, my ears ringing and legs stinging in a dozen places from bits of shrapnel thrown up from the strike.

The lights flashed from green to red. "The duel is concluded," said Portcon. "Worthy Challers Dizen has dropped his weapon, and conceded defeat. Worthy David Cross wins."

DAVID CAME to my chamber in the medical bay after they finished picking the bits of metal out of my legs and gluing me back together. His injuries were nothing more than bruises and scrapes, so aside from moving slowly, he didn't seem any worse for the experience. I, however, would be off my feet for at least twenty-four hours while everything knitted back together.

"Good duel," he said.

"You don't think I cheated?"

"Nah. I just said that to throw you off your rhythm. You were taking me apart."

I glared at him. "Setting your weapon on kill was a bit much, though, don't you think?"

"I wouldn't have aimed it at you. Just wanted to shake you up, take back the advantage."

"Yeah. Well, you did that."

Valka came to the door of the chamber, her face flushed from running. She took a second to take in the scene and pointed an accusing finger at David. "You! You almost killed him!"

He held up his hands. "I didn't."

"I should blow your throat out the back of your neck!" Her other hand was on her laser as she advanced into the room.

"Valka, stop," I said. "There's nothing to be gained."

She drew her weapon. "If I kill him now, he can't take you away."

"And if you shoot him like this, they'll either lock you in your pod for the rest of your life, or put you in the recycler."

She looked at me, voice trembling but jaw set in determination. "Then I'm coming with you."

"Sorry, sweets," said David. "No room left on the roster, and I've seen your scores. You're a halfway decent gunner and a better-than-average pilot, but not good enough for me to bump Krinna or Rendika to put you on the team. Sorry. I need Challers, but I don't need you. Now, are you going to put your gun away?"

She holstered the pistol with a "hmph" and leaned her butt against the bed. "Are you at least going to let him heal up before you drag him off to get killed?"

"I'm not the monster you think I am. You just watch. I'll bring him back, safe and sound."

I held up a hand. "David, could we have a moment?"

"Sure." He pushed past Valka and headed out to the corridor. "Have fun."

She turned and glared at me.

"I'm sorry," I said. "I really was doing my best."

"I know. And you had him too, until he pulled that dangerous, dirty stunt on you."

"I should have just kept shooting until he dropped his weapon. I let him snare me."

She bent down over me and kissed my forehead. "Don't wish you were that kind of guy."

"If I had been, I would have won."

"If you had been, I wouldn't have cared." She ran her fingers through my hair and frowned, finding the nearly bald patch near the crown of my head. "Wow. That was close."

"He was desperate to try for a head shot."

"I wonder why he wants you so badly for his team. There has to be something he's not saying."

I glanced down the hall. "He wants to figure out what's taking out the raiding ships."

"Well, that's a sure thing. Everyone does."

"No, I think he has some special plan in mind. Something he doesn't want to talk about, like it'll get back to someone."

"You think the Scouts have a spy here?" Valka cocked an eyebrow.

"It wouldn't take much to get one. All they'd need is one complete crew on their side to shuttle messages back and forth."

"Then I suppose we have to assume there is one."

"Is it me, or is this whole system set up to make it impossible to share information, to trust each other and cooperate?"

"It certainly doesn't make it any easier."

"Which explains why nobody seems to be interested in taking the fight straight to the Scouts. That would mean getting the whole fleet together rather than these little one and two-ship raids. They're just not used to thinking that way. And if someone did try to organize a major action against Scout Headquarters, the word would probably get out before they could get everyone organized."

"Someday. Let's just hope this whole thing doesn't come apart before then."

A doctor came in, checked the readouts on the display near the door, and nodded. "Ready to go back to your pod, Worthy?" He put his hand to the panel, and a whirring sound signaled the arrival of a robotic wheelchair. While Valka and the robot helped me off the table, the doctor gave his instructions. "You're going to need at least three days of bed rest, no strenuous activity." He gave Valka a pointed look.

"What?" she asked with a hurt tone.

"That means no sexual contact. No walking further than the hygiene station."

"Don't worry. I'll be good."

"See to it."

I settled into the chair and let it carry me to the elevators. The trip from the bed to the chair had worn me out and I wondered whether three days were going to be enough. The pain of my injuries was well muffled by the drugs they had given me, but that only made me want to pass out even more.

"Maybe I can find someone to take your place," said Valka.

"Please don't. Just don't. When I come back—"

"If you come back."

I leaned my head back against the chair's headrest and sighed. "I'm coming back, Valka. I promise it. I'm coming back."

chapter Twenty-six

Challers, Port

THE THREE DAYS of rest were welcome. The first was spent in a drug-induced haze. On the morning of the second day, I found some advanced reference materials on FTL mathematics and set up some simulations. If David wanted the best navigator available, and if it meant I would be more likely to come back in one piece, then I was going to make myself the best navigator I could be.

Valka checked in on me every few hours—either by stopping by the pod or by sending a message from wherever she was. By suppertime, I was starting to feel a little uncomfortable. The next morning, I woke up with a rigid erection and vague, fading dreams of Valka and Shirley having sex while I watched from outside the front windows of a raiding ship.

Around the middle of the light shift, Valka interrupted my studies with a message. "Put on my feed," she said. "Be quick." I suspended the simulations and switched to the live cameras.

She stood on a balcony, looking thoughtful, gazing out over the Boulevard without really looking at anything in particular. After a few minutes, she looked into the camera. "I hope you're watching, Challers."

I felt my cock twitch in anticipation. The show she had given me while shopping for underwear had been fun. This one promised to be even better.

"I've been thinking about why we became Worthies, and why we told ourselves we became Worthies. I think we didn't trust ourselves, for some reason, to do it because we wanted to get enough influence to be able to go back and save all those eggs from being turned into weapons. Somehow, we had to tell ourselves we were doing it for ourselves."

This wasn't going to be a show, I realized. It was a speech. I felt a bit disappointed, but I crushed the thought. This was important.

"But we both know that's a lie. Even if we do get enough credits for me to use the gentank, it's not going to give me my old body back. That template is gone, probably forever. I've been in this body now for long enough that it feels natural. I'm not sure I want to change anymore. I'm not sure it's worth the risk. I've decided I'm going to stay with this body. So that means I don't need to be a Worthy anymore. I can hang up my orgone belt, go back to my pod, and forget this all happened."

I shook my head, muttering to myself. This didn't make any sense. What happened to the woman who was so desperate to change her body, just a few days ago, who hated being an Ovor? Not only that, she had jeopardized our chances of achieving it by saying this where Wards and Worthies would find out about it. My stomach twisted around itself.

"Except I can't. There are thousands, maybe millions of lives at stake, and I can't lie anymore. There's a fight coming and I need to be ready for it. And so do you. I wish you didn't have to go on this mission, but my wishes aren't always what's important. You have to go. And I have to accept it." Her eyes sparkled. There were tears there, but they had yet to fall. "But I'm not going to let you go without something to remember."

She stepped through a doorway into a small rental room. It was done up all in rich reds and pinks, with a circular Scout-style bed on the floor. Its surface was sculpted into a low chair with a sloping back, a carefully created lump rising up from the floor. It was sitting at one side of the room, facing a floor-to-ceiling mirror. A small black sack lay on a corner of the chair. Vague shapes contoured its surface, inviting questions about its contents.

Valka stood in front of the chair and slowly undid the knot at one hip, and then the other, and shrugged out of her shirt. Underneath, she wore two flimsy black bras. She stroked the upper slopes of her breasts, looking in the mirror as she did so.

"I talked to Shirley yesterday. I wanted to see how she was doing, see if she needed anything."

Her hands drifted down over her body, pausing to caress each pair of breasts, until she came to her belt. She undid it and let it fall, revealing a pair of frilly black shorts made out of the same fabric as the bras. She slipped her feet out of her shoes and kicked the whole affair aside.

"She said something that has had me thinking ever since. She said that everything that happens to us, good and bad, goes into making us who we are. She was talking about Robert, but I think she was also talking about us. If we want to like who we are, then we have to accept the changes our lives have made...or else make new changes so we can like ourselves. The past can't be undone. Those changes can't be unmade. We can only make new ones."

Valka looked into the mirror. "I know you like this body, Challers. And as long as I take the pills that keep me from getting eggs, I've decided I don't really have a problem with it." She took off the bras and tossed them onto the pile of clothes. "So here we are. This is me. My body. And I'm going to love it."

With silent solemnity, she pulled off the panties, tossed the little scrap aside, and then sat on the wide chair. She rested her head back, still watching in the mirror, and began caressing her skin. Starting with her shoulders, she ran her hands down over her body in a slow, even motion, touching her breasts and ribs and belly on their way down.

I was getting my show after all! The doctor had forbidden sexual contact, but this would do in the meantime. I unbuckled my belt, slid my hand into my pants, and gave my cock a preliminary squeeze. Blood rushed in, rapidly filling my hand with flesh.

The holoscreens flickered, adjusting the view. One was from above and in front of her, probably from a camera installed permanently inside the room. Another one focused more closely on her body, the same one that had been on her on the balcony. I guessed it was one of the roving robotic cameras that buzzed around the Boulevard watching the Worthies.

Valka reached into the bag sitting next to her on the chair and pulled out a small bottle. She squirted some of the contents into one hand, and then set the bottle aside to rub her hands together. A slick, wet sound carried through and when she drew her hands across her skin, they left a wet shine. She spread the oil over her arms, her chest, her belly—even picking up her legs and coating them so her entire body gleamed. It looked wonderful.

It looked like it felt good too. Her chest and neck were becoming flushed and her nipples rose into tiny cones. She let out a little sigh as her fingers found her pussy and slipped between her lips. One hand rubbed it slowly while the other moved over her thighs, her belly, up onto her breasts, and then back down again.

It seemed like a long time since I had watched her masturbate, though it was really no more than a hundred days or so. Watching her brought back that moment—the first time I had ever seen her naked, the first time I had seen anyone naked, for that matter. So much had changed since then. My memories of that moment mingled with the images on the screens and a surge of nostalgia coursed through me.

The next item she took from the pouch was a white ovoid about the size of the palm of her hand. She squeezed the middle and a low humming sound came through the channel. I cocked my head to the side, confused, until she brought it down and pressed it to her pussy. The sudden gasp of pleasure told me there was something special about that little device. Was it electrically charged? Some kind of nerve stimulator? I couldn't tell exactly what was going on, but whatever it was, it must have felt good.

As Valka's ecstasy grew, my own pleasure followed along. I stroked myself as I watched, going slowly to make it last a good long time. I wasn't looking for a quick wank; I wanted to make this special.

But Valka wasn't delaying anything. She pressed the device deeper in between her pussy lips, and she arched her back and let out a cry of delight. "Challers...oh, I hope you can see me...I hope you can see me coming for you." Little spasms gripped her body and as they grew in intensity, her eyes clamped shut.

I couldn't resist any longer. I pumped my cock as hard as I could, my gaze fixed on the images hanging before me in midair. My breathing deepened, my vision started to blur, and then my fist was full of hot stickiness and my groan mingled with Valka's in the tiny room. I lay back to catch my breath with her gasping voice still echoing through me.

I looked up again to see her laying back on the seat, completely relaxed, hugging herself with a warm, contented smile on her face. She stayed there for a minute or two, quiet and still, and then opened her eyes. "I can't wait to be with you again, Challers," she said. "Put on your belt tonight when your time is up. I promise I'll be gentle."

I switched off the feed and sat in the dark, considering what had just happened. Everything she said made sense, but at the same time, it seemed like something in her had collapsed. I had done enough rationalizing to myself to recognize when someone else was doing it, and this certainly seemed like it to me. There wasn't time to deal with that topic right away, though. We would talk when I got back from the mission.

When I got back.

DAVID WAS KIND. He could have demanded my service as soon as the doctors cleared me; instead, he gave Valka and me a night together to say goodbye. It wasn't the most noteworthy sex we ever had, but after the priming she had given me on the holoscreens, it was probably one of the more enthusiastic sessions we'd had.

Afterward, we talked about the raid. She knew that sometimes the orgone collectors would need to be refilled, so she gave me formal permission to have sex with someone else if it was necessary for the mission.

In the morning, as I got dressed, Valka presented me with the eight plastic discs I had worn during the duel. "Take them. Wear them and remember me."

"I don't know," I said. "They do pretty well against these stunners, but I'm not sure how well they'd fare against a Scout mass driver. You'd probably better keep them, in case someone challenges you to a duel."

"All right," she said. "Then just take one." She pressed it to my throat where it became a skintight collar.

I touched it, feeling its paradoxical hardness under my fingers. "I don't need any mementos," I said.

"I know. But I feel better knowing this is going with you." She got up on her tiptoes and kissed me, wrapping her arms around me and pressing her body to mine.

"I will come back. I promise."

"I know you will."

I didn't have any gear to pack, aside from a couple spare outfits and my gun belt. Everything I needed would be waiting for me on the ship. David met me at the airlock, showed me where to stow my gear, and got me signed into my duty station on the bridge. Krinna and Rendika were already there.

I got settled in, downloaded some personal files to my console, and nodded to David. I was ready.

David raised his head. "Portcon?"

"What can I do for you, Worthy David Cross?"

"David's Destroyers are ready to depart. Aboard are Rendika Prelain, Krinna Lawson, and Challers Dizen."

"Worthy David Cross, your flight plan has been filed and crew readiness is verified. You are cleared for departure. Hangar doors will open after the all-clear."

We waited a few minutes for the alarms to announce that the hangar bay would soon be exposed to vacuum. As the air was pumped out of the hangar, we pulled away from the gangway and drifted slowly towards the doors. When they opened, Rendika fired the maneuvering jets and we were away.

Chapter twenty-seven

Challers, Pirate Corvette "Destiny Achieved"

DAVID GAVE me the coordinates for his first planned destination as soon as we were outside Port's warp field. While I verified them and began plotting the jump, I asked, "Portcon mentioned filing flight plans?"

"That's right," said David. "Every ship that leaves files a list of their planned destinations. That way, if someone doesn't come back, people who want to investigate what happened to them can find out where they went."

"Aren't you worried about that information getting back to the Scouts?"

"Not at all. By the time they could get it, it wouldn't be any use to them. All the flight plans are encrypted using a key available only to the highest ranking Cues.

"Cues? Who are they?" I asked.

"Cues. Haven't heard of them? Kensington Book is one. They're the people who own Port. Run the place, though they usually only intervene if someone really blows it in a big way. If you haven't had any business with them, that's a good thing. Anyways, they only decrypt the flight plan if a ship is more than two days late coming back. A raiding cruise is only two or three days. By the time anyone had the flight plan decrypted and sent out, it would be too late to do anything about it. We would already have been and gone."

"Jump coordinates engaged and local environment compensations are computed. We are ready for jump."

"All right. Do it."

I touched the ENGAGE button and the engines whined and thudded. The empty starscape that had surrounded us shifted, twisted, and reformed again as the sound wound down. Where there had been a vast expanse of nothing but starlight, there was now a sun and, straight in front of us, I could just make out a distant metal sphere surrounded by tiny work-drones and the fragments of asteroids they were working on.

"Begin infrared scan," he said to Krinna. "Challers, make ready a return trip just in case we have company."

"Scan initiated," said Krinna, hunched over her console.

"Course ready," I said. "We can jump anytime."

David leaned over in my direction from his command chair. "I hope there aren't any hard feelings about that business back in Port. You understand that theatrics like that really bring in the orgone."

I shook my head. "Look, just don't bother, okay? You put me through a lot and if it weren't for that duel, I'd say you owed me for all of it."

He smiled and leaned back. "You'll see. It'll all be worth it. This first trip is to make sure our little expedition makes a profit. Once we've got a hold full of saleable goods, we'll go on to our next destination."

"I hope you're right." I looked out the front window at the station. "So what's the plan here? We just fly up and threaten to start punching holes in the hull if they don't throw stuff out the airlock for us to pick up?"

"Oh, hardly," said David. "We've got a relationship with these people. Just watch, and play along."

"Infrared scan complete," said Krinna. "The system is clear."

Rendika turned to David. "Transmission from Rudjaroo Station."

"Play it."

A wide holoscreen appeared over Rendika's console, displaying a man's smiling face. "David! So good to see you again. I hope you have many treasures for me?"

"Of course! I can't wait to show you."

"Excellent. You have clearance to dock at Airlock Seven."

I gave David a quizzical look.

"Bring us in," he said, and winked in my direction.

A few minutes later, Rendika, David, and I emerged from the airlock into a wide balcony overlooking the Promenade. I felt an immediate wave of nostalgia. This was the same architecture as my birthplace, Stakroya Station. The shops were different, and the faces, but nothing could hide the similarities. I wondered what my mother was doing, whether she knew what was happening to me. Had the Scouts told her that I had been imprisoned?

Worse, had they punished her? Did they punish her when I escaped? I had never heard of anything like that happening, but after the atrocities I had seen at Headquarters, I knew it was not beyond them to take it out on her.

The smiling man from the message strode up to us—a shortish, narrow-faced man in a fine dress uniform. He greeted David with a warm handshake. "You have a new crewmember, I see," he said, nodding to me.

David turned and laid a hand on my shoulder. "Captain Sigler, I'd like you to meet Worthy Challers Dizen. This is his first trip. I hope you'll make him quite welcome."

"Oh, I'm sure, I'm sure." He shook my hand and then stepped aside to give us access to the ramp behind him. "If you'll join me in the conference room?"

"Of course."

We followed Captain Sigler down the ramp and across the Promenade into a room dominated by a large table. Two women stood nearby with serving trays holding bottles and glasses, and two men with towels. We seated ourselves at one end of the table and Captain Sigler took the other.

A glass appeared in front of each of us with an inch or so of amber liquid in the bottom. Sigler raised his. "To a fruitful trading session," he said.

David nodded to me and raised his glass. I followed along when Rendika raised hers with an eyebrow raised in my direction. "Indeed," said David.

We drank. It was fiery stuff, and I had a hard time not choking on it. There was a lot more alcohol in it than there was in the Brandywine back at Port.

"So what do you have for me?" asked Sigler.

"Two containers of high-protein powder, a crate of forty holdouts, and a crate of Firebelly, of course." David held up his glass. "I'd hate for your hospitality to be anything but warm."

"Excellent, excellent," said Sigler. "I can offer you two containers of titanium alloy, and another of aluminum ingots."

"You do know my ship can carry four containers."

Sigler smiled apologetically. "I know, but it is a bit difficult to divert that much product right now. You know how things are, I'm sure."

David nodded. "Of course. You can make up for it next time. I'll agree to the trade."

Captain Sigler sighed with relief. "I look forward to it. Now, I'll see to the cargo transfers. I hope you'll enjoy our continued hospitality." He rose from his chair, downed the last of his drink, bowed, and exited the room.

The servants put aside their accoutrements and moved closer to the table. Rendika glanced up at the two men flanking her, licked her lips, and nodded to the one on her right. He smiled back, bowed, and extended his hand.

David stood and looked over the two women. "You, I think," he said to the blonde.

"What's going on here?" I asked.

"Hospitality," said David. "Enjoy it."

The remaining servant, a pretty woman with shoulder-length red hair, smiled hopefully at me.

"What's your name?" I asked.

"Stella Dean, sir."

I stood up and shook my head. "Don't call me 'sir.' My name is Challers."

She nodded. "Challers. We have a room prepared for you." She stepped away and glanced down at the floor. It seemed like a needlessly humble gesture.

I glanced at David. He winked and put his arm around the blonde woman's waist. "Go on. See you in a couple hours. Have fun."

Stella led me up a set of stairs to a short hallway with four doors off of it, opened one of them, and gently pulled me inside. On Stakroya, these rooms had been storage, places to keep pieces of furniture and supplies that allowed the captain's conference room to be used for several different purposes. Here, however, it was a nicely appointed, if small, bedroom. A comfortable-looking chair sat in one corner, facing a narrow bed made up with clean pink sheets and a thin coverlet. The walls were covered with dark-red curtains.

When the door closed behind us, she touched the controls to lock the door, and then put her hand to her neck to unzip the front of her coverall. She kept her eyes on the floor, but behind her hair, I could see a flush coming to her face.

"Are you all right?" I asked.

She nodded and pulled down the zipper. Underneath, she wore a plain white pullover, and as she stretched to pull the coverall off her shoulders, I could see her small, pert breasts poking at the thin fabric. She pushed the coverall the rest of the way off, revealing a pair of utilitarian white shorts and slim legs.

I took her shoulders in my hands. "Stella. What's going on?"

She looked up and a flash of fear crossed her face and disappeared. "I am...available to you, Challers."

I shook my head. "Who is making you do this?"

"No one. I volunteered."

"You aren't acting like a volunteer."

"Please, sir. Don't ask questions. I don't want to make trouble, I don't. I'm giving myself to you entirely on my own. Nobody is making me do this." She sat on the bed and pulled her shirt up over her head.

The blush on her face deepened.

The morality here looked like it was about the same as it was back on Stakroya Station. Sexual contact was carefully controlled. Privacy was hard to come by, and there were rigid roles and expectations for everyone.

I put my hand gently on her cheek and raised her face to look at me. "Stella, have you been intimate with a man before?"

"No." She swallowed hard and I could see the beginning of tears in her eyes. "Please, sir. Don't send me away."

"I won't." I sat down next to her and took her hand between mine. "I don't want to do anything to hurt you, Stella."

"Captain Sigler said that there's someone left behind on your ship. He says that if we don't make you happy, you'll shoot. You'll kill everyone."

"Krinna," I said under my breath. I knew if anyone had the stomach to do something like that, it was her.

"Please, Challers. I'm probably already in lots of trouble just for talking about it."

"All right," I said. "If that's how things are, then let me make this as painless for you as possible. Maybe even useful."

She looked up and gave me a hint of an authentic smile, the first I had seen on her face.

"First, I want you to show me what you do when you touch yourself."

She squinted in confusion. "What?"

"When you masturbate. Give yourself orgasms. What do you do?"

She shook her head. "Orgasm?"

I brushed my hair back in frustration. It was an attitude I was familiar with. Stakroya Station had been full of it. Nobody ever told anyone anything about sex, except all the reasons not to do it—like it made women get pregnant and it was only for married folks.

"Then just lie down and relax. If I do anything that hurts, I want you to tell me, okay? Don't hold back. It's okay if you tell me. I really don't want to cause you any pain." I guided her down onto the bed. This wasn't exactly a mission-critical encounter, but I felt certain Valka would approve.

She lay stiff and straight, staring up at the ceiling and breathing, her arms at her sides and legs pressed together. "I'm ready."

I stood next to the bed. "Here. Turn over onto your stomach, okay?"

She shot me a horrified look, but it softened when she looked into my eyes. She turned over. I took her arm away from her body and began massaging her hand. As I moved up along her arm, gently squeezing the knots out of her muscles, I felt her slowly relax and her breathing smooth out. When I went around to the other side to work on her other arm, she turned her head my way and said, "That's nice. Nobody has ever made me feel like this."

I shushed her and began working on her arm. "Relax," I said softly. "Just imagine that you're safe, alone, someplace where nobody has any expectations."

"I don't know where that is."

"Then make something up. Your own spaceship carrying you away from everything threatening."

I moved down to her feet and dug my thumbs into her arches, provoking a deep sigh. I moved very slowly up her legs, alert for any sign that my efforts were making her more tense. Sure enough, as I started going higher than her knees, I felt a bit of a tremble and backed off. "I'm going to rub your neck and shoulders, okay?"

She nodded.

I climbed up onto the bed, straddling her hips with my knees. I held my body up above hers and leaned down to apply my hands to her shoulders. Starting gently, I gradually increased the pressure as I discovered one knotty lump of muscle after another. After working some of them out of her neck and shoulders, I shifted my position and dragged my thumbs down along her spine.

I climbed off the bed and knelt down at her side. "Are you ready?"

"Hmm?"

"I want to show you something, if you feel you're ready."

"Okay."

"Turn over."

She rolled over onto her back with a calm, slightly blissful look on her face. With a light touch, I rubbed her temples, next behind her jaw, and then drew my fingers down the cords of her neck to her collarbone. I watched her face as my fingers moved down over her breasts, but there was no apprehension in her eyes when I toyed briefly with her nipples. Keeping one hand there, I ran the other one slowly down across her flat belly toward the waistband of her shorts.

I paused there, glancing at her face. "Stella?"

"Mmm?"

"I'm going to touch your..." Crass language probably wouldn't have made things any easier for her. "I'm going to go inside your underwear now. Can you spread your legs a bit?"

"Mmm-hmm." She shifted her legs, hanging one foot off each side of the bed.

My fingers slipped under the elastic, probed past her thick pubic hair, and gently parted her lips. There was a catch in her breath and she let out a slight whimper.

"Should I stop?" I asked.

"No. You can...you can keep going. If you like."

Slowly, gently, I stroked her tender flesh, experimenting, my attention focused on her face. The best spot seemed to be a little bit beneath her clit, rubbing crosswise to bring each stroke into contact with her inner lips. She was warm and wet. Every passing second, every swipe of my finger, brought more color to her face, more depth to her breathing.

"Challers...I...oh, stop..."

"Does it hurt?"

"No...it feels...oh...funny."

"That's okay. Just tell me if it hurts." I moved again, gently squeezing her nipple between my fingers as my hand moved under her shorts. I dipped my finger deeper, briefly, and felt a thin yet resilient barrier. Her hymen. I retreated and went back to stroking further up.

"I'm...oh, Challers...I'm afraid."

I shook my head, silently cursing Captain Sigler to myself. How could he have assigned this completely innocent girl to this duty? Couldn't he have taken someone less unspoiled? "You'll be fine. What you're feeling is natural. This is what I wanted to show you."

She grabbed my hand, but instead of pulling it away, she held it close. I smiled a little to myself and pressed harder, moving a little closer to her clit. Tension gripped her body and, for a few seconds, she made tiny little noises through clenched teeth, and then relaxed, twitching, on the bed.

After a minute, she opened languorous eyes and smiled at me. "What was that?"

"That was an orgasm. You can do the same thing for yourself whenever you get a few minutes alone, like in the shower."

She closed her eyes, still smiling, enjoying the afterglow. "Thank you."

I rose from beside the bed and surreptitiously wiped my fingers on my pants. "Now that's done..."

"Oh, no!" She bounced up onto her knees. "I want to do the same thing for you."

"No, I can't. I don't want to take advantage of you that way."

"Please? I've...I've never been with a man. Ever. The reason I volunteered for this was so I would learn these things."

I thought for a moment, and then took the advice of my body. Through the entire affair, I hadn't gotten more than a slight erection. The thought that the whole reason we were being welcomed so warmly was because Krinna was back on the ship left a sour taste in my mouth. It wouldn't do any good for her to try to get me aroused and fail. I unlocked the door. "No. Today's lesson is over. Get dressed, Stella, and be glad David wasn't the one who chose you."

chapter twenty-eight

Challers, Rudjaroo Station

THE PROMENADE on Rudjaroo Station was both familiar and strangely alien. The shops and services available on either side of the lower level were the same sorts of things you'd find on Stakroya. Most places offered both new items and repair of old ones. Food was only available in the station cafeteria, but if you had a little ready cash, there was a bar for socializing and drinking the weak local beer.

Everyone was friendly, even obsequious about making sure I was enjoying my stay. Each one only made me more sick to my stomach. Finally, I could take it no more and I retreated back to the ship. I went to the bridge and sat down at my station, telling myself I would review the simulations I had downloaded, hoping that would clear my head a little.

"Back so soon?" said Krinna, watching a monitor showing the cargo sliding into the hold. She was leaning back in her chair, feet propped up on the console with the holoscreen projected in the air over her.

I swallowed and unclenched my teeth. "Not really to my taste."

She looked over at me and chuckled. "David was right. You really aren't cut out to be a Pirate."

"Is it a bad thing to want to avoid taking advantage of people?"

"You grew up on a station, Challers. Did Pirates ever show up there?"

"No. Back on Stakroya, it was always a threat that was on the horizon, the reason that the Fleet was nearby so often."

"Ah, and did you have any weapons there—things to use to defend yourselves if the Fleet decided it was time to purge the station?"

"What?"

Krinna cocked an eyebrow. "You didn't know? I suppose you wouldn't. Every so often, if a station starts making trouble, if it looks like they'll lose their hold, the Fleet comes in and kills everyone. They blame it on us and bring in a replacement crew from some other station. The holdout weapons we leave here won't show up on scanners and, if things go that way, at least they'll be able to fight back. You don't think the Merchants will sell them anything like that, do you?"

"Well, no, but..."

"And think about the food you got there on your station. My bet is you got soy cubes, vegetables, and teabulbs for most meals, am I right?"

"Well, yeah. That's the most efficient way to make food."

"Most efficient, but it's a very low-protein diet. It's designed to feed the largest number of people in the smallest amount of space. Did you get a good look at the people here?"

"Yes."

"Notice anything? Like, they're well fed? Healthy? That's because we bring dietary supplements. Things the Merchants and the Fleet don't let them have."

"But...don't they know? I mean, don't they know that the Pirates bring them these things? Wouldn't that make the Fleet come in and retaliate?"

"Unless they wanted to purge them all, they can't. If the Fleet tried to force the stations to treat us as invaders, then we'd respond in kind. We'd threaten to hole the station, and then we'd just take what we needed instead of trading for it. If the Fleet really wanted to keep us from visiting, they'd have to arm the station and that would mean installing orgone collectors and hyperbeams. Do that, and the station is able to resist the Fleet as well—not to mention, they could just fly off to some other location to get away. So they're stuck. As long as the folks in charge want to keep their relationship with the stations, they have to accept that we're going to be there as well."

"So if they were to put things on a more equal footing, instead of using the stations as human breeding grounds..."

"Then the stations would be allowed to trade with whomever they liked, manufacture whatever they liked. It would be a much better galaxy for everyone, but some folks just gotta be in charge, and they'll do anything to stay there." A beep sounded from the console. Krinna sat up and acknowledged it. "Hmm, looks like we have a visitor."

I looked over Krinna's shoulder. A holoscreen showed the area in front of the airlock.

"I'll go," I said. "I have a feeling I know what this is about."

I walked over to the airlock and made sure the interior door was shut before opening the outer one. "Hi, Stella."

She stood there in an ordinary coverall with a duffel slung over her shoulder. "I want to come with you."

I shook my head. "No, you can't."

"But when you told me to imagine being on my own ship, out in the void..."

"That's not what I meant."

"It isn't?"

"You don't understand what you're asking. You're leaving everything. You have no idea what it's like out there."

"It's better than here, I know that much."

A hand appeared on her shoulder. "You on a recruiting drive, there, Challers?" David swung past us into the airlock. "Come on in, kid. Let's see what you got."

Stella's face broke into a wide grin and she bounced into the ship behind David. I swallowed the sick feeling growing in my gut and closed the door after me as I went inside.

David turned with a dramatic gesture and smiled at Stella. "So here's how it goes, kid. You know that the ships are powered by orgone, right? And the most valuable form of orgone comes from sex. Different people are better or worse at generating orgone, and before we take you back to our base, we need to see how good you are at it."

She took a breath, and nodded. "I'm ready."

He gave a sideways nod of his head. "I'm sure you are, kid. Challers, will you do the honors? I'll go up to the bridge and monitor output, see if we've got a hot one."

The edge in his voice and the challenging stare he gave me ran hot blades through my belly. "I'm not really—"

"Or if you don't want to get her going," he said with a sharp grin, "I could do it, and you could take readings from the bridge. Up to you."

Stella turned back, looking at me over her shoulder, excitement filling her face. "Would you? Please?"

When she saw the troubled expression on my face, her excitement turned to fear, and then hurt. I couldn't turn her down, not when it meant putting her in David's not-so-loving hands. This whole thing made my initiation with the Scouts look tender and loving in comparison.

I pasted a smile on my face. "It would be my pleasure."

David nodded, smiling, and turned to saunter into the bridge. "Have fun, kids! See you in a bit."

The door closed behind him and Stella wrapped her arms around me and squeezed tight. "Oh, Challers! I just know this is going to be great!"

I put my hands on her hips and gently put some space between us. "I'm sure you'll do just fine." I led her to the orgone chamber and stopped her at the edge of the bed. "Let me get some preparations started, here." I bent down to the controls on the bed surface and programmed it to be a little softer and more comfortable. Its default form was basically a floor mat.

Stella put her duffel down behind the bench and kicked off her shoes. "This time, can I get the real thing?"

"I'm not sure I know what you mean."

"Sex. Real sex. You and me, together..."

"You said you'd never been with a man before."

She pulled off her jacket and flung it aside. "I haven't. I had that whole thing about saving it for when I was married, but all the guys here are idiots. I don't think any of them know how to make someone feel like you do. I'm never going back there. I don't care what they think."

There was a nervous thread running through her voice and I wondered how much she really wanted this, and how much was the enthusiasm of the moment. Still, I couldn't think of anything else to do but carry through with it.

Stella shoved her pants down and stepped out of them, and then bent down next to me and put her arm around my back. "Spoil me, Challers. Use me. Make me a slut."

I frowned. "Don't talk like that. Enjoying sex doesn't make you a slut. Everyone likes it. Some just don't have the freedom to express that desire openly."

She rolled onto her back. "Fine, then! Free me! Break these bonds that have held me to this stupid station and set me free!"

I turned from the little console next to the bed and knelt next to her, shaking my head. "Well, you've certainly got a good sense of drama. You'll need that, at least."

"See? I knew this was a good idea."

I kicked my shoes off and started undoing the knots on my shirt.

"Ooh, let me, let me," she said and got up to help. "I can't wait to see."

"All right." I held my arms up and let her work out the knots.

She spread the shirt wide and ran her hands over my chest. "Are all Pirates as nice as you?"

"No. I'm not bragging when I say I'm one of the more respectful ones." I tossed my shirt aside and worked off my gun belt. "Some of them can be quite abusive, in fact."

"Let me get the rest, okay?"

I lay back and stretched out my legs. She quickly pulled off my shoes, and then took a deep breath as her fingers closed around the waist of my pants. Clearly savoring the moment, she drew them off slowly, her attention fixed on the retreating fabric. I had never had anyone look at me so intensely and it made me tingle at the thought.

"You've really never seen a man naked, have you?"

"No," she whispered as I lifted my butt so she could pull my pants off completely. Her warm breath caressed my cock as she knelt, seemingly hypnotized as it twitched and pulsed with my heartbeat, gradually swelling and lifting up from my thigh.

"Vack," she said, awestruck. "Does it always move like that?"

"No," I said, trying to hide my amusement. "Only when it's getting hard."

"Can I...touch it? Will it hurt you?"

"Of course you can. Just don't do anything you wouldn't do to, mmm, your own finger." I couldn't believe this girl was so naïve. Had I ever been so ignorant?

Stella stroked it gently, fingers extended. It was a tentative motion, not one intended to stimulate but to explore. "Here," I said and wrapped her fingers around my cock. "Like this." Her movements were clumsy and a little over-enthusiastic, but at least she didn't cause me any injury.

"Is this good?"

It wasn't, but I wasn't going to tell her that. "Stella. We're here to see how well your body creates transcendent orgone. That means you're the one who needs to have an orgasm." I considered asking her to masturbate—the way Valka and I had when Masters and Shirley were trying us out on the way to Scout Headquarters—but I wondered if she'd be able to do it at all given her limited experience. "Just lie down here, in the center of the chamber, and let me take care of everything."

She quickly stripped off her underwear and lay down where I told her with a huge smile on her face, all innocence and hope. I lay down between her legs, stroking her pussy, intending to use my mouth to bring her to orgasm. I hesitated. As I stroked her, there seemed to be something off, but I couldn't say exactly what.

She got up on her elbows and looked at me crosswise. "What are you doing?"

"I was about to—ah—perform cunnilingus on you. Use my mouth."

"What? Eugh!" She put her hand down over her sex. "Do me the right way."

I shook my head. This was not going well. With a sigh, I crawled up alongside her. "Most of the women I know like that better than just about anything. And if this is your first time, intercourse might not be the best way to get the best results." I ran my hand over her body and felt a shiver run through her.

"I'm sure it'll be just fine."

I leaned down and kissed her lips, wanting more than anything to send her scurrying out the airlock before anything terrible happened.

But David was watching. I had no choice.

With one hand, I massaged her pussy, feeling her open up once again, while I kissed and licked her mouth, her earlobe, and then her nipple. She cooed and sighed as I explored her body, but with every breath, she begged, "Take me. Take me, Challers. I want you inside me."

That much, at least, she knew and she thought she wanted it. She thought it would be the greatest moment of her life. But we had covered the hymen and virginity in my Scout studies. I knew that for many women, it wasn't easy. When I realized she would be satisfied with nothing less, that she was holding back and waiting for me to fuck her, I tried to remember what I had learned about making the experience as satisfying as possible. The problem was that Shirley had been long past that stage, and I hadn't paid much attention.

I made sure she was aroused as I could get her with my fingers, and then situated myself between her legs. She looked up at me with half-lidded eyes, her mouth open, and chest flushed. I paused, overcome by emotion. How could I be doing this? I felt like I was taking the last fruit in the bowl, gripping it in my fist and squeezing the juice down into my throat. It felt like violence.

And yet it was what she wanted—at least, it was what she said she wanted—and who was I to gainsay that? She had made her decision. There was nothing else to do.

My erection started flagging so I gave it a few strokes to get it started again. Finally, I had to close my eyes and call up the memory of Valka masturbating in the orgone chamber of Shirley's Scout ship to get it hard enough.

I slid my cock inside, meeting resistance and pushing through. She gasped in surprise and pain, gritting her teeth. I moved slowly, trying to ease her past the pain. My instinct was to go harder and faster, but I resisted the urge. The only way this would work would be if I went slowly.

When the worst of it had passed, she opened her eyes and smiled up at me weakly. "Thank you."

I could only nod. I pulled out and went back to lying at her side. "How do you feel?" I asked.

She swallowed. "It hurts...but it's not bad, now."

"We don't have to go on, if you don't want to."

"No, please. Keep going. I need this. Please."

"Okay." I put my fingers back to work and bent my head to her neck again. Her hand found my cock, and I caught the slightest scent of blood in the air. My fingers felt sticky and I wondered how bad her bleeding was.

It took five minutes of constant work to finally coax a small orgasm out of her. By the end of it, my hand was cramping up so bad I thought it would freeze in place. I sat back and massaged my sore muscles.

There wasn't as much blood as I imagined—just a small stain on my hand—but it felt wrong just the same.

David opened the door from the bridge and shook his head. "Sorry, kid. It just doesn't make the grade. I'm afraid we can't use you."

chapter twenty-nine

Challers, Pirate Corvette "Destiny Achieved"

"YOU BURNER!"

Stella had fled from the ship crying and screaming, her clothes barely on, when David told her to go. None of her pleading had done her any good. And when she was gone, he looked at me with a smug smile telling me he enjoyed every minute of it.

"You knew that was going to happen!" I pointed at the open airlock door. "You've just ruined her life!"

"She'll get over it," he said and sauntered back into the bridge.

"I don't think my life is ruined, Challers." Rendika came up behind me and gave me a slap on the butt.

"I was talking about Stella."

"Stella?"

"The girl that David set me up with at the conference. She came back here and wanted to leave with us. That bastard in there had me 'test her out,' and then told her she didn't have what it takes!"

Rendika scowled. "That's a dirty trick."

"Dirty? It's criminal!"

The airlock closed and David called out from the bridge. "Time to be moving, folks. We're all loaded and secure. Never know when a Fleet battle cruiser is going to show up."

Rendika gave David a cross look as she passed him on her way to her console. I didn't look at him at all.

After a few moments work, there was a clank and a thump. "Airlock grapples released," David announced. "We're away." The station slowly dwindled as Rendika fired the maneuvering jets to get us to a safe distance where we could start the jump sequence.

I sat and fumed. I was so angry I contemplated pulling my weapon and blowing his head open, but I had promised Valka I would return to her.

"You'll find that the coordinates for our next destination have been sent to your console, Challers."

I pulled them up. "These are in the Rimward Reach," I said. "Pretty close to Scout Headquarters."

"That's right. We're going to a station that two ships recently tried to make contact with. A station we only recently got coordinates for. We'll need to be on our guard."

I calculated the course. "Ready for jump."

"Whenever you're ready."

I touched the controls, the engines thudded and whined to life, and we were there. This time, the star that burned before us was much smaller, a distant reddish thing.

"Starting infrared scan," said Krinna.

"What did those ships find when they came here?" I asked.

"I don't know," said David. "They never came back. Challers, plot a return course to Port."

I started the calculations. "That's your plan? To stick your fingers in the same hole that killed two other ships?"

"I have no doubts about the competence of my crew."

I slammed my hand down on the console. "This is suicide!"

Rendika looked up from her console, at me, and then at David.

"Relax, people," he said. "We're a hundred times further out from the station than anyone ever arrives. We're going to take a good long time at the scan and just wait and watch for a while. We're going to take it very carefully."

Krinna tapped her console. "Infrared scan contact." She created a holoscreen where we all could see the displayed data. "Warp-light distortion of six point four. It's a Merchant, outbound, probably on its way to Harginn Station if I'm reading the heading correctly. Looks like it left the system about twelve hours ago. Still scanning."

"Harginn? I know that name," I said, staring at the display in disbelief. "That's...you didn't."

David studied the screen. "That's right, Challers. This is Stakroya. It's common practice to visit the home station of new Worthies. We pick up family members and bring them back to Port for protection. Otherwise, there can be repercussions...retribution. That's why the other two ships came here. Really, Challers. You should thank me."

I turned and returned to my work, but I couldn't keep my eyes off the little blip that represented the place where I was born, wondering if what David had said was true. Wondering if I should thank him, or curse him. Wondering if my mother was all right. Wondering if Valka's parents were all right.

Valka's father. The thought of the man who had caused Valka so much pain living there, free and unpunished, put my teeth on edge.

Another blip appeared on my map about a light-second away from the station. "Hyperspace disturbance," I said. "Looks about two days old, maybe three." I pulled up the sensor readings to look them over, but they made no sense. "What does this mean?"

"It means there was a fight. A short one, judging from these readings. Dozens of scrambler beams fired in all kinds of directions. This doesn't look like any battle traces I've ever seen," said Krinna.

"Look for debris," said David.

Krinna shook her head. "Vapor. Dust. Nothing larger than a millimeter."

"Good."

"Good?" I asked.

"Right. The reason the Fleet uses scrambler beams is because they don't harm equipment—just people. Damages the nervous system. They want to capture our ships, learn the orgone storage technology. So we tie the ship's self-destruct charge to the shields. If the crisis orgone batteries are fully drained, the charge goes off automatically. Boom. No surrender."

"What kind of charge?"

"An old-fashioned fusion device. Nothing like a thermonuclear explosion to make sure nothing gets captured."

"Fun."

"Definitely keeps things interesting."

"And that's what happened here," said Krinna. "There are eddies in the interplanetary medium consistent with that kind of explosion. I'm going to try to do a reconstruction...figure out what happened to make these crazy traces."

"You do that, but kick that infrared scan up to a level-two search," said David. "Whoever won that battle could still be around."

I listened, staring at the little dot on my screen. My stomach gurgled and I forced down a belch. One, possibly two ships had already been destroyed here, but the prospect of being able to get onto the station to retrieve my mother and confront Valka's father— that was a strong temptation.

David got up out of his chair and went over to Krinna's station. "This is going to take a while. Go get something to eat. I'll keep watch here."

"Thanks." Krinna got up and went aft, towards the galley.

I finished the course calculation. "Course is programmed. Should be valid for at least an hour from this location. I'm going to go lie down for a bit."

David waved over his shoulder. "Have fun."

The little barracks was dark and empty. Nothing in the room said that people ever slept there, ever made it their home. It was just four bunks, two on the left and two on the right, with lockers underneath for stowing gear that nobody ever bothered to bring. I lay down on one of the bunks and stared at the tiny porthole at my feet, listening to Krinna banging around in the galley.

I could do the math. If the Merchant ship had left twelve hours ago, then it would have been in the system when the battle occurred. And a battle that involved the missiles we had tangled with escaping from Scout Headquarters wouldn't look anything like a duel with a Fleet battle cruiser. I doubted the Merchant ship would have those missiles on board, though. I couldn't see the Scouts letting anything as controversial as that out of their direct supervision. There was too much rivalry between the services for that.

"What's on your mind?" asked Krinna. She leaned against the doorframe and sucked something thick out of a cup through a straw.

"I think they're waiting for us," I said. "The Scouts. They know we're coming, because the Scouts know, or suspect, that I switched sides. If picking up family is as common as David says, then they knew we were coming. I think they've got some of those new missiles and they're using them to take down Pirate ships. "

She swallowed and nodded. "After seeing that battle track, I think you might be right. If it's true, then we need to gather as much information as possible before we act. What's the range on those missiles?"

"I don't know. The ones that chased us at Scout Headquarters could run for at least a few minutes. If they're powered by Ovor eggs, like I think they are, then they could conceivably travel for days at warp speed, then drop into hyperspace when they got close to their target."

"You told David about this?"

"Not yet."

"I don't think you should wait."

I realized I was hanging back because I wanted to see David need me. I wanted to see him confused and afraid, with me the one having the answers. It was a petty, immature feeling, and I was ashamed.

"You're right," I said, swinging my legs off the bunk.

David heard me out, listened to Krinna and Rendika back up my theories with observations, and then he grilled me on every detail I remembered from the escape from Scout Headquarters. We decided that if there were egg missiles in the system, they were either on the station itself, on the Merchant ship that just left the system, or on a Fleet battle cruiser hiding somewhere nearby. Of the three, the station was the obvious choice. They would be least likely to be discovered by someone who wasn't supposed to see them, and more likely to be ready when a Pirate ship showed up.

David stared out the front viewports and frowned. "We need to get on that station. Have a look around."

"No, we don't," said Rendika. "We need to get this information back to Port. We've already got our cargo. We've got our profit for the trip. We can't risk letting the data we've got on the battle track get lost."

Krinna shook her head. "And in the time it takes us to get back and convince someone that there's a danger, how many other ships are going to come out here, unsuspecting? If these missiles exist, and if they are on the station, then we need to find proof."

Rendika made a swooping motion with her hand. "Maybe we could buzz them, get them to launch the missiles, then jump out to a safe distance and watch."

"Risky," said David. "Very risky. Scrambler beams move faster than light. You don't know you're under attack until you've been hit."

"For that matter," I said with a sudden realization, "if we stay here long enough, they'll spot our infrared signature. They could launch the missiles just because, and we'd never know they were coming."

"Good point," said David. "All right. Plot a course for a point four light-hours away from the station. Make sure we're not on any of the navigation routes. Jump as soon as you're ready."

With a growing sense of urgency, I plotted the course and executed it, sending the ship out into deep space, well away from the station. Our infrared emissions, traveling at the speed of light, wouldn't reach the station for a third of a shift. We would be safe for at least that long.

David rubbed his chin and stared at the holoscreens. "We have to assume the missiles are on board the station, or close by. Either way, that's where they'd be controlled from."

I hesitated for a moment, and then said, "I have an idea."

"Tell me."

"I've been running some simulations. If we create a precisely plotted jump conduit, we could create an exit point inside the station."

"You want to try to send the ship right into the hangar bay? That's pretty damn audacious." David gave me an appraising look. "Your navigation would have to be spot-on perfect. Not only that, you'd need to know precisely how the station was oriented, or you'd come out in hydroponics instead of the hangar bay. The explosion would be extraordinary, but I doubt we'd live to enjoy it."

"Not the whole ship. Just one person. In a spacesuit."

"Ah...create the jump conduit, but instead of the ship going through it, a person does. The targeting wouldn't have to be as precise, but you'd still need to know the target's orientation."

"I believe I've got that worked out too. In order to reduce interior radiation, the station always keeps its hangar bays pointed away from the system primary."

"That only tells you two out of three axes of rotation."

"Yes, but the hangar bays are a ring shape. If we hit the right position, it won't matter what the orientation is. The exit point will wind up in one of them."

He shook his head, and took a deep breath. "That's still a huge risk. You could wind up in a bulkhead, or a ship docked there..."

"I've been in that hangar bay a hundred times. Remember, I grew up on this station. It's almost always empty. Merchant ships won't fit inside. They always dock to the exterior hatches. Since it's a trade hub rather than a manufacturing or mining center, it hardly has any work drones at all—just a few remotes for doing external repairs."

"I'll go," said Krinna. "I'm the best duelist here."

I shook my head. "If it comes to a fight, it's already lost. I'll go. I grew up there. I know my way around, know all the hiding places. Besides that, people know me. If I'm discovered, I have a better chance of either fitting in, or talking my way out of it."

David stood up and looked out the front viewport, as if he could see the station. "All right, so let's say you manage to get aboard safely and disable the missiles. How do you get an all-clear message to us that will arrive before a warp-powered missile attack?"

"After you drop me off, you jump to a position behind Kalther— that's the gas giant whose Trojan point the station is in. If they don't see you, they can't attack you. There are always some remotes out there mining hydrocarbons from the dust belt. Their sensors aren't good enough to detect you, but I can make one of them relay a signal you can detect."

David nodded. "All right, sounds like a plan. How long will those calculations take you?"

"For that level of precision? Ten minutes."

"Then we'll jump to fifteen light-minutes out from the station, and you can make your jump. The code for the all clear will be 'Chain Harvest Seven Kay.' Got it?"

I made a firm mental note. "Got it. 'Chain Harvest Seven Kay.'"

"We'll wait twenty-four hours for your signal, Challers, then we're going back to Port. There's no way I'm risking a fight shorthanded."

"That's fair. If it takes longer than that, something will have gone wrong in a big way."

"One thing, though. I'll have to take your belt. We can't afford to have that technology captured."

"Understood. David?"

"Yes?"

"No more games. No more manipulations. This is for real."

"Understood. Worthy Dizen , you may execute when ready."

I took a few minutes to get my gear in order, removed my orgone belt and strapped my laser to the outside of an emergency spacesuit. It was set on "kill." Once I had everything in place, I turned to my station and got to work. I had the first jump calculated in only a minute or two. I immediately triggered it. As soon as we were through, I began the second, paying close attention to the scanning data Rendika fed me on the station's position and orientation.

As soon as it was ready, I turned to leave the bridge. "It's all ready for you to trigger, David. When you see me out in front of the nose, hit the trigger. As soon as that collapses, trigger the second one. That'll take you to Kalther."

"Good luck, Challers."

I nodded, and stepped into the airlock.

chapter thirty

Challers, Stakroya Station

MY HEAD was killing me. I had landed on it when the jump conduit released me and it felt like it was ready to split open. The one thing I hadn't counted on was appearing a meter above the deck in full gravity. The helmet had taken most of the blow and, judging from the crack running through its surface, I was lucky I hadn't smashed my skull. I pulled it off and set it aside. It wasn't going to do me any good.

Even though I wasn't seeing precisely straight, I knew we had guessed right. There was a Scout ship sitting in the hangar bay not far from me. Nothing else looked out of place, however. The missiles we were looking for would be fairly large, ovoid shapes, three meters long and about a meter wide. They weren't here.

I had to get out of there. There was too much risk that the Scout ship had some sensors running, and even if they didn't have the data to figure out exactly what had happened, someone would be coming to investigate. I contemplated slipping on board the Scout ship, but there was no way the hatch would be unsecured, and I didn't have the tools to break in quickly. No, I needed to check the other hangar bays. That was where the missiles would be stored.

I got to my feet. At least I wasn't dizzy. "No concussion, let's hope," I muttered to myself and moved quickly toward the main hatch.

It opened just before I arrived. I was surprised to see a female station security officer—they were never women—next to a man in a white sleeveless uniform. I recognized it immediately and all thoughts of the security officer were meaningless. This was a Scout. There was something familiar about him, but there wasn't time to puzzle it out. I drew my pistol and fired.

The shot blew open the front of his shirt and threw him back into the corridor behind him. Underneath his shirt was nothing but bright red. He was down.

"Hold it!" I said, covering the female security officer. "Don't make me kill you too."

She held up her hands and stared in disbelief. "Challers?"

I didn't recognize the officer and that bothered me. There shouldn't be any strangers on the station. I knew everyone, by face if not by name.

"Challers, it's me, Horren. Horren Parl."

Horren was Valka's father. From having been transformed into an Ovor for a while, I knew what a man's voice sounded like after the change. That was what had happened to Horren. I stared at her. Part of me was gleeful to see Horren humbled like this, made the victim of the Scouts. I had wanted a confrontation with Valka's father to exact retribution for the childhood stolen from her.

But I had a more important mission. I shook my head. "There's no time for that now. The Scouts installed some missiles. I need to know where they are, so I can disable them."

"They put a cargo container in Hangar Bay Three. Put a seal on the hatch. Said no one was to go inside."

"That'll be where they are then. Go on. Lead the way."

She turned, arms still raised above her head, and stopped with a confused grunt. I looked past her.

The Scout was gone.

"Move!" I said, advancing close behind Horren, and plucking the stunner from her belt. We moved out into the service corridor, but it was deserted. There was no time to lose. I had to get to those missiles. Once I disabled them, I could deal with the Scouts.

I leaned in close to whisper in her ear. "Horren, I need you to do something for me. For Valka's sake. If you do this, I swear, you won't regret it. This will end the war. End the oppression of the Scouts, and the Fleet—all of it."

"What? How?"

"That shipping container is full of missiles, each of which contains an Ovor egg for power. Firing it tortures and kills the egg. That's why they turned you all into Ovors...to make eggs for the war."

"You're lying. Nobody would be that...That's...terrible." I heard a tremble in her voice—whether it was fear or what, I couldn't tell.

"Believe it or not, some people will do anything to a child. Even just an egg. If that means anything to you, then as soon as you can, transmit a code out to all the remotes for them to broadcast. The code is 'Chain Harvest Seven Kay.' You got that?"

"But the comms are offline."

"Then do it when you get them back. 'Chain Harvest Seven Kay.'"

She nodded.

"Do it when you wake up." I shot Horren in the back. The stun dart pierced the fabric of her uniform easily, delivering a combination of a powerful electric jolt and a dose of knockout drug. The jolt would keep her down long enough for the drug to work. Unfortunately, the sensors in her belt would report that she was down and draw more attention.

I sprinted down the corridor toward Hangar Three. The hatch was closed, but through the windows looking out onto the hangar, I could see the hangar doors were open and the only thing in it was one shipping container, its open side pointed at the void. Cables ran from the container to the wall, probably linking it to the station's computer network.

I heard footsteps approaching at a run. I had only moments to spare. I made sure the pistol was set on its highest setting, aimed through the window at the spot where the cables ran into the container, and fired, hoping that the infrared pulse would pass through the armor glass.

I was wrong. The panel shattered, leaving a gaping hole in the window. Atmosphere streaming out made a vortex of vapor on the other side. Immediately, klaxons sounded and red lights flashed along the wall. Bracing myself against the rim of the window, I fired through the hole, blowing the cables free. They flailed, spraying vapor in every direction. But they weren't cables; they were hoses, bringing fresh water and air to the living, human creatures inside the box.

"Hull breach in Hangar Bay Three," said a voice. It seemed thin and indistinct. "Bulkhead doors closing in five seconds."

I fell to the floor and crawled for the nearest bulkhead, fighting against a tremendous flow of air. Behind me, I heard the damaged window cracking. If it failed, the speed of the air going past me would increase twentyfold, and then my chances would be slim indeed. My ears popped madly, but I fought on, moving around the curve of the hallway towards a bulkhead door that was sliding down to cut off my escape.

Two security officers, both of them women, waved me forward, gripping the edge of the doorway. "Come on! Come on!"

A third arrived with a safety line and threw it to me. As soon as I had a grip on it, they all hauled on it, pulling me under the bulkhead door just in time.

"Get him up," said a man's voice.

Two of the security officers hauled me to my feet. The male was the Scout I had shot, the one I thought I had killed. His shirt was shredded from the middle of his sternum down to his belt, but the red I had seen underneath wasn't blood—it was a smooth, shiny covering of red plastic that flexed as he moved.

"Ah, I see you're admiring my new armor. It's quite remarkable, is it not? Designed specifically to defeat those nasty lasers you Pirates like to tote around. But we're not here to play with my toys. We're going to discuss the location of the Pirate stronghold." He nodded to the third security officer. "Stun him. Strap him down to a table in the medical bay. Let me know as soon as he wakes up."

She shot me without a word or even a second glance, and my consciousness dissolved in a burst of white-hot electric pain.

chapter thirty-one

Renedy, Stakroya Station

I DIDN'T KNOW what it was, but I knew something was happening. My cat-and-mouse game with the Scouts was coming to an end. The wrenching howl the station structure let out and the weird vibration that shook the walls had been like nothing I had heard before. It felt like the end of everything.

I checked the camera network. They had been installed to keep track of us station folk, but before they could catch me, I had taken control of the system and locked them out. And now, I used it to keep track of the Scouts. I knew from their confused reaction—grabbing security officers and barking orders—that something big had happened.

A door opened, and I was pleased to see one of them thrown to the deck with what looked like a bloody wound in his chest, but when he got up shortly thereafter and scuttled away, I cursed.

Then I got a good look at the man who had wounded him.

Challers.

It wasn't easy to sit and watch when the Scouts finally caught him, but by then, I knew I was on his side. The Scouts had been talking about him nonstop since the Merchant ship had left. It was pretty easy to figure out that he had defected to the Pirates. And if he was here, then there was a good chance there was a pirate ship nearby, and if I could get him on board, then they'd have to take me, too. I had a chance. Shaunson was in with the Pirates—at least a little. Challers was too. If they were in, so was I.

It was a simple matter to unlock the comm system and send the message he had given to Mr. Parl. The communications system was one of the first things I had made sure I could access. No doubt that would summon Challer's Pirate friends.

If he was going to escape, though, I needed to get him out of the infirmary, and that would mean leaving my hidey-hole and risking the corridors. The station folk were about evenly split on how they felt about me. Some, I'm sure, were jealous that I had managed to escape the forced transformation. Others were glad someone was doing something to make the Scouts feel unwelcome. They especially liked the program I had running on every console, causing the screen to shut down as soon as they got within a meter. I had discovered that each one carried some kind of transponder, making it a trivial matter to track their movements. Star was the only person I trusted with even a few of my secrets, so I gave him access to some vital functions so he could take care of emergencies while I slept. Aside from that, I owned Stakroya Station.

It would have been easier if I could wait for the dark shift, but I needed to get to him sooner than that. If their interrogation went poorly, he might not survive. I wouldn't be responsible for letting anyone else get killed.

I checked the cameras one last time to make sure my chosen route was mostly clear, then started out. Moving quickly, I hustled through maintenance corridors and side passages until I got to the hallway leading to the infirmary. My tracker told me that the Scouts were only just across the hall, so I had to move fast. I wiped my sweaty palms against my coverall and poked my head out into the passageway. Everything looked clear.

Heart thudding, I crept toward the infirmary. This was the closest I had been to my enemy since they arrived. I watched the door where I knew they were, ready to dash away if it even looked like it would open. I had no intention of letting them put a hole in me.

Finally, my back was to the infirmary door. I touched the control plate and felt it slide open behind me. I got a pang of regret, seeing the familiar infirmary, and the emotional baggage of the past few days weighed heavily on my mind.

No time for that now, I chided myself.

I crossed to the door to the examination room. Some of that weight fell away when I saw Challers lying on the bed, straps around his wrists and ankles, unconscious. I leaned in close and whispered in his ear, lightly shaking his arm. "Challers...Challers. Wake up."

He groaned.

"Come on. Wake up. We gotta get you out of here."

His eyelids fluttered, but he stayed solidly asleep.

The door behind me opened and I spun around. "A bit of bad timing on your part, I'm afraid," said the Scout standing in the doorway, his pistol aimed at the center of my chest. "I made sure he got an extra dose of anesthetic. You've led me on quite a chase, Miss Jawmet, but it's over now."

I set my jaw, refusing to let him see the rage and despair coursing through me.

"So, first things first." He gestured toward the console to my right. "Remove that silly program of yours and surrender control of the station's network to me."

"Never."

"Oh, don't be silly, Miss Jawmet. The result is going to be the same either way. If you cooperate, you both live. Otherwise, I kill you, and we take the whole network apart and rebuild it. No good for anyone."

"I don't care."

"No?" The Scout shifted his aim. "Then how about if I start with your Pirate friend here?"

I swallowed. "You wouldn't. You haven't interrogated him yet."

"My, my, aren't we plucky? Yes, well, I guess you called my bluff." The pistol shifted back and, once again, I was staring down the barrel of his mass driver.

The console came up by itself and Star's face appeared on the screen. "Renedy? Are you there?"

"Answer it," said the Scout.

I stepped over to the console and thumbed it. "I'm here, Star."

"I've got an incoming signal from a ship. They want to talk to Challers."

The Scout cocked his head. I could faintly hear the radio in his helmet talking to him, but I couldn't make out the words. Then he took out a small injector and tossed it to me. "Give this to our friend here."

"And what if I don't?"

"I'm sure you don't want to see the poison that's keeping him unconscious do any more damage, now do you?"

"You're bluffing."

"Try me."

I growled and put the injector to Challers's neck. He moaned, tried to sit up, groggily looked down at the straps holding him to the bed, then lay back again.

"Your friends are calling," said the Scout.

Challers grunted and shook his head slowly.

"Take the call, Renedy."

I sent the acknowledgement, and the face and upper body of a sharp, dark-haired man appeared on the holostage. He wore a loose Pirate-style shirt. His face paled. "Challers? We got your signal."

"Things...didn't go as planned. You have to get out. Now. Jump while you..."

Alarms blared on the other end of the connection. The man's attention was diverted left, then right, then down, then he sat back with a grim expression. "I'm sorry we weren't there for you, Challers."

"My fault," he croaked.

"Good luck," said the man on the screen, and the signal cut out in a burst of holostatic. The explosion felt so close I could feel it through the hull.

"You fired the missiles," said Challers. "You killed them...just like that."

"Burner," I said. "You void-sucking burner!" I could feel the blood rushing to my face. I wanted to rip the self-satisfied grin off his face, grind him into bloody pieces, and blow him out the airlock. "You used that channel to get them to hold still long enough for the missiles to hit!"

"Of course I did! After the damage your traitorous friend here did, they only had a few more hours of viability anyways—might as well use them. Now then." He raised his weapon and aimed it at my head. "Your usefulness has come to an end."

I closed my eyes and waited for the shot.

I heard the door open, and the voice of the other Scout, a woman. "Hasn't there been enough death? Let her live. She can't do us any more damage."

I opened my eyes. She wasn't particularly tall, but she had the biggest breasts I had ever seen except in that Merchant sex holo. There was a haunted look to her, as well, like something within her had died. I wasn't sure whether I should be relieved or even more scared that she had intervened. Watching her through the cameras had given me the creeps; seeing her in person only made it worse. There was something seriously wrong with that woman.

"You're right, Trace. No reason Miss Jawmet can't finally begin making her contribution to the war. Take her down to the ship and get her processed." He tossed her a roll of medical tape. "This ought to hold her."

Challers scowled, staring at the woman. He knew her.

I could have fought her, but it would only have gotten me shot. The woman wrapped layers of tape around my wrists, binding them together, then drew her pistol and aimed it at me.

"Let's go," she said.

chapter thirty-two

Challers, Stakroya Station

THE SCOUT moved in close and I finally remembered where I had seen him before. It was only once, and it seemed a lifetime ago, but seeing Trace, and hearing her name brought it all back.

"Umber," I said. "I knew I didn't like you."

The tall, square-jawed man was Trace's mentor, the one who had put her in a gentank to give her those enormous breasts she didn't want. What had he done to leave her so beaten down?

He ran a hand through his short-cropped blonde hair. "Ah, I'm flattered! You remember me. I certainly remember you, Challers Dizen—given that you are one of the most wanted criminals in the galaxy right now. Recapturing you is going to get Trace and me our old bodies back."

"So why are we here and not in your ship? You've already killed my friends."

"Here's how things stand, Challers. I'm ambitious. I don't just want my body back—I want the location of the Pirate fleet. We're bringing this war to an end, Challers."

"Vack you."

He smiled. It was a vicious smile, all teeth and no eyes. "Oh, this is going to be fun. Now, I don't have the sophisticated interrogation setup they have back at Headquarters, but I've been briefed by people who've studied the recordings. I know what it takes to break you."

Renedy, Stakroya Station

I FOULED UP. I had totally fouled up. How did I ever think I could do this? I was never a solider or a spy. While we paused at the elevator, I looked back in the direction of the infirmary.

"You're Trace, right?"

She nodded.

"You know Challers?" I asked.

"Yeah."

"Is he your friend?"

"Used to be," she said.

"Doesn't sound 'used to be' to me."

"He betrayed the Service."

"And that's a bad thing?"

The doors opened. "You don't understand."

I walked in and leaned back against the wall, trying to look casual—like my hands weren't bound behind me, like she didn't have a pistol out, like we weren't captor and captive. "So tell me."

"The Scouts have something of mine. This is the only way I can get it back."

The elevator lurched and started down towards the hangar bay. "What's that?"

"They have my old body. When they made me like this, they recorded what I had been before. They can put me back."

"And that's worth Challers's life."

She set her jaw and looked down. "I did what I could."

The doors opened on the hangar deck. To our left, wide armored windows looked out onto the hangar bay where the Scout ship waited. "You can do more," I said. "Let me go. Better yet, let's turn the tables on that bastard up there, and get Challers out of here. The war needs to be over, but it's the Scouts who have to lose."

She waved her pistol in the direction of the airlock leading to the hangar bay. "I'm sorry. I just can't do that."

"Yes, you can! Vack, how can you be so selfish?"

She raised the pistol and pointed it at my leg. "Don't make me shoot you."

I turned and walked towards the airlock. "I can't believe you're being so selfish."

Trace thumbed the lock and the doors opened. "Shut up."

I turned and shouted. "I will not shut up! This is wrong! You've seen what's happening here. You've stolen the bodies of almost everyone on board the station, and you're about to steal mine the same way the Scouts stole yours!"

"Quiet!" A tear rolled down her face. "Don't make me shoot you!" She shoved me through the airlock.

I stumbled and fell, landing painfully on one shoulder.

Trace stood over me, gun pointed at my head. She blinked fat tears and choked out her words. "Don't make me shoot you."

Challers, Stakroya Station

MY HEAD SWAM. My body tingled. The drug Umber had given me cruised through my mind, shattering my thoughts into evaporating wisps as it found them.

"Challers." His voice echoed in my head. "Can you hear me?"

"Un-huh."

"Good. Focus on my voice, Challers."

I couldn't do anything else. My own thoughts couldn't put themselves together. There was only the voice. "Your voice."

"Think of the Pirate fleet, Challers. Where is it? Where is the Pirate base?"

"Pirate base." The image sprang to mind of that huge ship floating between the stars.

"Where is it? What are the coordinates?"

"Coordinates." Numbers flashed in my mind, slowly shifting second by second as Port's powerful warp drives took it on a gently curving course between the Old Stars and the Rimward Reach—a course chosen to avoid any chance of encountering another ship.

"Yes, Challers. The coordinates. Last position of the Pirate fleet."

"Last?"

"Yes. When you left them. Where were they?"

The numbers ran backwards. My navigational display aboard the *Destiny Achieved* appeared in my memory, sharp and clear, with Port rapidly shrinking as we readied for jump. More numbers. It would be easy to just read them off. So easy.

"The coordinates, Challers. Tell me the coordinates."

"N...no."

A sharp pain flared in my side, shattering what little resolve I had managed to muster.

"Tell me the coordinates of the Pirate fleet."

"Five...seven..."

"Start with the referent, Challers. What referent were you locked to?"

"Special referent."

"Not galactic core?"

"No. Something else."

"What is it?"

"Don't know."

"All right, then give me the coordinates for Stakroya Station on that referent."

I read off the long string of numbers that appeared in my mind.

"Good! Very good, Challers. Now give me the Pirate fleet last time you were there. Shouldn't be too hard to figure out what your referent is."

Something wailed inside me, helpless and hurting, trapped behind a wall of chaos and confusion. It screamed that I shouldn't do this, that doing so would destroy any possibility of bringing down the Scouts and their terrible hold over the galaxy. But it couldn't stop me. I couldn't stop myself from listing off the long chain of numbers. "Seven...three...two...eight...five...five..."

Renedy, Stakroya Station

SUDDENLY, the Scout wasn't there. Something hit her, something big, moving fast. Another face appeared above me, a woman. The helmet of her airsuit was flipped back. "Are you all right?"

"Yeah. Just bruised."

"I'm Rendika Prelain. We're here to help. Can you stand up?"

"I think so."

Rendika put her arm around my shoulders and helped me to my feet. "I'm going to cut that tape from your wrists."

My hands tingled as the blood returned to them. "Renedy Jawmet," I said.

"Do you know Challers Dizen?"

"Scout has him. Up in the infirmary."

Rendika looked to her right and nodded. A huge woman, maybe two meters tall, was on top of Trace, holding her in a painful-looking arm lock with one knee planted solidly on her spine.

"End this one?" said the big woman, drawing a nasty-looking pistol from her belt.

"No!" I said. "She saved my life."

"Besides," said Rendika, "it'll be easier to take their ship if we have one of them with us."

"All right. You get the two of them aboard. I'll go get Challers."

"Be careful," I said. "The Scout with him has some kind of armor under his clothes that protects against your guns."

She took Trace's pistol and looked it over. "Does it protect against theirs?"

"No, but you won't be able to fire it. I saw someone try; Paul Fischer tried to steal one of them. It wouldn't work, and he got killed trying. I think their weapons are keyed to only work when they're in their hands."

She grunted and frowned. "Well, I guess I'll just have to find another way."

Challers, Stakroya Station

"PICTURE THE HANGAR BAYS, Challers. How many corvettes are there?"

"Seventeen."

"Is that typical?"

"I...don't know."

"And how many hangar bays are there in the ship altogether?"

"Six." Despair gnawed at me. I was spilling everything and there was nothing I could do about it. Everything that came to mind just tumbled out of my mouth. "I hate you," I said, mumbling.

Umber chuckled. "Yes, I imagine you do. How many troops are on the base?"

"No troops."

"All right, how many people who could fight if it were invaded?"

"Don't know. Maybe a thousand? Lots."

He chuckled. "Yes, quite a large number indeed," he said, sarcasm twisting his tone.

The door opened. Umber scowled, turning to look over his shoulder. "I left explicit instructions that I was not to be—"

There was a bang, the sound of a Pirate laser hitting its target, and Umber stumbled forward against the bed. Then another bang, and another, and he fell against me with his full weight. Rolling sideways, shielding his face with one arm, he grabbed at his pistol with the other.

My mouth might not have been under my control, but my hands were. They were bound to the side of the table, but he had rolled against my right arm as he maneuvered to bring up his weapon. I grabbed him, taking hold of his wrist before his pistol could clear the holster.

"Agh! Let go, you stupid—"A shot hit his unprotected head and he fell, lifeless, onto the floor.

Krinna holstered her laser and picked up a scalpel. "Come on, Pirate. Let's get you out of here."

I blinked, wondering if I was hallucinating. "Krinna! But...you're dead!"

She cut the strap on my wrist and smiled. "David was suspicious when the signal was sent by someone other than you, so as soon as we jumped in, he sent Rendika and me through a jump conduit into the hangar bay."

"So David...he faked his death, right? Ejected the self-destruct charge and jumped out of range when the missiles closed in?"

"No." She gave a heavy sigh. "That...wasn't part of the plan."

"Then he's really dead...? I'm...sorry."

She shook her head and cut the rest of the straps. "There's no time for that now. We have to get out of here, and there's only one ship left with a jump drive."

"I've got blood on me," I mumbled.

"Oh, vack, what did that burner give you?"

"He drugged me. I don't know what it is."

Krinna shook her head and helped me to my feet. "Do you think you can stop talking?"

"No, I don't think so."

"Wonderful."

"Isn't it?"

chapter thirty-three

Renedy, Stakroya Station

I LOOKED OUT the front window of the Scout ship's tiny cockpit at the hatch where Rendika's partner, Krinna, had disappeared. "I need to go."

"You're staying here? Not a good idea, sister," said Rendika.

"No, I need to bring someone with me."

"Not happening. It's going to be cramped enough with five of us in here. I don't know if the life support system will take that—much less six."

I thought of Star and Nella, stuck here while I escaped. Nella had lost everything, and now she would be losing me as well. "Promise me I can come back for her."

"This mission was originally to try to get Challers's family. We'll be back for another try most likely so we might be able to get your friend then too. "

I set my jaw. My relationships weren't important enough to risk everything for it. "All right. Let me at least send her a message."

"Sure. We'll transmit it as soon as we're away." Rendika gestured to Trace, who touched a few controls.

"Recording," she said, her tone beaten, flat.

I turned toward the hologram showing my face. "Nella, I'm sorry I have to leave you here. The Pirates seem to be doing the right things. I'll try to get back for you. But...if I don't, if something happens...thank you. For everything." I nodded to Trace, and the device shut off.

The last thread binding me to Stakroya Station had been cut.

Krinna came through the doors, half carrying Challers, and she helped him up the ladder and into the ship.

"Can you open the hangar?" asked Rendika.

"Yeah, most likely," I said. "Just give me a remote login on the station network."

Another display appeared in the air near me. I entered a few commands, and within minutes, the great doors yawned open and our stolen ship backed out of the hangar bay into open space.

"Go on back and help Krinna and Challers," said Rendika. "I've got things up here."

Down a narrow passageway, I found Krinna laying Challers down on a bench on one side of a wide circular floor. "Renedy, right?" she said as she straightened up.

"Yeah."

"Hi, Renedy!" said Challers. He was smiling broadly and his head seemed to have come a little loose, the way it was waving around.

The woman held out her hand with a quick smile. "Krinna. Everything secure up front?"

"Rendika has everything under control."

"Under control! That's Rendika. Always under control." Challers lay down and started whistling.

"Okay, then I guess it's you and me getting us out of here."

"What?"

"You and me. We need to get back to base as soon as possible, and that means you and I are going to have a good time." She glanced around the chamber. "Been a while since I ran one of these things. But I suppose you never really forget."

"Okay, explain in language a stationer like me will understand."

Her smile turned a little softer. "Sorry. I forgot. Here's the thing. These Scout ships? Basically, they run on sex. You can't really go anywhere without folks humping bumps here in the orgone chamber. It kind of works with one, but it's really designed for two."

I blinked. "You have to be joking."

"Nope."

Rendika's voice came over the intercom system. "I hate to rush you, but things have gotten complicated. There's a blip on the infrared scan. A Fleet cruiser is on its way in-system. If it figures out what's going on, they're going to hit the hyperdrive and they'll be here before we know it. Now's the time."

"Okay, you got a reprieve, sweetbud," said Krinna. "I'll go solo to get us out-system, then we'll have a go together once we're clear." She undid the seal on her airsuit and pulled it off, tossing the bulky pieces to the side. Underneath, she wore nothing more than a tiny pair of bright blue flimsies that barely covered anything. She looked like a cross between a Fleet Marine and a regular woman; every muscle seemed three times bigger than it ought to be. She pointed to another bench. "Have a seat."

I sat where she pointed.

She knelt in the middle of the room and gave me a stern look.

"Now this is a delicate piece of machinery, so I need you to just sit there...wait...never mind. Do what you like. If you feel like touching yourself, go for it. We could use the extra power."

My mind was reeling. Was this really how the Scouts got around? I looked over at Challers. He was muttering to himself and staring at the ceiling.

When I looked back, Krinna had her eyes closed and her hands were roaming over her body. They quickly drifted to breasts and crotch. Her fingers slipped down through the thick blonde fur covering her pussy, and in only a few minutes, I could see, hear, and smell the signs of arousal.

I wasn't the only one who noticed. The quiet mumbling monotone Challers had been doing changed and he turned his head, watching Krinna. "Can't touch," he was repeating to himself, "can't touch, can't touch, can't touch, can't touch..."

The whole experience was just too bizarre. I wanted to run away, to go back home; it was too much weirdness, too fast.

And yet, somehow, watching Krinna pleasuring herself was getting me excited. At the sight of her hand on her breast, I imagined her hand on mine; her hand in her pussy almost felt like it was in mine. Finally, I had to just let go of my fears and let the moment sweep me along; it was either that or break down completely.

Cries of pleasure sounding more like growls than moans, came from her throat and her limbs trembled with gradually increasing spasms. After a few minutes, she fell onto her back and let out a long, wounded moan. Throbbing vibrations ran through the ship in time with a hammering noise coming from every wall. For a second, I thought the cruiser had finally caught us, but Rendika's voice broke through the rumbling. "Here we go!" she said with a whoop, and the noise rose to a peak with Krinna's orgasm.

The noise faded. "Okay, we're safe," said Rendika.

Krinna sat up and smiled at me. "Got it now, sweetbud? That's how it works. But it works much better with two, and danger-boy over there isn't in any shape to do the job." She nodded at Challers.

He smiled faintly and went back to mumbling.

"It's just a lot to digest all at once, you know?"

She got on her feet and took my hand. "Look, we just put a half a parsec or so between us and that cruiser and they've got no way to track us. So we're not going to get ambushed anytime soon. But we still need to get back to the fleet, and going solo isn't going to do it." She nodded in the direction of the cockpit. "Now, if you'd rather, I could go switch places with Rendika, and send her back here..."

For some reason, I didn't want to insult Krinna by agreeing to that.

She didn't look like someone I wanted angry with me. "No, that's fine," I said. "I guess I'm just kind of overwhelmed."

"I gotcha, sweetbud. Would it help if I told you I'd be gentle with you?" She cocked her head to the side and gave me a surprisingly gentle smile. It looked alien on her harsh features, but at the same time, it did soften her image.

"Yes, actually, that does help. I'm not exactly an expert at this." I kicked off my boots and set them behind the bench I was sitting on.

"Are you a virgin?"

"Almost," I said. "I've only done it three or four times, and only once with a woman."

"You're doing pretty well then. I think most station folk would be climbing into the ventilator by now."

I swallowed and pulled down the zipper on my coverall. It was caked with grime and my body underneath wasn't much better. "Ugh. I've been hiding out in the maintenance tunnels for days. I'm not really fit for this."

"All right then. Let's get you washed up." She stripped off my coverall the rest of the way and marched me to the ship's tiny fresher.

"Whoa, you are pretty smelly," she said, pushing me under the spray. She doused me with various cleaning solutions and lathered me up, her hands going absolutely everywhere, and I was mostly clean within a few minutes. The feel of her strong hands in my hair and on my skin made me feel small and weak, but protected and treasured at the same time. It was a warm, comfortable feeling, especially after the constant anxiety of the recent past. She was, after all, saving me from Stakroya Station.

"There we go. Feel better?" she said, rinsing the soap from my body.

"Yeah, I guess, but—"

"Good." She guided me out of the shower and took out a towel to dry me off. The vigorous rubbing she gave me left my skin tingling, and my body felt better than it had in weeks. I realized I was avoiding her gaze and forced myself to look into her eyes; I needed to see something there before I could give myself to her the way she was asking me. I wasn't sure what it was I wanted to see, but when I looked up, I saw it.

Lust.

Her eyes were intense, sparkling, and wide with anticipation. "Relax," she said. "This is going to be fun. I'm going to do stuff to you I bet you've never felt before."

My skin dry and pink and tingling, she led me out to the circular chamber. She did something with the controls and a rectangular shape rose up out of the floor.

"Lie down."

The platform was just big enough for me to lie down on with my legs hanging off one end. My pulse ran hard and fast in my ears as I did what she told me. I expected her to bend down between my legs the way Nella had, but instead, she lowered herself astride one thigh, placing her warm cleft on my leg. She was still wet. I wondered how much of that had been from the masturbation, and how much from giving me my shower.

Her hands roamed over my body, gently caressing every little patch of skin in no particular order. I could feel a sense of anticipation growing, a want that turned into a desire, and then a desperate need. I had been afraid before, but that trembling doubt fell away in the face of that urgency.

Her fingertip trailed over my lips. I kissed it, wishing she would bring her own lips down to mine, but that wasn't part of her plan. She dipped her finger down between them and I sucked on it, tasting her skin and the faintest aroma of body wash.

She smiled down at me and I took that as an invitation. I put my hands on her ribs, her arms, trying to work up the courage to touch her breasts. The muscle underneath her skin was solid. I wondered whether she would be as hard inside as well.

Her eyes stayed with mine as her hands moved over my collarbones, shoulders, and up onto my breasts. Compared to Krinna and Rendika, I felt skinny and weak, but she lavished attention on me like I was the most attractive lover she had ever had. Any doubts about whether I was pretty enough faded with each stroke and squeeze.

Then she shifted forward, sliding her body up until her thigh made contact with my pussy, and ground her body against mine. There was no comparison to the one time Nella and I had been together. This was way more raw. More direct. I found myself thrusting against her to increase the friction.

"That's it," she said in a growly voice. "Like that."

My clit wasn't directly touching her, but the movements of our outer lips together felt great anyways. I could feel that tingly, warm sensation building inside me, spreading out through my body.

Krinna had most of her weight on her legs. I could feel them flex against my skin as she moved. The power of this woman felt barely restrained, as if at any moment she might burst open. I almost feared seeing another orgasm like the one I had just witnessed.

"Touch yourself," she breathed. "It'll work...better that way. Trust me."

She brought her own fingers down between our bodies, between my thigh and her clit, and I could feel them dance between us as we moved. I did the same, letting her movements push them down into my slit, moving with her rhythm.

"Tell me," she said between gasps, "when you're close." Her throat worked a swallow and she arched her back, putting even more weight on our bodies, pressing our hips together like she wanted us to melt into each other.

"I'm...almost..." The ship was vibrating, pulsing, just like it had with Krinna—only far more intensely. I got a prickly sensation over my skin. "What's happening?"

"Don't worry," she said with a relieved sigh. "Almost there. Come with me. Come now."

The command cut some barrier inside me and the orgasm burst through me, erupting from my mouth and my eyes and my fingers and toes and tits and cunt and belly and the ship hammered around me like it was going to come apart.

Krinna collapsed forward, stopping herself from landing on top of me by gripping the platform on either side of my head.

"Congratulations," said Rendika's voice over the intercom. "You just brought us the whole way in one jump. We're here."

chapter thirty-four

Challers, Port

VALKA CAME to me as soon as the doctors would let her in. "Challers!" She flung herself onto me, pushing past the medical equipment to wrap her arms around me. "Are you all right?"

I smiled and gave her a big, sloppy kiss. "I'm fine. Just had to purge a nasty drug the Scouts pumped into me. How have you been?"

"It's been...lonely."

I took Valka's face in my hands and looked into her eyes. "I'm glad to see you again too, but there's something important I need to say to everyone."

She pulled back and nodded.

"Portcon? Please give me a display showing the number of Wards watching my feed."

A holo display appeared, showing a fairly respectable number. It wasn't the whole ship by any measure, but it was a lot. I hoped it would be enough.

I addressed the holocam nestled up in the corner of the room. "Wards and Worthies," I said, getting up from the bed, "not too long ago, my friends and I tried to tell you about a new weapon that had been developed by the Scouts, a missile that used innocent human beings as power sources. You chose not to believe me, and rightly so. All you had was my word and, as an ex-Scout, that word was not worth much to you.

"I've returned from the station where I was born with technical details about this weapon and sensor records of their use. This data was on board the Scout ship we used to escape from Stakroya Station. These files have been posted on the public data store—ask Portcon if you wish to review them."

I glanced at the numbers. They were all zero. "Port? What happened? Where did all the viewers go?"

"Your feed has been cut, Ward Challers Dizen. Your presence has been requested on the command deck. The Cues wish to speak with you."

I swallowed hard. "What do they want?"

"That is not a question I am qualified to answer, Ward Challers Dizen."

"Well, if I'm going to see them, it's not going to be as a Ward. I don't care who they are...I'm getting a replacement orgone belt first."

We went up to the boulevard and stopped off at Vivian's shop for a new belt. There was no need for a fitting since measurements were kept on file. As it was being prepared, Valka said, "I'm coming with you."

"No. I need to do this alone."

"Challers!" She stood in front of me.

I looked up at the corner of the room, near the ceiling, where the holo camera was almost certainly watching us. There may not have been any Wards, but I would bet every credit the Cues were watching. "No."

She caught my glance, and nodded. "Right."

As I stepped down off the dais, she kissed me long and hard. "Good luck, Challers."

THE COMMAND DECK, it turned out, lay at the forward end of the Boulevard, past a huge pair of sliding transparent doors. A messenger in a pale-green uniform I had never seen before met me there. "Follow me, Worthy Challers Dizen," she said.

I nodded and fell into step behind her down a long, gently sloping corridor. We passed a half dozen doors on either side until we came to a heavy hatch closing off the end of the corridor.

"Now what?" I asked.

"We wait until they're ready."

"If they weren't ready, then why did they send for me?"

She gave me a scowl. "I don't think you understand how much trouble you're in, Worthy."

"Fine." I looked around for someplace to sit down, but there was nothing nearby—not even a potted plant—so I stood, and then paced, and finally sat down against the wall to see if I could get some sleep.

After what had to be hours, the woman put her hand up to her ear, and then turned and nodded at me. "They're ready for you."

The hatch opened with the deep drone of heavy servos and I went in.

There were about twenty of them, sitting at a half-circle-shaped table that was raised up three meters from the floor where I stood. Lights shone down on me from every angle, making it impossible for me to see anything but dark silhouettes. The hatch closed behind me.

"Worthy," said the man in the center. "We would like to know what you meant to accomplish this morning." His voice was old, like he was fifty or sixty, and deep. My stomach wanted to crawl up my throat. Was that Kensington Book, the man who had welcomed me to his tavern when Valka and I became Worthies?

I took a deep breath and let it out slowly, expelling as much of the tension as I could. I spoke calmly, in an even, confident tone. "We need to strike at Scout Headquarters now. For one thing, there are probably Scout spies out there, and we need to attack before—"

"There will be no attack, Worthy Challers Dizen. An enterprise like that would require the presence of a sizable proportion of the fleet. We cannot risk making ourselves that vulnerable. It is totally out of the question."

My reserve was weakening. Panic and rage surged in my stomach. "What? No! Don't you understand? These missiles are powered by Ovor eggs! They're almost babies! How can you sit there—"

"The Scouts have developed 'secret weapons' before. We have always developed countermeasures. Worthy Dizen, you underestimate the ingenuity of your fellow Worthies. The system is designed—"

"Vack your system! Are you listening to me? They are putting babies in missiles out there and shooting them at us! We have to stop them!"

The man waved his hand in my direction. "Deal with him."

Two large men emerged from the darkness, coming up on either side of me. "No!" I shouted, backing towards the hatch. "No, you can't do this!"

"I assure you, Worthy...we can."

The men grabbed my wrists and shoulders, and a rectangle of pale orange light opened in the floor. It was a doorway of some kind, one I was certain I wouldn't come back from. I screamed and fought and kicked, but I was a child in their grasp.

The hatch opened. The men holding me turned to look, and then fell to a flurry of laser blasts from the crowd of Worthies coming through the door, with Valka in the lead.

"With all due respect, sirs," she said, tossing me a pistol, "we're going. And if you know what's best for you, you'll come with us."

I strapped the gun to my waist while the faceless figures leapt to their feet, shouting in confusion. We left them there, arguing, while we ran to the hangar bays.

"The Cues tried to shut down Portcon, so we couldn't get the word out," said Valka. "But they couldn't stop Rendika and Krinna and me from going out and talking to people. They knew your feed had been cut, but they didn't know what had happened. So we fanned out on the Boulevard and showed folks what we found. There was a lot of arguing at first, but as soon as word got out about what they were planning on doing with you, that was it."

"So what's the plan?"

"I don't think there is one. But we've got the coordinates for Scout Headquarters. Actually...the Pirates have always had them. So that's where we're going."

I shook my head in disbelief. "They've always had the coordinates?"

Valka shrugged. "Well, yeah, of course. We're not the first to defect from the Scouts, not by a long shot. Happens all the time, from the Worthy bios I've seen. They just never wanted to actually go there."

I imagined a hundred Pirate cruisers jumping out to the Scout base...and who knows how many missiles fired at them as soon as they showed up. "If we try to make this a conventional attack, we're going to get slaughtered."

"You want to try to organize this mob?"

"I have to try." I pushed to the front of the group we were in, making it to one of the hangar bays ahead of most of the crew. I climbed up onto a cargo container and shouted, "My fellow Worthies! Give me a few minutes, if you please!" There was some murmuring and bumping around, but I managed to get their attention, at least momentarily.

"In a few minutes, we're going to show those Scouts what we're made of...but if we don't do it right, we're not going to get very far. I've seen what those missiles can do, and you know that if they have them anywhere, they have them at Scout Headquarters. But I have an idea that will take them to their knees. We've got more Worthies than we need to crew all these ships anyways, so the ship I'm on is going to have plenty of extras. We're going to need them. We're going to jump to a spot one light-hour from Headquarters. Once we're in position, we'll get a good fix on the ring, then plot another jump inside the station."

"Inside? That's insane!" Dissent rumbled through the hangar. "The mass differential will shatter the hull!"

"I've done it!" I shouted above them. "I plotted a course inside the hangar bay of Stakroya Station. You just have to take your time, pay close attention, and send in only what we absolutely have to...our extra crew, in airsuits, armed to the teeth."

"Without a ship?" someone cried out.

"I've done it. It's not fun, but if you hit the center of the ring, there's a river running down the middle to land in. They won't know what hit them, but we have to move fast. There may be traitors among us who will warn them. So who's with us, Worthies! Who is with us?"

A huge cheer went up, and we piled into the corvettes, grabbing all the airsuits and weapons we could muster. As soon as we were out of the hangar bay, the transmissions started flying to the other ships coming from the other hangar bays, and by the time we jumped, at least half of them were in on the plan. If there were traitor ships amongst the fleet, it didn't matter; even if they plotted their course to within a few hundred kilometers and immediately warned the Headquarters, there was little they could do.

The plan was foolproof.

My calculations had to be perfect. Everything was all riding on me. Hundreds of lives were at stake and there was a limited amount of time to make it work. Luckily, I had a dozen or so highly skilled navigators to check and double-check my work while I was doing it. After about forty-five minutes, we had the numbers worked out, and each ship slotted their version into the drives and fired them up. My crew got into our airsuits, climbed out the airlock, and dove through the jump portal.

There were six of us in all: Krinna, Rendika, Valka, an ex-Scout named Pollard, and a couple of brand-new Worthies named Yassiv and Trook. None of us had any real history of fighting beyond duels, but Yassiv and Trook were even worse—they had only just gotten their orgone belts that morning when they heard about the egg missiles. They were enthusiastic, but completely unprepared.

THE PORTAL came out about three meters above the water. We had compensated for the rotation rate of the station, more or less, in our calculations. "More or less" turned out to be a significant velocity and we did not land gently. Hitting the water felt like being thrown against a wall. When the six of us managed to pull ourselves out, we did a quick status check right there on the side of the river. All of us had various bumps and bruises, but thankfully, we had escaped serious injury. Flashes of blue going off in the distance heralded the arrival of other teams. I hoped they had been as lucky as we had been in landing. We shucked our airsuits and hid them under some bushes. They wouldn't do us any good as armor and they would only slow us down.

"What's our objective, chief?" asked Krinna.

Somewhere along the line, I had been elected squad leader; it wasn't a job I wanted, but it would have made more trouble to argue about it than it was worth.

I remembered the disk-shaped flyers from my time at Scout Headquarters that would make it easy for Scouts to move quickly in the huge, open space of the oxygen deck.

"First thing is to get under cover," I explained. "We're too exposed here. Then we'll see about tracking down the exterior defenses, see if we can make things easier for the folks who decided to do this the hard way."

Rendika smiled. "In other words, we're going to fly by the seat of our collective pants."

"Yeah, that about sums it up. Let's go."

Valka clapped me on the back. "Right behind you."

There was a grove of trees nearby, so we hustled in that direction, scanning the air around us for signs that the Scouts had noticed our arrival. I heard the whine of engines approaching before I saw its source and shouted "Run!" and dashed for the trees. I didn't wait to see where they were coming from or how many of them there were. I just ran.

The sharp crack of their mass driver weapons sounded before we reached the trees. Yassiv shrieked in panic, but I couldn't look back to see whether he had been hit. I put my back to one of the trees, hoping it would be enough to stop one of their bullets if they decided to shoot through it to get me.

Trook reached the cover of the canopy and nearly collapsed, while the others scattered to find other trees to hide behind.

"Trook!" I shouted. "Just because you can't see them, doesn't mean they can't see you!"

"Oh! Right!" He stumbled toward me, clearly intending to take cover behind the same tree I was using, in spite of the fact that it wasn't wide enough for both of us. Vack, it wasn't even big enough for me, really.

"Over there!" I pointed in the direction of a tree that wasn't occupied, trying to locate the flyer by the sound.

He lumbered toward the tree just as the bullets began hitting the ground. Rendika came out from around her tree with a huge weapon held in both hands and fired. There was a sound like a thousand tiny explosions and tiny shreds of leaves fell down out of the tree where her beam had blasted its way through. The whine of the flyer's jets spun and faded.

But it was too late. Trook lay in a spreading pool of blood.

chapter thirty-five

Challers, Scout Headquarters

WHILE RENDIKA kept watch, Krinna leaned down, picked up the outflow tube for his orgone belt, and hooked it up to hers, draining his supply to replenish her own.

"How can you tell where they are?" I asked Rendika.

"Sonic locators," she said, tapping her goggles.

"How far are they?"

"I think they landed about 500 meters that way," she said, pointing in the direction we were headed.

"All right, then we're going to angle away from them. I don't want to lose anyone else. Everyone, keep your eyes open." I made sure everyone was with me, and then struck out between the trees, taking a shallow angle running almost parallel to the buildings that made up the side wall of the oxygen deck.

It took us a while to reach it, but the path kept us from running into any more patrols, and soon we were moving along the edge of the oxygen deck. After a few minutes, we found a door, forced it open, and closed it behind us again.

The space beyond was a maintenance bay with racks of spare parts, a couple of half-disassembled agriculture robots, a rack of tools, and lots of grime. The sight made me think of Joco Gata, the maintenance guy who had been killed for what he knew about the Scouts' plans.

I looked back out the doors at the greenery outside. "Rendika, how would you and Yassiv like to stay here and guard this door, while the rest of us have a look around?"

She gave a sharp salute with her crooked smile. "Nobody gets past us."

Yassiv looked relieved.

Valka was already looking over a data terminal hooked up against the wall. "Needs an identity chip," she said. "Gotta get someone with access."

I turned to Pollard. "You got any tricks for breaking into the Scouts' network without an ID chip?"

He shook his head.

"Okay, then we're moving on."

Krinna showed us the best way to advance through room-to-room while fighting. She had been in a few fights aboard space stations and knew the drill. It wasn't really necessary, however. Beyond the maintenance bay, we found a fabrication shop, its robots working but idle, ready to make whatever parts needed to restock the repair bay it was connected to. Beyond that was a small warehouse for the raw materials to run it, and then a terminal for the rapid transit system that permitted access to the rest of the ring-shaped station. There hadn't been any side passages along the way to the station, but there were many portals along the platform.

Pollard pointed to one of them. "If there are any egg missiles here, they're probably going to be that way."

"Why do you say that?"

"That door leads down. The outer docking bays will be in that direction. It would make sense to install them there, especially if that bay is empty."

"All right, let's have a look."

Just as we were about to start moving into the system, air started rushing through the station. "Take cover! A car's coming in."

We had only seconds to prepare. Several of the doors wouldn't open quickly, so Valka and I found ourselves on either side of the door leading down, while Krinna and Pollard took another one. We prepared our weapons, set them to the highest power, and waited. The car arrived, the door opened, and small white spheres rolled out onto the platform.

"Grenades!" shouted Krinna. "Take cover!"

We ducked away from the door, but instead of explosions, there were just a few quiet pops.

"Gas," I said. "Vack!" I pulled Valka back from the doorway and retreated down the ramp. Without any breathing gear, we were completely vulnerable to whatever that gas was. We ran until we found a pressure door, sealed it, and blasted the controls behind us. I had seen that in an adventure holo once; I hoped it would slow down our pursuers.

The room had another wide hatch just like the first, but it wouldn't open.

Valka opened a locker. "Look! Airsuits!"

"Great. I guess I shouldn't have destroyed the controls."

We found suits that would fit us well enough and pulled them on as fast as we could. Just as we were getting the helmets fitted, the door we had come in from shoved open a few centimeters and another white ball bounced into the room. I motioned to Valka and we flattened ourselves on either side of the door as the sphere popped open, releasing a thin blue gas. The portal opened a little further and a Scout in a white uniform, wearing a breathing mask, squirmed through the gap. He saw me, raised his gun, and I raised mine. I stared into his eyes, and hesitated...it was only a moment, but it should have been fatal. He should have shot me.

Valka didn't hesitate. She put her gun to his head and fired. His head exploded, splashing gore everywhere.

I stood there, stunned.

Without a pause, she lunged forward, firing her pistol through the gap. I heard running footsteps of another Scout retreating back the way he had come. She tried to push past, but the doorway was too narrow for the airsuit. She pulled back in and shrugged.

I was ready to vomit and she was acting like nothing had happened. "Valka, are you okay?"

She smiled, her bright-white teeth standing out against the dark red splattered across her face. "Fine, and you?"

"You just killed a man."

"He was about to shoot you, Challers! You didn't want me to stop him?"

"Well, yes, but...I mean..." I sighed. There would be time for examination later. "Let's not use the suit communicators. They can probably listen in."

She nodded.

I pointed to the corpse's hand, and then the console in the corner. With the ID chip embedded in the dead Scout's hand, we could see what the network could tell us. We pulled the dead Scout over to a data terminal and propped him up so his hand would be close enough that the console would activate.

I went to keep watch at the door. After a few minutes, she tapped me on the shoulder and pointed to the hatch on the other side of the room. I opened it, we went through, and closed it behind us. We were in a huge hangar bay, big enough to hold a whole Merchant ship. We pulled off our helmets so we could talk; if any gas leaked into the huge space, it would be too diffuse to affect us.

She walked towards me. "The Scout that got away reported in. There's another squad on its way here. I managed to get our ID chips reinstated locally, but that's the best I could do." She pointed to a container hanging from supports on the high ceiling of the chamber. "More egg missiles."

"We need to deal with them," I said.

"Yeah. They've already fired a bunch from other bays around the station, but it looks like these are being held in reserve."

I drew my pistol and thought about the missiles on Stakroya Station. Merely disconnecting them from the support umbilicals wasn't enough. They would be used against the other Pirates and had to be destroyed.

Or did they?

I ran over to a console, waved my hand over it, and was glad to see that it started up normally. A handle slid out of the console as a giant robotic arm emerged from the ceiling—a cargo-handling waldo arm. I had never actually operated one myself, but I would just have to learn. Valka got started on another console, blocking local connections so that network administrators elsewhere would not be able to interfere.

Just as I was getting started with the arm, another door opened, and Pollard stepped out, pistol drawn.

"Pollard!" I shouted. "You know how to operate one of these things?"

He aimed his weapon at my chest. "Hands up where I can see them," he said. "You too, Valka."

I groaned and put my hands in the air. "You burner." Valka did the same.

"You're lucky I don't just gun you down. But we've got orders to take captives."

I shook my head. The reason was obvious. "Because they don't have enough people. Every captive they can turn into an Ovor is another missile factory. Innocent lives for war."

"I'm not going to argue politics with you. Come out from behind the console."

I complied, but I wasn't going to give up trying to convince him he was wrong. "This isn't politics! It's about using defenseless lives as weapons!"

"We've always been weapons. We've never had any more ability to choose our paths than the eggs do. Now Challers, pull your weapon from its holster by the butt and set it down on the floor, nice and slow."

A klaxon split the air and a loud female voice boomed throughout the docking bay. "Emergency decompression beginning in thirty seconds. All personnel clear the area immediately."

Pollard was distracted, just for a moment, and I drew my weapon and fired. The blast ripped open his chest and sent him flying. He wasn't wearing the red underclothes; the scarlet splatter across his chest was real.

Valka shouted. "Challers! They're going to fire the missiles!"

"Not if I can help it." I turned back to the console and grabbed the control stick. I didn't have time for finesse. Under my guidance, the arm took hold of the container, ripped it from its moorings, flipped it over, and put it back where it had been—except its firing ports were now aimed at the ceiling. The clamps engaged, holding it firmly in place.

Valka used another console to sever the arm's connection to the outside network. When I had finished disabling the missiles, she yanked some cables out of the main console to shut the whole system down.

"That's it!" I shouted. "Come on, let's get out of here!" The hatches were closing by the time we got there, but we managed to get through before the countdown finished. "We gotta go find the others," I said.

Valka nodded. There was a fierce look in her eye. Last we saw Krinna, she was taking cover with Pollard. Her chances didn't seem good.

The hatch Pollard had come through led to a storage bay for construction pods, and from there we found a passageway leading back up to the transit station. The car that had brought the Scouts before was gone and the area was deserted. We made it back to the door where we had left Rendika and Yassiv, but they were missing too. The only evidence of fighting was expended gas grenades lying about.

"Looks like they captured all of them," I said.

"Then we need to get them back. Maybe they took them to that prison complex we were in."

"Are you ready to go back there?" I shuddered at the mere thought of it.

"Oh yeah," she said. "I'll follow you anywhere."

I scowled. Her enthusiasm was welcome, but it was worrying too. "Do you have any ideas about how we get there?"

"There are those construction pods," she said. "Some of those ought to be flyable."

It took some doing, but our ID chips still worked, and the network disruption Valka had thrown up around the area kept anyone from trying to change it. Along with the pod we were in, we activated the whole fleet of them, opened the hatch to the docking bay, and floated out with the other pods' robotic brains slaved to our controls.

I expected the chaos of a space battle outside, but the limited sensors of the construction pods couldn't see any action. There were occasional distant flashes of light, but there was nothing but eerie silence around us.

We cruised along on the pod's slower-than-light thrusters, skimming the outer surface of the station in case there were any weapons that could track us.

"That's interesting," said Valka, pointing at a spot on the hull that was glowing bright white.

"Scrambler beam," I said. I recognized it from the simulations I had done at Port. "They must be firing at Pirates out there. I'm going to stop it." I set one of the unmanned pods to independent operation, cranked its thrusters up to maximum, and sent it down into the glowing spot. There was a silent explosion, a jet of atmosphere, and the spot was reduced to a jagged hole. We continued on.

The construction pods didn't have a lot of data on board, but they did have a basic schematic of the Headquarters. It wasn't hard to find the airlock the Robert had used to break me out of the prison what seemed like a lifetime ago. I sent the other construction pods out in all directions, hoping to confuse anyone watching us, while I deposited a hull-welder in the airlock, and then turned the construction pod around to dock.

"Are you ready?" I asked as I climbed into the little space and hefted the heavy hull-welder over my shoulder. It wasn't really designed for interior work, but I had a feeling we would need it.

"Say the word," said Valka with a strangely neutral tone.

"Let's go."

There was no point in stealth. The only thing we had going for us was surprise. I was pretty sure it would be a suicide mission, but if I was lucky, the Scouts would be shorthanded. They couldn't be leaving too many people behind to guard the prisoners, and they weren't likely to be holding prisoners anywhere else—not when they had this facility already. We ran down the wide, circular ramp leading down to the prison as fast as we could.

We passed pockmarks along the walls and floors, artifacts of the running gun-battle of my escape. None of them had been patched or painted, though the bloodstains were gone. Adrenaline surged through me remembering that day, and for a moment, I mourned the innocence I lost when I first took a human life.

The guards at the front doors were wary, but they didn't have their weapons ready and both of them fell to a barrage of laser fire as we came around the corner to their post. The front doors were closed and locked, but the hull-welder made short work of it and there was no one behind them. We cut our way through all of the doors, finding two or three of our compatriots behind each of them.

Krinna, Rendika, and Yassiv were there.

It felt good to finally get a break. We looted the place of weapons, finding captured Pirate lasers and Scout mass drivers. After a bit of work to get the ID-locks undone on the Scout weapons, all of us were armed. We swarmed out onto the oxygen deck and found a Scout patrol landing with a couple more prisoners; their guards fell quickly and we commandeered the patrol craft to take us to the command center.

There was no command at that point—no controlling what had become a howling mob. Heavy fire came up at us from the main doors, smacking into the bottom of the craft within seconds of sighting the doors, ripping through the skin and machinery like it wasn't there. Several fell, injured or dead, before we were able to set the machine down in some heavy vegetation. We fanned out and assaulted the doors en masse. More fell, but we took the gates.

We screamed through the complex, cutting down any Scouts we found, until we had control. We shut down the exterior defenses, the scrambler rays and hyperbullet cannons, and sent out a signal that any Pirates remaining in the system should come in, dock with the station, and assist with the assault.

THERE WAS FIGHTING inside the station for several days, but the outcome was never in very much doubt. The last pocket of resistance surrendered less than a hundred hours after the assault began.

We won.

The victory celebration spilled out of the Academy, into the bars on the Promenade, and out into the oxygen deck, but I brought Valka to a quiet side passage and down into a long-shuttered laboratory. There, in the center of the room, diagnostic displays shining in the darkness, sat an operational gentank.

I took a memory card out of my pocket and held it out to her. "We found your original template recording today."

"But Challers, I don't want that anymore. I like being like this." She squeezed her boobs and smiled at me. The smile was foreign, almost creepy. "And I know you like this body."

"No," I said. "There's something wrong. Something about this body took something away from you. I don't know what it is or how it happened, but at least I can give you back the body you were born with, instead of this baby factory the Scouts created."

"But Challers! You told me you liked me like this." She moved in close, running her hand over my chest. "Remember that time in your pod? When I sprayed milk all over? You said you liked that. I could do that again, you know. There are treatments I could take."

"No, Valka, listen..." I grabbed her wrist. "There's something wrong, don't you understand? You've changed!"

"There's nothing wrong! Please, Challers, I'm allowed to change, aren't I?" She tried to grab the memory card out of my hand.

I closed my fist around it. "Yes, but people aren't allowed to *change you*. The Scouts did this to you. Please. For me. Get in the tank."

"No!"

I took her by the wrist and dragged her over to the tank. She didn't put up much of a fight. I slotted the memory card, and while it downloaded, I opened the lid.

She squirmed in my grasp. "Challers, please. I like myself. Don't make me go back. Please don't make me go back." There were tears behind her voice.

I set my jaw.

She cried as I took off her clothes. "Challers, I'm afraid! I know so much now. I know I love you. I know that I can be with you forever. I don't want to go back to being broken."

I fitted the breathing mask over her face and lifted her in my arms. She had stopped struggling and was sobbing quietly into my chest. As I lowered her down into the glowing pale blue gel, I said, "When you come out, you might not be happy, but you'll be fully human again. And if you were thinking straight, that's what you would want too."

I closed the lid and started the cycle.

epilogue

Renedy, Port

THE FACE I had been told belonged to a system called "Portcon" appeared on the holoscreen above my chair. "Welcome to your assigned pod, Ward Renedy Jawmet."

The Pirate fleet, along with Challers and Valka and everyone else I knew, had already left on their quest-mission-thing, whatever it was. I wished them luck. They had taken the fight to the Scouts, somehow, and that was just fine with me. The Scouts had twisted everything I had ever valued to their own ends, and I wanted them to pay.

"What am I supposed to do?" I asked.

"You must remain in this pod. Entertainment and life support will be provided."

"Uh...okay. So it's a prison?"

"Not at all..." Portcon explained to me about my status as a Ward, how I would be fed and clothed and housed in exchange for my orgone. That was kind of weird, just in itself, but with the reserves having been taken by the fleet, the need for that energy was greater than ever.

I settled in and started figuring out exactly where I stood. There was a lot of information available to me, even more than when I had been in the communications cluster on Stakroya Station.

The gossip channels were full of speculation about what would happen next. Would the fleet return to Port laden with plunder? Would they take possession of the Scout Headquarters instead and make it their new base of operations? Nobody seemed to know, but everyone agreed on one thing.

It was going to be exciting.

Read on for a preview of:

HUNTERS
book three of the Orgone chronicles
by Nobilis Reed
Coming soon to Logical-Lust Publications

chapter one

Valka, Port

The worst part wasn't watching it happen. The worst part was that I couldn't do anything to help.

She was beautiful in the way Challers found women beautiful; wavy brown hair that begged to be touched, full breasts with brown nipples that stood up when they got hard, and a nice, soft, grippable ass.

The first part of the interview actually went quite well. While they took off each other's clothes and explored each other's bodies, she asked easy questions about his background. He told her about growing up on Stakroya Station, about being selected for the Scouts, about his training on Scout Headquarters, about looking into the disappearance of another cadet, and his defection to the Pirates.

That's when things started to get nasty. They were already fucking by then, with him trapped on his back, and her hands on his shoulders. Most of the viewers would know about his career as a Pirate anyways, so there weren't a lot of questions about those things. Instead she came out of nowhere with an attack.

"So how many credits did you actually make in the raid? Five hundred thousand credits, something like that? How many credits does that make per Pirate that died in the assault?"

One of the cameras focused on his face. I could see it in the monitor hanging from the ceiling over the studio. He blinked and scowled. "What?"

"Well, there were twenty-four casualties, plus eleven who were badly enough injured that they'll never be able to operate as Worthies again. That works out to—what?— fourteen thousand per life destroyed?"

"I wasn't doing it for the credits," he said. His cock was still inside her pussy but his hands dropped from her breasts to her thighs. "We had a job to do. We still have a job to do. And the Pirates who died or were injured in that assault were mostly—"

She cut him off with another question. "So what do you intend to do with your newfound wealth, Worthy Challers Dizen? You've easily got enough to buy yourself a share and become a Cue. It's what every Worthy dreams of."

"I think I can accomplish more as a Worthy. We've done some real damage to the Scouts. As soon as we've made repairs and decrypted the information—"

She interrupted him again. "So you intend to lead another suicide mission into the teeth of our enemies? How noble."

"It wasn't a suicide mission!" Challers gritted his teeth and arched his back. He was close to orgasm. I knew because I had seen that face many times myself. At the same time there was the raw edge of anger to his voice, and hearing it made me grit my teeth in sympathy.

"It was for Jennifer Beenz. Did you know she had only just become a Worthy that day? She took the orgone belt so she could follow you to Scout Headquarters."

Challers growled and flipped the interviewer onto her back. He spread his legs for purchase and thrust into her hard, making a slapping noise as their flesh came together. "They...were...using...human...beings...as...weapons!"

The woman didn't let up. "And the Worthies you used in your attack are different because they were grown people rather than Ovor eggs?"

She was remarkably collected for someone who was getting the pounding of her life, but from what I had seen, this was pretty standard for her interviewing technique. I suppose after a while you can develop the skill.

"They're different...because they had...a choooice...." Challers's body went rigid, every muscle in his beautiful body stood out under his skin, and then he collapsed like a deflating balloon, only just barely holding himself up off of her.

"Thank you," said the interviewer, climbing out from under him. "Ladies and gentlemen, Wards and Worthies, I've been talking with Worthy Challers Dizen, leader of the devastating attack on Scout Headquarters the day before yesterday. Thank you for pulling up Pillow Talk." She accepted a towel from an aide and began wiping herself off. "Watch again tomorrow, I'll have an interview with Carino Beenz, the life-partner of Jennifer Beenz, to talk about how he is coping with the loss of the love of his life."

The "recording" signs all over the studio went out, and I rushed onto the stage to help Challers clean up and get into his clothes. He was shaking with rage.

"I didn't do it for the money," he said, through gritted teeth.

"I know. You did it because they were making babies into weapons."

"I'm glad someone believes me."

The interviewer had already left the stage. We were quickly becoming the only people in the room. "Come on," I said. "Let's go get some lunch."

Just outside the door, Renedy Jawmet ran up to us, panting slightly. "I saw the feed," she said to Challers. "You got fucked over in there."

"In more ways than one," he said with a dry smirk.

About the Author

Nobilis Reed is a husband, father, and companion to rather a few cats, living in a quiet Northern Virginia suburb. For many years, he recorded his stories privately, but a few years ago he decided to see whether anyone else wanted to read them. To his surprise, he found that there were more than a few who were interested. When the concept of "podcasting" came along, he jumped in, and has now been producing audio fiction for more than three years.

Visit his site at www.nobiliserotica.com

Other Titles From Logical-Lust Publications

www.logical-lust.com

Scouts

2011 EPIC eBook Award™ finalist for Best Sci-Fi Erotic Romance

EPIC's
eBook
Award
2011
Finalist

An overpopulated space station threatens to separate two young loves. At any moment, Challers Dizen could find himself conscripted by the Fleet and forced to become one of their lethal, over-muscled Marines, while Valka Parl could be taken away by the gluttonous Merchants. Their only hope to stay together is to join the mysterious Scouts.

$12.99 US, £9.99 UK, $3.99 eBook download

Future Perfect – A Collection of Fantastic Erotica

Speculative erotica at its best from author Helen E. H. Madden, from the adventures of a sexually obsessive superhero to the best orgasm you'll ever have – at the end of the universe.

Helen takes erotica to a whole new level in this astounding collection!

$11.99 US, £8.99 UK, $3.99 eBook download